Heart
OF A
Duchesse

KATE JENKINS &
MORGAN MOREAU

Heart
OF A
Duchesse

BOOK 2

VASSETRE

To Morgan, who puts up with all my awful ideas and
sometimes even goes along with them.
To my mom, who is so very supportive even
while sitting there clutching her pearls at the very
idea of her daughter writing smut.
To Kala, for consistently asking when this
book would be done, but in an encouraging way.

~ Kate

To Kate, one of my favorite world builders.
Who knew elves could be so insatiable?
To Grey: "I feel like I just found my new best friend." –
Blackbeard, and "It's about belonging to something when
the world has told you you're nothing." – Izzy Hands.
And Rhys Darby. Quit being so freaking charming.

~ Morgan

Table of Contents

Cast of Characters xi

Chapter One 1
Chapter Two 6
Chapter Three. 15
Chapter Four. 22
Chapter Five 28
Chapter Six 34
Chapter Seven 42
Chapter Eight 47
Chapter Nine 60
Chapter Ten. 67
Chapter Eleven. 77
Chapter Twelve 83
Chapter Thirteen 90
Chapter Fourteen. 98
Chapter Fifteen. 119
Chapter Sixteen 137
Chapter Seventeen 143

Chapter Eighteen 149
Chapter Nineteen 155
Chapter Twenty 164
Chapter Twenty-One 175
Chapter Twenty-Two 188
Chapter Twenty-Three 195
Chapter Twenty-Four 203
Chapter Twenty-Five 213
Chapter Twenty-Six 220
Chapter Twenty-Seven 226
Chapter Twenty-Eight 230
Chapter Twenty-Nine 239
Chapter Thirty 246
Chapter Thirty-One 251

Book Club Questions 263
Author Bios 265

Other Locations

Azmarin Empire: A country to the north.
Dathria: A country to the east.
Myrefall: County in Coralia.
Quenall: The capitol of Coralia.

Dom

Fythias

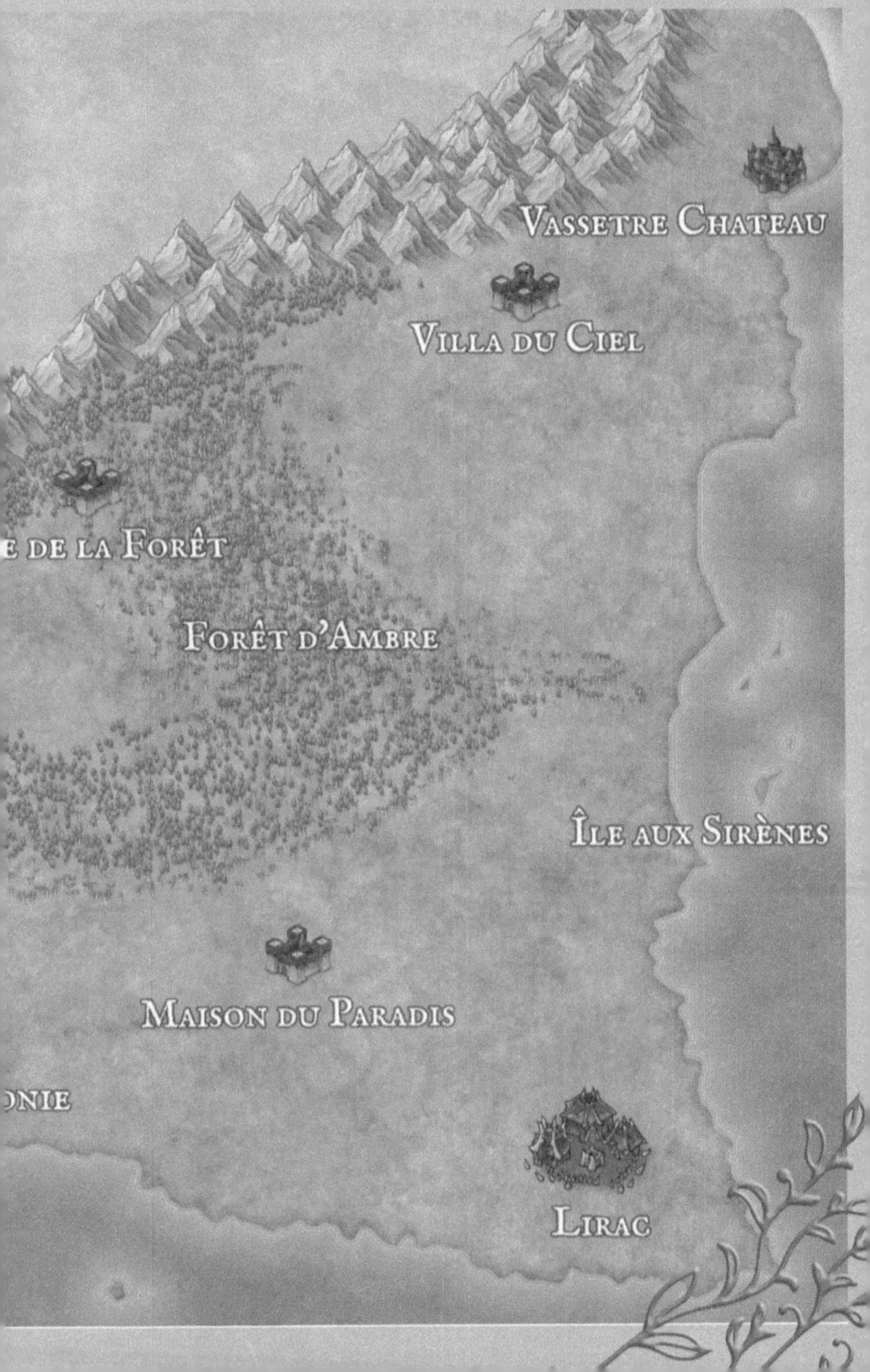

Vassetre Chateau
Villa du Ciel
E de la Forêt
Forêt d'Ambre
Île aux Sirènes
Maison du Paradis
ONIE
Lirac

Cast of Characters

Alain: Human. Deceased king of Fythias.

Alaoin: Human. Child of Eloise and Louis.

Phineas "Finn" Allard: Human. Steward of Vassetre Chateau.

Anaise: Half-Human, Half-Sirene. Member of Sabine's guard.

Tristian Anouilh: Human. Comte du Ciel.

Aphros: Nereid. King of the Nereid People.

Eloise Aresenault: Human. Princess Consort. Wife of Prince Louis.

Grégoire Arsenault: Human. Prince. Middle Child of King Rodolphe

Louis Alaoin Arsenault: Human. Prince. Youngest Child of King Rodolphe.

Avana: Elf and Dwarf Hybrid. Failed Assassin.

Brielle: Human. Guard Captain of Prince Louis.

Claudine: Human. Caretaker at an Orphanage.

Baron Cyrille: Human. A Minor lord sent by Prince Grégoire to ask for Sabine's suit.

Dion: Human. A Fythian Comte.

Lisbeth Dubois: Human with magic. Personal companion of Duchesse Sabine.

Meri Dubois: Human with magic. Former guard captain, current head cook.

Elodie: Human. Head over the Weavers Guild

Faron Istro: Elf. Personal Guard to Sabine.

Glaucus: Sirene. Local Merperson.

Henri: Human. Baron and suitor for Sabine

Jacqueline: Human. Caretaker at an Orphanage.

Marcelle: Sirene. A Vassetre Chateau Guard.

Hugo Onfroi: Dwarf. Retired Guard Captain

Peronelle: Human. Steward of Prince Louis.

Phindel: Elf. Friend of Faron from Coralia.

Raidne: Sirene. Local Merperson.

Thaumas: Sirene. Local Merperson. Former lover of Sabine.

Sabine Vassetre: Human. Duchesse Vassetre.

Chapter One

Finn sighed as he took in the gathering of staff, all crowded around his office desk. Unlike his usual relaxed expression, the chateau steward surveyed the group with exhausted determination. His handsome, tanned face marred with a creased brow and dark circles beneath his eyes spoke of a man who still needed some sleep. "Thank you all for gathering," he said over the hum of voices.

Sabine kept staffing numbers on the smaller side compared to some noble estates, but at least twenty people stood along the walls of Finn's usually accommodating office, so quieting down took a moment. Faron, who was crammed in the back, knew not everyone was present, though he supposed a skeletal crew would be needed to keep things running while Finn provided them with morning updates. Faron assumed Avana was with the guards since she wasn't here, but he honestly didn't know.

"Her Grace has made a decision which will impact the estate, at least for some weeks, and I wanted to deliver the information as soon as possible."

Faron tilted his head to the side as he studied Finn. The steward's countenance felt unreadable. A negativity sat in the hunch of his shoulders, the way his fingers tapped against his leg. More than that, whatever news Finn had to share had Meri and Lisbeth both very, very apprehensive. Both women sat in chairs closer to the dark stained desk, Lisbeth's hands folded into her lap while Meri's dark brown eyes bore holes in the wall behind the steward. He would have to talk with them once Finn had his say.

"What is it?" Marcelle asked the steward from his position by the door. As usual, Marcelle's golden hair was tied back and his arms were crossed. Normally a bright, vivacious man, the young Sirene seemed to pick up on Finn's mood, and his solid black eyes somehow exuded concerned uncertainty.

"Her Grace has decided to visit the Comte du Ciel," Finn said bluntly, keeping his gaze focused on the crowd but on no one in particular. "She has her reasons, of course, and she will personally meet with those who need to be aware of her actions and motivations before we set off, which I have been told will be in a few days' time."

"She's not accepted his proposal, has she?" Marcelle asked, eliciting gasps of protest and horrified shock from around the room.

"Not that I am aware of," Finn replied shortly. "But I do wonder if the visit might result in some arrangement. We know the prince has been pressuring her for some time, and the comte had proven interested in Her Grace." Finn held up his hands to quiet the group down, though this took time and an irritated clearing of his throat. "I know," he said bluntly. "I know. This was not an event any of us could anticipate, but she has agreed to visit, and given the state of things, I think it is wise to approach the visit with caution."

Faron felt terribly confused. He couldn't fathom why Sabine would wish to visit Tristian. She disliked the man and all he stood for. She had expressed many times how boring, unintelligent, and potentially dangerous she found him to be. She'd also made it clear there was something about him that made her feel unsafe. She'd had Faron place guards on the doors to the wing of her side of the chateau, yet she would agree to go and visit the comte? With marriage a possible outcome? No, something was wrong.

"When did she decide this?" Faron asked, suddenly aware that of all the people in the chateau, his position should have made him among the first to know. He was her personal guard, and he had been acting as the guard captain since his arrival. He should have known.

"Late last night," Finn replied with a sigh. "She sent word via letter this morning to the comte's estate declaring her intention to visit."

Faron's eyes narrowed as he recalled the prior night's discussion between Sabine and himself. He wondered if she'd already planned the visit before they had spoken, and if so, had her ultimate coldness before he'd been dismissed been the result? But no. That didn't sound right. Sabine never took her frustrations out on her people. He would have to speak with her when the meeting was done. He waited for whatever else Finn had to say, fighting the urge to get up and go.

"I will notify those chosen to accompany Her Grace to Villa du Ciel as soon as I have been informed of Her Grace's choices," Finn said as he brushed his red-brown curls from his face. "Until then, please proceed with your morning duties."

Faron waited as the staff filed out of the office, noisily chatting and gossiping over the news before striding to the door, purposeful in his steps. That was until his arm was grabbed and he suddenly found himself face-to-face with Meri. Her gold eyes narrowed into fury and her short dark hair seemingly stood on end.

"No," she said, her voice firm.

"No, what?" he demanded.

"No, you will not demand answers from Her Grace, and do not try to tell me you weren't about to do that, because I can read it on your face. She must have her reasons to decide on a visit, and your intention to go demand them of her is disrespectful. Leave it be, Faron." Meri released his arm, a flash of her gold bracelet showing before a sleeve covered it.

Faron rubbed his arm, still feeling every spot those small fingertips had pressed against his skin. He'd be surprised if no bruises formed. "She had no intention of ever stepping foot on the comte's estate yesterday. Something must have happened."

"Obviously something happened, but going and demanding things of Her Grace won't make her tell you. If anything, it will get you fired," Lisbeth said as she joined the group. Her gingery curls, pinned out of her face, bounced obscenely, too joyful to be of use to Faron or anyone else given the occasion.

Finn appeared soon after, coming to join the little group. Thankfully, the corridor was empty now. "Does anyone know anything?" he asked quietly, glancing around the hall before looking back to the group. "Her Grace was short on details when she spoke with me this morning."

"No," Lisbeth said, shaking her head, her orange curls still swaying. "Other than deciding to visit Tristian since some-time last night. She won't say why."

Finn sighed and glanced up at the ceiling. "I'll see what I can find out. She cannot stand to be around Tristian. She doesn't trust him."

"She seemed alright last night, if distant," Faron said thoughtfully.

Finn raised an eyebrow and exchanged looks with Meri before looking back at Faron. "Did you perhaps say or do something to upset her? Did she say anything to you? Usually, she's forthcoming with her plans."

"No. We were just talking," Faron said with a shrug.

"Right," Finn said with a sigh. "Well, I've got a visit to organize. Even a short visit requires an excess of planning. The three of you should try to figure out what happened if you can, whenever you see her."

Faron nodded, deciding he was going to go see Sabine and figure this out on his own if he had to. He moved to go only to have Meri block his path.

"Leave her be right now unless she calls you. You're upset and not in the right headspace for a productive discussion, and your attitude may leave her unwilling to answer questions. For now, go get the guards ready. Some of them will need to accompany us when we leave."

"Spirits, fine!" he exclaimed and spun on his heel to head to the barracks. Faron knew his reaction was over-the-top, but his willingness to act rationally never seemed to work where Sabine was involved. He didn't even know why he felt so disconcerted over the decision to visit the comte, and examining his response felt dangerous and unnecessary right now.

"Ten silvers this is his fault," Lisbeth said, not hiding her words at all.

Faron threw a rude gesture back at her before rounding a corner.

Chapter Two

Sabine didn't miss the glances from her staff or the whispering that came to an abrupt stop anytime she walked into the room. She knew her decision to visit the comte, to try to discover what he knew and was thinking, would go over poorly. She knew her staff would not understand. In truth, the Duchesse Vassetre only understood a need for decisive, productive action since her confrontation with Faron the night before.

Thankfully, she'd ignored her initial idiotic impulse of agreeing to marry Tristian. The letter, hastily penned through heartbroken tears, had been tossed into the fire less than a half hour after its composition. Still, as she sat up afterward, contemplating how she wanted to proceed, she had to admit there was some usefulness in taking up one of the many offers to visit. She needed information. She needed to know more about the connections and promises between Tristian and Grégoire and how those plans tied to the spread of the Merscale trade and Coralia. So, her plan had changed.

As she walked through the corridor on her way to her office, no one could guess the duchesse had not slept or that she had spent several hours the night before crying angrily over Faron's rejection. Her light caramel hair sat beautifully arranged as always, a mix of twists and braids adorning her head like a crown. Her vivid sea green eyes somehow escaped the expected puffiness, and her lightly tanned skin glowed. What a lovely façade she'd conjured.

Of course, she owed no one her façade. She had a right to be unhappy. To feel used, unsupported, and unloved. A woman in her position often had to accept she would always feel the sting of those thoughts. Still, she felt a little selfish about the limited wallowing in self-pity she'd permitted for herself. It wasn't as though Faron owed her anything. No matter what fantasies she'd created in her mind, he'd never promised her more than a few stolen hours. He never claimed feelings beyond a mutually pleasurable time, and there was no denying how pleasurable those hours were. She'd been stupid. She'd forgotten herself. She wouldn't anymore.

Grateful that no one waited for her when she arrived in her office, she gladly closed the door behind her. She made it as far as her desk before she was forced to take a few long moments breathing deeply, eyes closed, to prevent herself from falling apart. Her hands rested on her chair arms, fingers pressed so firmly into the fabric she might have injured the poor thing had it feelings or the capacity to bruise.

You are in an unhealthy frame of mind. Now is not the time to make any visits. You could change your mind. You just sent the letter informing Tristian of a visit. You can reverse your decision or delay the meeting. No one could say or do anything about it.

The thoughts had her reaching for a quill, but her fingers curled away, and she shook her head, resolved. Her hand returned to the chair arm, and she rested her head against the back of her seat, ignoring her stinging eyes.

"No," she told herself firmly. She wasn't allowed the freedom of falling apart because Faron did not want her. She had too many people relying on her and far too many responsibilities. She had a country to help guide, to hopefully unify under Louis. And she could only do so by doing her duty and getting useful information to pass along to the youngest prince.

Her hand rose again, plucking up parchment, quill, and ink, and she began composing a letter. Instead of penning an explanation of her coming plans to Louis, she instead composed a letter to Faron, detailing her decision to reassign him to guard captain rather than her personal guard. His current salary and his accommodations would remain the same, but his responsibilities would change. Knowing Faron would not like the change, Sabine offered a severance: the remainder of his yearly salary and funds to cover lodging and travel until he secured a new position. When her note was done, she put it aside so the ink could dry, feeling as though this letter would be discarded in much the same way the late-night proposal acceptance had been.

A tentative knock sounded at the door, a sound unfamiliar to her given the way those who could freely access her there usually knocked. Finn's announcement clearly created some negative feelings. "Come in," Sabine called out.

Lisbeth entered, a small, very tentative smile on her face. "Good morning, Your Grace."

"Good morning," Sabine greeted, returning a tired smile. She straightened in her chair, not wanting to add to the ongoing worry she knew her people felt. "You're usually overseeing other things by this time in the day," she commented.

"I wanted to see if there was anything in particular you wanted me to pack for your trip?" Lisbeth's voice was soft, concern lacing her voice and features. "I do not know your plans for your time at the comte's, so I wanted to check."

Sabine sighed and sat back in her chair, too physically and emotionally spent to put up much effort in her demeanor. "I've not given the matter any thought, in truth. Not beyond deciding on a visit. I suppose if you want to pack, start with the basics, and I'll figure out the details after."

"I'll try not to pack anything too fancy. I haven't heard of the comte hosting a ball in some time," Lisbeth said more to herself before she bowed. "I'll take care of everything, Your Grace." She turned to go, her hand outstretched to grasp the doorhandle, before turning to back to Sabine. Taking several steps toward the desk, Lisbeth's face grew thoughtful. "Do you know who you're bringing with you?"

Sabine suspected Lisbeth's question wasn't what she'd wanted to ask, but the differences in their positions sometimes resulted in Lisbeth feeling as though she needed to tiptoe around subjects before finally arriving at the point of concern.

"I have some people in mind, though I have not settled on a final group," Sabine replied. She wondered if Lisbeth thought of Faron. She and Meri, after all, had encouraged her involvement with Faron, though she believed they thought he must have felt a mutual attraction toward her that spanned beyond the physical. Sabine now knew he did not.

Lisbeth gave her another small smile. "I am sure whomever you pick will be best to handle anything that should come up while visiting with the comte." Lisbeth tried but couldn't keep the disdain from her voice at the mention of Tristian.

A tired chuckle left Sabine. "He annoys me as well, and I will be the one speaking with him. Spending time with him. You should all be doting upon me for undertaking such hardship."

Lisbeth finally laughed, her voice and expression sounding more like herself. "Oh, I know I will, and if you're taking Meri, she's already sworn to make all your favorite foods. I don't know about anyone else," she said, her grin getting larger before it slipped off her face completely. "You don't have to go to the comte's. Your dislike of him is well known, and I doubt you would enjoy even a minute of your time there. We could claim you're sick."

"We could, but I think I would like to see and hear whatever information there is to gather from a less familiar place." Avana, she thought, would make a useful addition to the travel party. Sabine would need to let her come along.

Lisbeth made an understanding noise. "So, you're not planning on marrying Tristian? Just seeing if he knows what the prince might be planning?" Lisbeth asked, sounding hopeful.

"Spirits, no! It is likely I will never marry, but if I did, it would not be to someone like Tristian," Sabine assured her, though she surprised herself with the declaration of never. Yes, her heartbreak was clearly dominating her behaviors this morning.

"I wouldn't say never. You don't know what could happen. If you choose that path, you have our support. You have done a wonderful job as Duchesse Vassetre. Meri tells me consistently how proud your parents would be. You don't need a husband, no matter what Comte Tristian or the prince think." Lisbeth gave Sabine a dazzling smile.

"Why would you think I would ever consider the comte?" Sabine asked, mostly as a distraction.

"There is a rumor going around that we are only visiting the comte so you can marry him," Lisbeth explained, shaking her head. "Would you like me to put a stop to it?"

"Who decided I was marrying him?" Sabine asked, though she thought she could likely name suspects with some accuracy. "I suppose it doesn't matter, but I would not subject myself to such a fate. Just because Tristian is the only one claiming to want me doesn't mean I have to go along with it."

"Marcelle is the one who brought it up at Finn's announcement, and you know how the rest of the staff love to gossip." Lisbeth rolled her eyes. "I think I'll let the rumors continue and allow the rest of the staff to realize how stupid they're being on their own. Perhaps if anyone is around gathering information for the comte, it will help with your snooping." Lisbeth gave a delicate shrug. "I might tell Faron though. He seemed concerned."

Sabine snorted, unable to help herself. "Faron does not care. He's made that abundantly clear."

Lisbeth visibly flinched. "He what?" she asked in confusion.

"It doesn't matter beyond knowing that what was happening between Faron and I is no longer happening," Sabine explained, shrugging as though she did not care. "I would not worry about what he thinks about my decisions or any surrounding rumors either way."

Lisbeth nodded, an unhappy expression etched into her pretty features. "Well, if he screwed up the best thing in his life, he can continue to think you're marrying the comte," she huffed.

"Good plan." Sabine glanced back to the letter she'd penned before Lisbeth arrived. "I was actually thinking of appointing him as my new guard captain and reassigning someone else as my personal guard."

A dark cloud crossed over Lisbeth's face as she realized how badly Faron had offended. Thankfully, she didn't automatically side with Faron, something Sabine had worried about given the connection between Lisbeth and Faron. "Marcelle would be a wise choice. Most thought you would pick him and were surprised when you hired an unknown instead." Several other emotions crossed Lisbeth's face before she continued. "I'll let Meri and Finn know Faron should be in your presence, especially alone, as little as possible. If you're alright with that. I know how overbearing he can be, especially when he thinks he's innocent of whatever offense led to your decision."

"You're welcome to." She finally looked back at Lisbeth. "Though I think doing so would simply cause more questions."

"I'm sure we can come up with something." Lisbeth observed Sabine with undeniable pity before coming around to the other side of the desk and enveloping her in a rather awkward hug since Lisbeth was standing and Sabine was sitting. "I'll make his life awful for you if you want," she said softly.

Sabine gave a sad little laugh, appreciating the brief reprieve from her broken heart. "Recruit Avana into your cause," she suggested as she returned the hug. She needed the affection more than she realized. "She knows how to effortlessly annoy Faron."

Lisbeth laughed. "I can do that, but I'll have to put down some boundaries with her, or she might poison him. Avana is very attached to Meri and you. If we're punishing Faron on your behalf, she might go overboard."

"I have noticed her attachment," Sabine replied. She liked the young elf, even with the feral streak running through her. "Though, I think she will delight in tormenting Faron."

"Oh, she will. Meri explained to her what it means to tease someone for fun last week. She thought Meri was being mean to Finn when they were joking around about his cooking skills, and it upset her greatly. Avana has been trying her hand at it and not doing very well, so this will be good for her. She needs to learn not everything has to end in murder and such." Lisbeth started to pull back from the hug, but a good look at Sabine's face had her leaning back in, giving her an even tighter embrace.

"I promise I'm okay," Sabine told her old friend. "Today is not the worst day of my life. Not even close."

"I'll take your word for it, but if Meri serves you a lot of comfort foods today, it's not my fault," Lisbeth said, pulling away from the hug completely this time.

"I will not oppose good food. I am tired, and I have a long day ahead of me." Sabine couldn't say she felt better, but she felt as though she'd manage through her heartbreak with more ease than she'd believed late last night.

Lisbeth rose and tapped her chin thoughtfully. "If it's alright, I'm going to look over your schedule with Finn. I'm sure we can pencil in a nap or something if you're tired. We aren't going to see the comte for a few days, and you'll want to be at your best to handle him."

"I will manage my schedule," Sabine replied. "I'm quite skilled at it, you know."

"I know, but sometimes you work when you should rest." Lisbeth gave her another smile. "If you don't want to schedule some down time, however, I completely understand. There are times when one needs to remain busy."

Lisbeth bowed then headed for the door. "I'll go pack your clothes and talk to Meri about food. Not in that order."

"No, we wouldn't want to keep you from Meri for too long," Sabine teased.

"You know I can't go half an hour without seeing her. I'll perish otherwise," Lisbeth threw back dramatically, and she went out the door. Poking her head back in she added, "I'm here if you need anything, okay?" Her earnestness, an endearing trait Sabine adored, left the duchesse a bit less sad, at least for now.

"I know," Sabine returned.

Lisbeth gave her a small wave and left, the door closing with a soft click behind her.

Chapter Three

Faron paced the length of his room, confused, hurt, upset, and not sure what to do about those feelings. A quarter of an hour earlier, Finn dropped off correspondence from Sabine. The steward made it very clear Sabine did not wish to see him and implored Faron to listen. He assured Faron the reason Sabine was going to see Tristian had nothing to do with accepting the marriage proposal and to please give Sabine her space. She would tell them her plans when she was ready.

Faron had done his best to comply, but after reading the letter—which now lay on his mantle instead of tossed in the fireplace where it belonged—he felt hopeless and argumentative. The letter advised Sabine's decision to replace him as her personal guard and explained the ongoing tension with the prince. She wished him to take the position of her guard captain. The position, Faron knew, needed to be filled, but it was also not the position he'd signed on for. He would obviously take it if left with no other choice because he worried what would happen if he didn't.

With hard work—not just his but Avana and Marcelle's, as well—the guards had come a long way, but they were recruiting more guards who would need training. If he couldn't guard Sabine directly, then this would be the best way to keep her from harm.

It would also allow him more time to figure out if his confession from the night before in her bathing chamber was part of the reason for her decision to visit Tristian. Faron knew she wouldn't agree to consider the comte's proposal, no matter the current speculation. She just wasn't that rash or impulsive, even if she hadn't liked what he'd admitted. While he now held guilt for how he'd confessed, Faron also knew his assessment of their relationship hadn't been wrong. They hadn't known each other long enough for their feelings to be love. Could what they share eventually turn into love? Of course, but he also wasn't willing to let that happen. Their lifespans were so very different, and as selfish as he knew he was, he didn't want to go through the pain of losing someone he knew he could love so ferociously.

Less selfishly, Sabine was a noblewoman with great influence, power, and even greater responsibilities. Marrying a lowborn elf of Coralian ancestry wouldn't be allowed, and the mere suggestion would bring about a confrontation between Sabine and Grégoire, Faron was sure. Sabine had enough to contend with, and he wanted to limit the risk of conflict between the two as much possible, at least where he was concerned.

No, it was best for them to keep whatever was between them to the bedroom. Though, with his dismissal from her chamber the prior night and the removal of his position as her personal guard, their more private time together might be at an end, which might be for the best before one of them did fall in love.

And yet, it hurt, the possibility of not being able to be with her, and not just sexually.

He took a breath, shaking the thought away. He could go over the reasons she was reassigning him all day. What he should be focusing on was her visit to the comte. What possible reason could she have to visit a man she despised? Did the comte have something on her? Did the prince? Outside of blackmail, he could think of no other answer as to why Sabine would put herself in reach of people she did not trust let alone like. There had to be something foul afoot.

Deciding it didn't matter if she wanted to see him or not, Faron strode to his door, intent on seeing Sabine. A part of him knew he shouldn't, that he should give her the space she requested, but if something had happened, he needed to know. He doubted she would keep it from him or the others if a threatening letter had appeared, but it could happen depending on the leverage they might have. Also, if he was forced to take the position of guard captain, this might be the last time they had to truly talk. So maybe, other than just checking on her, he could ensure he hadn't completely ruined everything and possibly explain himself better.

Faron had taken only a few long strides from his chamber before he heard approaching steps. Turning around, he spotted Marcelle. The usually affable Sirene's mouth was set in a grim line, no doubt caused by the news of Sabine's plans. "You seem as happy as the rest of us," he commented as his steps brought him beside Faron.

Faron hated to admit it, but he didn't know the Sirene very well. They had talked a few times but mostly during and about training. So, to see Marcelle now seeking him out was very concerning. Was he there to keep Faron away? "It's been one of those days," Faron answered.

"That's one way to put it," Marcelle said with a sigh. "I don't think anyone feels comfortable with Her Grace's decision to visit the Comte du Ciel, especially when she's traditionally been quite firm about not going there. Were you going to try to figure out why her mind changed?"

"There are a few things I wanted to discuss with Her Grace," Faron said before considering his words. Sabine never seemed bothered by the staff gossip, but this entire situation was far from normal, and he knew there was a chance anything he said here would get circled around. So, he decided to make his answer vague. "I've considered asking. However, I want to judge her mood first. It's possible some of the others might have approached her already. I don't want to put her in a foul mood on accident."

"Good point," Marcelle said with a nod. "Still, she likes you. She takes your counsel. She might listen to you, open up to you."

Faron wasn't sure if that still held true after last night, but he nodded all the same. "I'll see what I can do. I doubt she plans to marry him, but something else could have come up."

"That's all you can do," Marcelle said. The two men kept their pace down the corridor, Marcelle neither confirming any sort of watch nor providing an explanation of what he was doing. When they reached the corridor where Sabine's office resided, Marcelle spoke again. "I shall let you be on your way. I have much to do."

Faron gave Marcelle a small smile, more of a grimace, and bid him farewell before continuing to Sabine's office. He strengthened his resolved to talk to Sabine, if not about them, then about the visit to Tristian's. He knew Sabine may not be happy to talk to him about it, especially since he wasn't supposed to be there. However, if the rest of the staff was worried enough that Marcelle had sought him out, then he would have to press the issue, even if he asked her to talk to one of the others instead of himself. Arriving at the door of Sabine's office, he knocked and waited for an answer.

Movement from inside alerted Faron of her presence, though several long seconds passed before she replied. "Come in."

Faron didn't take a deep breath, nor did he steel himself. He just walked in, knowing if he thought too hard about it, he might change his mind. Sabine sat at her desk, head bowed over a leather-bound ledger, delicate fingers trailing slowly down the page.

When she looked up at him, beautiful as she ever was, she gave no sign of warmth or pleasure in seeing him, though she also offered no hostility. "Yes?"

Faron was suddenly very aware that he shouldn't have come. It had been made very clear Sabine didn't want to see him, and her cold reception made it clear he wasn't welcome. However, he was here now and retreat was not possible. "Your Grace, I came to speak to you about the letter I received today."

She nodded. "What questions did you have about your new assignment?"

"I was curious as to who my replacement is?" he asked.

"I have not decided yet, though some have suggested Marcelle."

Faron ignored how her words felt like a punch to the gut as the truth settled in fully. "Marcelle would make an excellent personal guard." His words came out more strained than he wished.

"I think so. He was under consideration last time. I have not made my final decision, though," she repeated. She did not look away or shun him, but a definite coolness remained in her address.

Faron nodded at her words. He hadn't realized how valued Marcelle was, but he could understand why given the man's skill and sharp mind. If he could somehow fix all the things he'd broken, Faron thought to make better use of Marcelle's skills in the future. Still, Sabine's indecision over the position gave him the courage to speak. "I would like to put in a formal request to stay as your personal guard."

"Why?"

Although her "why" didn't sound promising, it was better than an outright refusal. Faron could work with it. "I enjoy being your guard. It is fulfilling work, ensuring your safety and getting to spend time with you." Faron knew he shouldn't have said the last part, not when he wasn't sure if he was the reason she was planning to visit the comte. "I worry for your safety, and while I know I can do good as your guard captain, I would rather be your guard."

She didn't answer him at first, though she tilted her head in silent contemplation. "You are good in the role," she finally conceded. "But is remaining in the role the best decision?"

Faron wanted to say yes, but he knew he couldn't just shout out an answer. Sabine was asking for him to honestly consider her question, so he did. He thought about the days spent waiting outside her door, the walks they took together, the night when Avana first arrived, and all the other moments they'd shared. He avoided thinking about the sex or how much he wanted her even now and instead considered his time with her guards and the need she had there. In the end though, after moments of contemplation, the answer was still so simple. "Yes."

"Why?" she asked again.

Faron sighed. "Of all the duties in your chateau, ensuring your ability to carry on with your work unharmed should be everyone's priority. I cannot speak for everyone, but I can assure you it is mine. I do not overlook or disregard your desire to aid Fythias, and I hope you recognize my own desire to keep you safe while you carry out that most important task."

Thankfully, her eyes left her work and met his own, vividly green as always but filled with unspoken sadness. He stepped forward, finding himself kneeling by her chair. He'd have reached out and taken her hand in his, but somehow, he knew the gesture would be unwelcome. "Please, let me remain in my current position, Sabine. I could not stand any other."

She glanced down, breaking the eye contact they'd shared. Faron didn't know what thoughts swirled through her mind, and he didn't have a right to ask more of her than he already had. "Faron," she began, though both sharply turned their heads to her office door as Meri burst into the room, breathing hard and leaning on her cane.

Faron rose to his feet since whatever Meri had to say seemed urgent. She wouldn't have interrupted without invitation otherwise.

"Your Grace, we are getting reports of a merchant in town selling Merscales. He's brandishing a letter from the prince, claiming it says he can sell here."

Faron's face drained of color as Meri's words registered, and his head snapped to Sabine.

Sabine grew flushed as anger set into her expression. Her brows narrowed and she stood. "Faron, gather our best soldiers and meet me in the chateau entryway in ten minutes."

"Of course, Your Grace." He turned on his heels and ran to the barracks.

Chapter Four

Livid did not describe Sabine's mood as she, Faron, Marcelle, and a handful of her guards made their way down to the village. Granted, she had not been especially cheerful, but the audacity of selling the body parts of Merpeople on land she managed, land she cared for, made every personal woe less important.

The village appeared no different than usual. Merchants hosted booths, carts, and shop fronts for their wares, and they waved at the group as they proceeded to the market square. Faron walked just behind her, and she could feel the tension radiating from him.

"Once we confirm the presence of Merscales, the supplies will be confiscated," she said quietly. "What happens after will be determined by how the seller behaves."

A murmur of agreement sounded as Faron stepped up beside her. "Do you think the prince was stupid enough to grant a merchant permission to sell on your lands, or are they possibly lying?" Faron asked Sabine in a low voice.

"I don't know," Sabine replied. "And I'm not sure what the better explanation will be. If Prince Grégoire is truly involved, I might be prompted into starting a war." Though her clipped words could be taken as light frustration, Sabine was willing to take a hard stance against the atrocities against Merpeople entering Fythias. She'd provoke the wrath of every royal on the planet if it meant keeping her people safe.

"The cruelty associated with the Merscale trade is something worthy of going to war over," Faron said, his tone harder than Sabine had ever heard it.

"It is," she agreed. She looked up at Faron, seeing the hard set of his jaw, the severity of his feelings evident in every line. The urge to comfort him swelled, but there could be no comforting. Not now, anyway.

The offending booth came into view just past the center of the market square. Merscales twinkled in the bright sunlight without shame, a merchant smiling broadly and waving people over. The booth, decorated with bright banners made of fine materials, was poised to attract customers.

Sabine wanted to be sick over the display, but she took a breath, fortifying herself for the confrontation. "Ask for his license and authorization of goods," she told Faron.

Faron nodded and stepped forward, doing nothing to make himself less intimidating. The merchant—a larger man with slicked-back blond hair and peach fuzz craving to one day become a mustache—sneered at him as he approached. A stupid thing for him to do, clearly, when Faron towered over him by a good foot.

"I have already told the others," he waved a dismissive hand at the glaring merchants at their stalls, "I have permission to be here from the prince."

"And I am here on behalf of the Duchesse Vassetre to ask for your license and authorization of goods." Faron's tone was professional as he motioned back to where Sabine stood.

The sneer faded from the merchant's face, but his eyes took on a more calculated quality as he handed over the information requested. "Advise Her Grace that I also have correspondence between her prince and my lord if she needs them."

Faron just nodded and walked back to Sabine, holding out the license and authorization of goods.

She plucked the items from Faron and read through them. The first she tore up without much examination. "Your lord cannot grant you permissions on my land, regardless of any other circumstances, so you have no permission to sell anything based on the license you obtained elsewhere." Sabine did not bother to raise her voice. The second item she studied more thoughtfully. "This authorization of goods is not viable, even if we ignore the illegal contraband," she replied. "You have not obtained permission or membership from an appropriate guild."

The merchant turned a nasty shade of red as he stepped out from behind his stall. He moved as if he planned to get into Sabine's face, or worse, strike her, but he stopped when Faron and the others drew their weapons. "The soon-to-be king granted me permission to sell here without the need to go through something as antiquated as a guild." He sneered again before a smirk landed on his lips, as if he knew something Sabine didn't. "As to my goods being illegal, well, sweet girl, that is simply not the case. Merscale trade is legal in Fythias and has been for almost a fortnight now by order of your prince. I'm not sure how a…" He paused and examined Sabine from head to toe. "Noble of your standing wouldn't know this already."

She almost laughed at the fool. He thought he was out-smarting her, talking down to her. She simply lifted a brow. "I don't know why you smirk. The king cannot unilaterally change those laws without approval from Parliament, of which I am a member, and Prince Grégoire is certainly not king," Sabine replied icily. "So, no. Even if Prince Grégoire thinks he can permit you, he does not have the power, which means you are in possession of illegal goods, which I have half a mind to lock you up for."

The merchant's eyes narrowed. "I was told to watch out for you," he sneered, his voice lowering before he turned back to his stall. "It doesn't matter. I was told to start here and move to the comte's lands if there were issues. He is apparently sensible about the newest trends. I'll pack up and be on my way." He looked back over his shoulder and added, "Your Grace."

Faron moved to take a step forward.

"Confiscate his goods," Sabine redirected.

"With pleasure," Faron said and stepped forward as the merchant started sputtering.

"You can't do this!" he screamed and moved as if to approach Sabine, only to find Faron's sword at his neck.

"You will find she can and is," he growled, his head jerking to the stall. Marcelle and the others quickly moved forward, grabbing bags they found behind the stall as they loaded up the items.

Sabine watched in disinterested fury as the merchant complained and yelled, nothing deterring the soldiers from gathering items as had been directed. She had to say nothing to show her power, to demonstrate why she was better posi-tioned. The merchant and, no doubt, any he worked with held much different expectations for how this confronta-tion was meant to go.

"Once his stall is emptied, someone escort him from my lands. He is not to return. If he is found on my lands again, arrest him."

Faron nodded before roughly grabbing the merchant and shoving him to Marcelle. "You're in charge of this. If I have to do it—" Faron cut himself off, but all present understood Faron was beyond enraged at the moment. The merchant wouldn't make it to the border if Faron was in charge.

When the merchant's items were collected, Sabine looked over the remains. "The scales should be given to the Sirene," she said, pointing to two of her well-trusted guards. "Their ruler will see the items returned to the proper people. Stop by to see Glaucus if you need someone to act as a middleman."

The guards answered in the affirmative as Faron moved back to Sabine's side, his eyes not leaving the merchant as Marcelle and another guard drug the man, still screaming, away from them. "I hate this," he muttered.

"As do I," Sabine agreed. "This was bold."

"Very much so. I don't like any of it, especially the part where he's claiming the prince made the Merscale trade legal. If the prince is claiming such a thing..." He looked to Sabine in concern.

Sabine shook her head. "I will not let it come here," she promised softly.

"I know you won't," Faron said with conviction.

She wanted to hug him, to reassure Faron she would never allow Fythias to become a new Coralia, but she could not offer him the comfort. Not when he'd made his thoughts concerning her so clear. "I am going back to the chateau. Someone should check around the market. Make sure everything is still fine."

Faron looked down at Sabine, his eyes full of something unidentifiable. "May I walk you back?" Relief spread across his face after she nodded. "Thank you," he said earnestly then offered Sabine his arm.

She took it despite thinking she should not. The new line between them dictated more distance, but Sabine thought it made more sense to allow for the visual protection of her guard in the public settling.

Chapter
Five

As they walked back to the chateau, the silence between Sabine and Faron was not as strained as it could have been. Sabine thought it might have to do with Faron being on alert, glancing around, his other hand on his sword. She noted he didn't relax until the doors of the chateau closed behind them, and even then, the tension in his shoulders and face lingered. She did not relinquish her hold on him until they were safely inside her office, the safest location for her within the chateau. "I think I shall be fine now."

Faron nodded, his mouth still set in a firm line. Sabine watched as he closed his eyes and let out a deep breath, before between one breath and another, she found herself pressed against the wall, Faron's body against hers as he kissed her. "You were breathtaking," he said between kisses. "Utterly brilliant in how you handled that." He kissed her again. "No one in Coralia or Fythias could stand against you."

Despite the foolishness, she kissed him back, her hands pulling him closer. She was hurt by his words the prior night, certainly, but right now, she wanted him, the comfort he gave her. One of Faron's hands moved to the nape of her neck, cradling Sabine's head, while the other moved from her hip to her ass. He lifted Sabine so she could feel him against her center, and her legs went around him, securing her in place.

"You're stunning," he said as his lips moved from hers to below her ear.

"Show how much you think so," she replied.

Faron nodded against her skin, kissing and nipping down her neck. "Hands or mouth?" he asked.

"Cock," she replied, already breathless with need.

He growled in response then bit her on the shoulder, sucking the skin in a bruising manner before lifting his head enough to speak. "Are you ready for me?" he asked, his hot breath making her skin pulse with need. He moved the hand behind her head to under her skirts, letting it travel along her leg.

"Spirits, yes," she said as his nails gently grazed her thigh.

A couple of Faron's fingers ran along her center and slipped inside of her, pumping in and out several times. "Yes, you are," he said in a rough voice. He withdrew his fingers, and after freeing his straining cock, Sabine felt him press into her. An arm went around his neck as she inhaled. No matter how many times he'd filled her, every new encounter felt perfect.

Faron slowly entered Sabine until their hips connected, then he stilled, resting his head on her shoulder. "You're amazing. Everything about you is incredible."

She didn't believe him. Not after last night. He'd made his feelings clear, but right now, she wanted to ignore the truth and her broken heart and just focus on the two of them. She received no warning before Faron began thrusting, the pace he set hard and deep, making her cry out in sheer pleasure.

Her grip on Faron tightened, keeping her upright as she met each deep move of his hips. Faron shifted slightly, lifting her a little higher, while having her fall forward more fully against him. The subtle adjustments changed the angle of his thrusts to hit that one perfect spot, picking up his pace even more.

Sabine's whole body pulsed with great shocks of visceral pleasure, and her fingers tangled in his long wavy black hair. "Harder," she nearly begged.

"Whatever you want," he murmured against her skin.

His pace grew near brutal as he bit down on her shoulder again, bringing his name to her lips. Sabine couldn't get enough of the elf, and she wanted his hands and mouth all over her, even as she drew closer and closer to falling apart.

"Sabine," Faron moaned before kissing her hard, leaving her breathless as she finally fell over that pleasurable peak. Her limbs still trembled with aftershocks as Faron's thrusts grew erratic, before he gave into his own pleasure.

Without separating from her, Faron carried Sabine across the room and settled into her large desk chair, Sabine straddling him. She could feel him growing hard again, his elven blood enabling him to reengage much more quickly.

"I wish to have you again. Please. Right here, in your chair," he asked.

She looked down at him, their positions changing her usual perspective. She took in his dark brown eyes glazed with lust, the shadow of beard growth, the pout of his lips. She loved every inch of him, and again, she debated ending this, knowing indulging in more of him would only cause more pain. Instead, she cupped his jaw, letting her thumb smooth along his cheek. "Have me."

Faron's hands drifted to her hips, grasping them as he gently thrust up into her. Sabine gasped, still a little sensitive from the last round, even if she relished the feel of his thick erection buried in her, responding to her with rapt attention.

Faron's hips continued thrusting in a slow, lazy rhythm, his eyes on her face watching her every reaction, drinking her in. She rose and fell to meet each movement, the pace slow, deliberate, and thorough. The hand on Faron's cheek slid down to the side of his neck and then to his shoulder. Faron sighed into her touch, and she wasn't sure what he was enjoying more: being inside of her or her caresses. Either way, she leaned in to kiss him again, hungry for him, for everything he represented and she could not have. Sabine groaned against his mouth as one of Faron's hands clenched a handful of her hair, pulling her deeper into the kiss.

Even when the kissing ended, Sabine stayed close, her forehead pressed against Faron's as she chased her climax. Faron's movements became more erratic, though she felt his tense fight to keep his pace as slow as possible. He was close, as was she, and Sabine sucked in a breath as she made a last valiant effort to push them both over the edge. Faron held her close as they both fell apart, Sabine desperately preventing herself from collapsing on top of him.

As their bodies quieted, Faron's arms draped around her, pulling her gently against his chest. Sabine allowed it, knowing she would never again find herself in the same position. She took in the scent of him, the feel of his warmth, the way his heart beat a little faster from their recent activities.

Faron laid a kiss upon Sabine's head and adjusted his hips so his softening member slipped from her. "I don't think you want a third round," he said softly.

"No," Sabine agreed. She carefully sat up, though she did not leave his lap just yet. She didn't want to, even though she needed to. "I don't think this can happen again."

Faron looked down, and for a moment, Sabine thought he looked regretful. There was also something else in his expression she couldn't name. "Alright. If that's what you want, I won't fight you. But know I'm here for you in all ways. Not just like this."

It wasn't what Sabine wanted. Didn't he understand? She'd never wanted anything less, but he'd been the one to draw lines the night before, and Sabine couldn't allow herself to go further down this path knowing she would never really have what she wanted. "I know," she replied softly.

Faron brought a hand up to caress her cheek just once. "I still want to be your personal guard. I can, and will, keep my hands to myself, but I need to be able to protect you, to keep people like that merchant from carrying out their sick fantasies."

Sabine believed him, despite how he stated he felt, so she nodded. "If that's what you want," she agreed, her voice quiet.

Faron opened his mouth to respond, but instead, he just held Sabine close to his body. She allowed him to hold her there for several long minutes, her eyes closed to ward off tears she knew wanted to spill. Eventually, though, she sat up, pulling herself from his arms before rising from his lap.

Faron removed a handkerchief from a pocket, cleaned himself off and tucked himself away, stowing the handkerchief out of sight. "Do you need assistance cleaning up?" he asked her.

"No. I'm going to bathe then spend my afternoon planning the visit to Tristian's estate. I think the encounter in the village more than demonstrates urgency to go."

Faron nodded in understanding. "Thank you for dealing with the merchant as swiftly and decisively as you did. There is no question about what you will and will not allow here. I think the villagers are thankful."

"I told you: I won't allow the sale of Merscales in Fythias. There are so many who are relying on those of us with money and power for protection. I'm simply doing my part."

"Still, it needs to be said. So again, thank you."

She nodded in acknowledgment, though Sabine felt she'd always maintain her stance.

Faron stood. "I will let you get cleaned up." He stepped up to Sabine as if to kiss her before pulling back. "I will come back and stand guard when you're ready."

She nodded, and since she thought she might do something very foolish if she remained huddled up in the office with Faron, Sabine turned from him and walked out, heading in the direction of her suite.

Chapter Six

Faron sat on the stone bench overlooking Lisbeth's gardens. It was a beautiful garden, useful with its vegetables and bountiful fruit trees but also pretty with ornamental plants, single bloom roses, and others he couldn't identify.

He knew he should be packing to leave. Sabine had let him keep his job, so he assumed he would be accompanying her to the comte's place of residence. He just didn't feel up to packing, and the calmness of the gardens helped settle his thoughts.

His stolen moment with Sabine in her office had been… Well, there was really no word for how it had felt, or not a word he was willing to use, at least. Even now, with an hour since he'd left her, all Faron could think about were her vivid eyes staring into his soul, the way her hands caressed his face and neck, the way she'd kissed him as though her very ability to breath relied solely on his focus. He felt the same way about her.

Their time together—bittersweet and perfect—left Faron with the knowledge of how hurt she'd been the night before.

The look in her eyes, the way she had said they couldn't be together again, left him feeling empty but resolute. He didn't believe Sabine could love him, even knowing she did have feelings for him. Whatever their feelings were, they weren't love, and he wouldn't let it get to that point.

Faron remembered his time with Phindel in the village, watching the way he consistently looked around for his now deceased wife, how he repeatedly turned as if to tell her something before a deep well of sadness formed in his eyes when he realized, once more, she was gone. The long, silent sadness helped to drive home for Faron that he could not be with Sabine. No, she needed to find a nice human noble, one with similar values, and live a good long life surrounded by her husband and children. The knowledge that those children wouldn't be his, that he wouldn't get to grow old with her, was like a stab in the gut, but he knew he was making the right choice for both of them.

Faron sighed, burying his hands in his hair as he looked down at the damp grass under his feet, only to give a start a second later as Lisbeth sat down next to him. He'd been so focused on his thoughts he had missed hearing her footsteps.

"What are you out here moping about?" she asked, giving him a small, concerned smile. Her shoulder-length curly ginger hair appeared messier than normal, and her freckles stood out against her bronze skin in the sunlight. A dirty smudge on her chin let Faron know Lisbeth had been working on another part of the garden before spotting him.

"I'm not moping. I'm just thinking," he replied.

"No, you're definitely moping," said another voice from the ground on his left.

Faron's head whipped around to see violet eyes peering up at him from a heart shaped face. Ash blonde hair cascaded down Avana's back as she lay stomach down on the grass. Faron had often wondered why her former master had allowed Avana to keep her hair so long, but he thought better than to ask outright.

"How long have you been there?" he asked Avana.

"Oh, about five minutes before Lisbeth showed up. I wasn't even being particularly quiet when I got here." She looked back down at the pile of daisies in front of her. "I was going to make a flower crown and see if you'd notice if I slipped in on your head, but now I'll make one for Lisbeth."

"Thank you, Avana," Lisbeth said.

Faron rolled his eyes. He wanted to be upset he hadn't noticed her, but it wasn't worth worrying over for now. "I would have noticed," he told the other elf.

"No, you were too busy sulking. You wouldn't have," Avana replied as she started weaving the stems together.

"I wasn't—" Faron cut himself off with a sigh. "Is there a reason the two of you are out here?"

"I was tending one of the other gardens. Her Grace has six different garden areas if you haven't forgotten. While this one is my personal garden, I am in charge of the others as well when not helping Her Grace," Lisbeth said.

"I'm allowed outside," Avana added, as if that was reason enough.

"So, what are you moping about?" Lisbeth asked again.

Faron knew he had to tell her something, or he'd never be left alone. He also knew he could talk to her about Sabine, but it seemed a complicated feat. There were his feelings for the duchesse—not love—and his concerns he'd ruined everything, including their friendship. He hadn't been able to keep his hands off of her since he'd met her. The differences in their lifespans never left his thoughts, nor did the notion of how she couldn't marry a commoner such as himself. He chose to address none of it. Lisbeth believed in love conquering all, and she would encourage him to pursue Sabine, something he could not do. "I'm concerned about the trip to the comte's estate."

Lisbeth reached out and laid her smaller hand on his. "We all are, but it's going to be okay. I'm going, as is Finn, and Meri has already decided she's going and nothing will stop her." Lisbeth laughed. They both knew after the night where Faron and Meri had almost gotten fired, that if Sabine said no, Meri wouldn't put up too much of a fight.

"I'm going too, but I don't know if Marcelle is," Avana said with a slight pout.

Faron opened his mouth to question her discontent, but Lisbeth squeezed his hand, shaking her head slightly, so he let it drop.

"I believe Sabine has decided on going so she can gather information. After what happened in the village earlier, I know this is for the best. I worry the comte will see it as Sabine having an interest in marriage," Faron admitted.

Lisbeth bowed her head at the mention of the Merscale merchant. "Spirits. I can't believe one of those monsters was here in our village. How can the prince think it's acceptable to sell Merscales?" Lisbeth asked. Her cheeks, flushed with rage, and furrowed brow spoke of Lisbeth's anger. Lisbeth wasn't really looking for an answer, though, and Faron didn't provide one.

"Everyone has been talking about what happened in the village, but I don't get why everyone's upset. Wasn't he just selling jewelry?" Avana asked, her violet eyes wide.

If it wasn't for the confusion coloring her face, Faron may have snapped at her. The Merscale trade had always been cruel and unethical, and the changes in the system which encouraged the capture and maiming of Mers only made it more so. Still, as sheltered as Avana had been, Faron somehow doubted she understood what was involved.

So, he answered her question while reminding himself to maintain patience. "Some Coralians believe it's acceptable to maim Nereids. Nereids are a type of Merperson who have thick, hardened scales which are as beautiful as precious stones. Some humans like to capture them, rip the scales from their bodies, and use them to make jewelry and other items. It's horrifically painful for the Merperson, and most don't survive the process. Those who do usually don't last more than a few days afterwards," Faron explained, watching as Avana's eyes grew round as horror crept onto her face.

"That's… That's terrible. No wonder everyone's upset." Avana looked back down at the flowers in her hands. "I'm upset now too."

"Well, I didn't mean to upset you, but you did ask," Faron pointed out, giving Lisbeth a look when she smacked his arm.

"The trade used to be less violent," Lisbeth added. "Mers who grew the desired type of scale would trade scales they'd shed for goods and money."

"It was still a dirty business," Faron said. "Look where it led."

"I know," Lisbeth replied. "King Sargarus from Coralia is the first person who openly encouraged mass abduction and violence, though it surely happened on a smaller scale. The economy slowly grew dependent on the trade within a handful of years." Lisbeth sighed and brushed dirt from her hand.

"A pitiful excuse if ever there was one," Faron grumbled. He nodded to Avana. "Do you still question the problem of the Merscale trade?" he asked, scowling as Lisbeth smacked his arm once again.

"Faron, you should show more patience when she asks questions. Avana didn't know what the trade entailed," Lisbeth insisted.

"No, he's right. I did ask. I will not be asking questions in the future, though," Avana declared, shaking her head.

Lisbeth sighed in defeat and nodded. "I suppose we must wonder what the comte knew of the merchant. I assume he would be made aware since the Merchant talked about going to his village?"

"I think it likely he knew before the merchant had a chance to set up his booth," Faron said. He frowned at the memory of the encounter and the way the man strove to physically intimidate Sabine. She'd looked on, unimpressed with the efforts, but the threat of someone of no consequence toward the most powerful non-royal in the country left Faron with an unease separate from the more immediate physical threat.

"Did Her Grace know about the merchant beforehand?" Avana asked. "Or, at least, had she heard rumors?"

Lisbeth shook her head. "If she'd known someone was in the village with illegal contraband, she'd have been down there much earlier." She touched a finger to a nearby clover, which not only grew larger and greener but multiplied across the ground surrounding her and Avana. The young half-elf grinned and began adding clover to her flower crown.

"The Merscales and the claims made by the merchant will undoubtedly become part of the discussions she intends to have with the comte," Faron added. "Though he probably thinks she's sprinting into his arms because she wants to accept his proposal."

"If the comte thinks Her Grace is stupid enough to marry him, well, that's his own fault," Lisbeth said with a roll of her eyes.

"It is. However, I've wondered about something." Faron emotionally braced himself for what he was going to say next. "Out of Sabine's suitors, were there any she was even remotely interested in?"

Lisbeth shot him a suspicious look. "I can think of three off the top of my head, but one was already in a committed relationship."

Faron nodded. "Well, if the other two aren't, maybe Sabine can convince Tristian she's thinking of taking one of the other two up on their offer should he try to push her into marriage. Maybe he'll even invite them over while we're visiting. It may get Tristian to back off." And if it put Sabine in proximity of someone in her own social standing, someone whose lifespan matched hers... Well, the thought hurt, but having her with them was better than Sabine being tied to Tristian.

He glanced at Lisbeth and saw her lips were pressed tightly together. Her green eyes narrowed as she nodded. "I'll talk to Finn about it, and we'll take your idea to Sabine if he thinks there is good reason." Lisbeth pressed her lips together tightly once more before adding, "If she doesn't like the idea, then we'll explore other options."

Lisbeth stood up from the ground, brushing her backside free of dirt and grass, though Faron guessed she would change once back inside the chateau, especially if she would be tending to Sabine once more. "We could always tell the comte she's with you if he starts pushing matrimony, though I hear we've made it clear you're not." The look she gave Faron stopped his protest dead. "We'll talk more about that later. I'll go find Finn now. Enjoy Avana's flower crown," she said cheerfully as she strode off, leaving Faron upset and confused, until he felt said flower crown drop onto his head.

"Now you're the prettiest idiot in the kingdom," Avana said flatly.

Faron thought he might deserve that.

Prince Louis,

Forgive the hastiness in which I write. A merchant sent by your brother arrived in the village by my estate, selling Merscales. He came armed with documentation showing Grégoire's approval, and he openly tried to challenge me before I had the contraband confiscated. I also had him escorted from the village.

Your brother is escalating, threatening our people with the horrors plaguing Coralia and Azmarin. We cannot allow it to come to Fythias. Even with my considerable power and wealth, I cannot keep it at bay for long.

Yours,
Sabine, Duchesse Vassetre

Chapter
Seven

Plans to visit Comte Tristian solidified in the following days, with Tristian sending numerous letters detailing his excitement over the visit. Sabine wondered if he thought she'd relented and would either agree to accompany him to Coralia or, if not, marry him. Neither thing would happen, and Sabine didn't intend to be forced into such an agreement. She couldn't be, not with the number of guards she intended to bring with her.

While her staff worked to finish the last-minute details associated with packing so they could leave first thing in the morning, Sabine had ventured out to the beach with Thaumas, who she hadn't been able to spend much time with in the past few weeks. Of course, ever since his marriage and the birth of his child, he'd had less time for her in general, a practical fact of life.

The Sirene looked a bit grimmer than usual, though Sabine wasn't surprised. The presence of a Merscale trader in the village had many worried, although the correspondence she'd received since the event had applauded her for decisive action. Still, she knew the act had signified an undeniable truth. Fythias was in danger, and there were only a few people who might be able to do something about it.

"I can't say I'm glad you're going to Tristian's," Thaumas said as they walked along the shore, briny water brushing along their feet as waves rolled in. "But I know why you're going. Fythias doesn't need the taint of Merpeople massacres."

"I was going before the Merscale trader showed up," Sabine reminded him as she watched a tiny crab pop out from under waterworn pebbles and wade farther into the water. "I don't downplay how terrible he was, but there have been signs for months. I knew, once I was told to go to Coralia, we needed to act. Acting means getting whatever information I can. Visiting him is the best thing I can do."

"Just make sure you bring your giant guard with you," Thaumas said firmly. "I know Marcelle and some of the guards are staying behind, which makes sense, but I don't trust Tristian to keep his hands to himself around you."

Usually, Thaumas would follow up such sentiments with a witty quip or joke, but none came now. Given the growing dangers, Sabine understood. She wished she could promise to fix everything, but even though she had every intention of doing what she could to resolve the very real threats posed by Grégoire and Coralia, she could make few promises and even fewer which did not involve bloodshed.

"I'm bringing Faron," Sabine assured Thaumas. "There's no denying his skill and dedication when it comes to his job. I doubt anyone would be able to do so much as look at me without incurring his wrath." Being around him still hurt far more than she wanted to admit, but he would reliably protect her.

"Good," Thaumas said, and he put an arm around her shoulders. Though Thaumas's lean frame put no additional weight against Sabine, their height differences forced both to adopt a less natural gait. "You're making faces I don't like to see on you, Bine."

"I'm fine," Sabine assured him.

"You aren't," Thaumas countered, tugging her a little closer. "Talk to me. Tell me, what did the elf do to you?"

Sabine thought about dismissing the worry, but honestly, on top of everything else she was dealing with, she didn't want to. Not with Thaumas, who she knew would repeat nothing she shared. "He said he didn't love me," Sabine shared. "Which is unfortunate, given how I'm certain I love him."

Thaumas cursed, something he usually avoided. He cleared his throat before offering her support. "The elf is a fool and unworthy of your affections. I know my words don't mean much now, given how things changed so quickly between us, but you need and deserve more than someone who had the choice I did not that can so easily dismiss you. I know you know that."

"I do," Sabine confirmed with a nod. She lifted the hem of her skirt as another wave rolled in, covering part of her shins in icy salt water. "But still, I cannot deny how he made me feel, even if I made him feel something much shallower in return."

Thaumas brought them to a stop, and he pulled Sabine around to face him. As always, at least since he'd married, his touches were respectful, even though his fingers brushed against her cheek. "You do not inspire anything remotely shallow in anyone you come across. That's why you have so many who love you, who would do anything for you, and others who fear you. Whatever stupid notion Faron has regarding you speaks to flaws in his character, not any deficit in you. I will not hear otherwise."

Sabine appreciated the thoughtfulness, the care her former lover showed her after years apart. He was more of a peer than anyone in the chateau, even though Lisbeth, who suspected what Faron had done, had been willing to keep her company and keep her spirits up. Having someone to vent to, even for a minute, felt good. "I think you're right, even if I hate the way I feel now." The waves rose again, and Sabine forgot to lift her skirt. Both she and Thaumas ended up wet up to their shins. Sabine didn't care. Wet skirts were hardly concerning given the possible horrors awaiting them all.

"You could lure him out here, and I'll drown him," Thaumas offered as he let his hand drop from her face. He took her hand in his, and they began walking again.

"You'll give into the stereotypes?" she asked with a playful grin.

"Only for you, Bine. Only for you." He gave her a sly smile. "Might need to recruit a couple of others to help, though. He's a tall one."

"Whatever you do, don't tell me who and when. I want to be able to deny knowledge of your deviousness."

"And here I was, counting on you to tell everyone I was with you when the drowning happened," Thaumas replied.

Sabine laughed, feeling temporarily better. Nothing but time would heal her broken heart, and honestly, she knew she had no business worrying over Faron when she would depart for Tristian's home in the morning.

"Do you need to head back?" Thaumas asked after they'd walked for a while longer. "I don't wish to rid myself of your company, but I know you have a journey ahead of you."

Sabine knew his words did not indicate a rush to end their time together or a push to make any particular decision. Thaumas had always been aware of how her time was divided amongst her responsibilities, and he always checked to make sure he wasn't taking up too much for himself. Knowing she wished to stay behind, Sabine nodded. "I probably should, but I'm not ready yet. Let's keep walking."

"Absolutely, Bine."

Chapter Eight

The imposing figure of the Villa du Ciel greeted the Vassetre party long before they arrived in the village. Unlike the peaceful coastal views of the Vassetre Chateau, the gray stony facade of Tristain's estate sat with its back to the northern mountain range, leaving Sabine feeling caged in. Two rows of round towers, connected by curtain walls and battlements, framed the estate, creating a rectangular exterior. The keep, a large building rising above the corner towers, stood in the middle of the grounds, protected by a drawbridge and a second interior wall.

As her carriage drew to a stop, Sabine heard her accompanying staff moving quickly to dismount from the front. Her carriage door opened, and a footman extended a hand to help Sabine down. The ground just inside the drawbridge—a combination of dust, mud, and straw—had Sabine carefully holding up her skirt so the hem did not become dirty.

Glancing up, Sabine saw that the front two towers served as watchtowers where soldiers stood ready, though she was left less than impressed with the youth of the individuals she saw.

Lisbeth stepped up next to Sabine, her ginger hair brighter than normal with the angle of the sun. "Why does this place look more like a prison than a chateau?" she asked quietly as Avana came to stand beside her. Without hesitation, Lisbeth put an arm around Avana.

The young half-elf's lips pursed as she glanced around. "It definitely feels like a prison," she murmured.

"I imagine the Comte du Ciel runs it as such," Sabine replied just as quietly.

Finn joined them from a second carriage, and he also took a moment to look around the courtyard. "Did we bring enough of our people?" he asked.

"I think so," Sabine said. "Pay attention to Tristian's numbers. If you or Faron determine we don't have sufficient numbers, we'll send a couple of people back home so they can send more support."

"I think we should be okay. The man's dull not stupid," Meri said as she joined the group. She was dressed in a guard uniform, her walk smoother than normal, but Sabine knew her cane was packed in one of her bags. Meri had refused to be left behind, stating while Faron and Avana were more capable, she had more experience if something went truly wrong.

"I don't think he's as dull as he puts on," Avana said. "If he were, the prince wouldn't want anything to do with him."

Sabine nodded. "He's far too invested in my actions, and he's been of enough help to Grégoire to be included in whatever plotting they've been doing."

"True," Meri replied as her eyes narrowed.

"Hello!" a voice called out, and Tristain was seen walking at a brisk pace through the gate leading into the keep.

He looked happy to see Sabine, his boyish grin and bright red cheeks reminding Sabine of a child. She half expected him to hop up and down while clapping his hands in delight, but as Faron stepped up behind the group, she saw Tristain's gaze narrow in apparent displeasure.

"Good afternoon, Comte Tristian," Sabine greeted as though she did not notice. She gave a brief nod of respect, though her higher ranking did not require her to provide her host with the acknowledgment. She thought he would appreciate the compliment and thus be more compliant. "Your home is beautiful. I do not believe I've been here since I was a young girl."

Tristian held out his hand for Sabine to take, bowing enough to lay a rather wet kiss on her pale hand before releasing her. "You do flatter me, Your Grace. My home is much as it always has been, but I am delighted you remember your long ago visit. I do have my own vague memories of you being here once. I think you were seven, which would have made me ten." He gave her a would-be charming smile, but it was honestly too wide and showed too much gum, while his eyes held none of the warmth one would associate with such a gesture.

"I think you are right. Our parents went on a hunting trip," Sabine added, withdrawing her hand as soon as it was acceptable to do so. "Then I believe they cohosted a ball."

"Yes. That sounds correct," Tristian agreed after a moment's thought. "Our families received quite a few compliments. It's a shame they never shared another." He smiled blandly and looked around, his eyes widening as though he just realized she'd traveled with her own entourage. "I'll send my people to help yours unpack." He offered Sabine his arm to escort her inside. "My people will show yours to their quarters in the servants' hall, and I'll show you around if that sounds appealing?"

"Oh, I would love a tour," Sabine said as she took the offered arm. "Finn, will you oversee the unpacking, please?" she asked.

"Certainly, Your Grace," he replied, bowing.

"And Lisbeth, would you mind being my escort while Comte Tristian shows me around? I would hate for terrible rumors to befall us."

"Of course, Your Grace," Lisbeth said and moved closer to Sabine. "I'll be just a step behind you." Her voice was cheerful, though her eyes were guarded.

She smiled up at Tristian. "I would protect your honorable reputation as much as my own."

"How thoughtful," Tristian replied with barely concealed disappointment. Sabine had no intention of being alone with the comte if she could help it.

As the trio began walking, Sabine saw Meri snag Faron's sleeve as he moved to follow them. It was for the best, as she knew Tristian did not care for Faron.

Tristian glanced back, and Sabine swore the smile on his face was sharper than before, if only for a moment. "Would you like to start with the gardens or the chateau itself?"

"Oh, I would hope you'd show me whatever you deem most impressive," Sabine replied.

"Let us start with the garden, then. I know you have a woman on staff with magic who tends to yours, so I doubt the gardens here, tended by regular people, will measure up. One can hope though." Tristian gave her an insipid smile.

Sabine did not look at Lisbeth or do anything that might confirm her identity. Surely, some of Tristian's people could point her out given their willingness to attack Lisbeth during the comte's last visit, but Sabine didn't want to make it easy for him. "I am certain your gardens are beautiful."

Tristian's smile grew a bit warmer as he walked her down the cobblestone path, pointing out different flowers or bushes he was proud of, such as the water lilies floating in a manmade pond, lilacs and lavender and rose bushes of a variety of colors. All of them in neat, tidy rows along the path, with large grassy areas for people to have a picnic on or benches for lounging.

"I admit, I don't spend a lot of time outdoors, but my visitors enjoy the gardens. Prince Grégoire particularly enjoys the hedge maze." Tristian pointed in a vague direction, and Sabine could just make out what she presumed to be the maze.

"And what does His Highness enjoy about the hedge maze?" Sabine asked.

Tristian gave a small shrug. "He likes to go for walks, for whatever reason. Sometimes he says he uses it to think through difficult problems facing the kingdom. I think he just enjoys the outdoors. You know what the prince is like."

Sabine nodded, her eyes turned toward a lovely flowered tree, though the plumage was the last thing on her mind. She wondered just how frequently Grégoire visited and if his visits ever brought him closer to her estate. "I am glad he has a friend in you. No matter the differences he and I might have over certain topics, I can imagine being prince is a lonely position."

"He visits often enough, either with me or a few of the other lower nobles, though I doubt he stays lonely for long. He does often complain about how lonely his large estate is with his wife now passed on, Mother keep her soul. It's too bad she took the baby with her when she passed. An heir will be needed when he takes the throne, lest it go to his younger brother's whelp." Tristian shook his head as though he found the very thought disgusting. "Who knows what they're going to fill the infant's head with as he grows."

Tristian pulled out a handkerchief and wiped his forehead, which had grown damp with sweat. He'd been truthful when he said he didn't spend much time outside. She observed the comte and couldn't help but compare his softer midsection and weak shoulders to Faron's broad and rather muscular frame.

"They'll probably fill the boy's head with this Spirit of the Forest nonsense instead of worshiping the Mother as he should. Honestly, what has gotten into people? To worship a forest spirit instead of the woman who sacrificed herself for all of humanity? It's horrendous." He looked at Sabine as if expecting her to agree with him.

"I thought only Coralians had such an interpretation of the Mother," Sabine replied, then she lifted her shoulders in a delicate shrug. "Not that it matters. It behooves all members of the royal family to learn about the different spiritual beliefs of their kingdom, no matter what they personally believe. I know it helps me in my position."

He patted her hand in a way that reminded Sabine of an amused parent trying to avoid laughing in the face of their child. "Our prince has friends and acquaintances in Coralia, as I'm sure you know. They've discussed spiritual ideology and other topics, as one does with friends. Prince Grégoire then brings those ideas here. We banter back and forth over drinks about it all. I've even been gifted with the chance to read some of the prince's correspondence where they discuss and argue the theology."

Tristian chuckled and shook his head, leaving Sabine feeling as though he expected her to be impressed by his friendship with Grégoire. Somehow, she doubted the prince felt any affection toward Tristian, but she couldn't deny the comte might be useful. "And what sort of arguments have you been privileged to read?"

"Oh!" Tristian replied, delighted. "The interpretation of the Mother as a bringer of peace seems central to all, but how that peace arises is where we diverge. You see, the Mother meant for humans to serve as the leaders of people, with elves, Merpeople, dwarves, and others falling in line in the hierarchy beneath them. In truth, as soon as I became aware of the arguments, I began to accept them as true. I've been slowly implementing changes to our spiritual centers in my village by introducing the texts with the correct interpretations from Coralia. I suspect, once he is officially crowned, Grégoire will begin making widespread changes. But enough about that. Politics of such nature must bore you to tears. Why don't you tell me how things have been on your estate since that messy business the last time I was there?"

Frequent visits and systematic changes through bastardized religion would, Sabine thought, be an effective way to implement change, and after the Merscale merchant's appearance in her village, she knew more instances would arise. She'd have much to do once she was home.

Ignoring his sexist digs, she pasted a smile on her face. "Thankfully, my grounds have been restored to their original state since our unfortunate last visit."

"I'm glad to hear it, and I hope it brings you more peace to know I disposed of the men that caused you distress. I won't go into the details. I wouldn't want them to frighten you, but those men will never bother another."

Again, Sabine made a point of not looking at Lisbeth, though she was certain the older woman heard every word. "Let us not discuss such things, as you suggest."

"I apologize. I forgot how delicate women can be with such matters." He gave her a dismissive smile and continued their walk.

Tristian pointed out a few fountains and some fruit trees showing the promise of a late-season harvest before steering them back toward the chateau. They hadn't even seen close to half the garden, but Tristian's red face and sweaty brow confirmed he was more than ready to be done with the tour. "Let me show you the interior of my estate, then I'll escort you to your rooms. You must need a rest after traveling here."

"Would you mind terribly if I were to retreat for some rest now and you show me around your estate later?" Sabine asked. She saw the out, and she would grab for it. "Less than a day's journey between our homes, and I feel as though I spent days on the road."

Tristian gave her a sympathetic look. "Of course! How remiss of me. I'll escort you to your rooms now."

Servants opened the large ornate doors to the comte's home, and Tristian guided her toward the west end. The interior of the manor went largely unnoticed, as Sabine saw nothing but endless dull browns and creams occasionally interrupted by a portrait filled with people who looked like Tristian.

Eventually, they arrived outside of the suite designated for Sabine. "I thank you for your hospitality and the tour of your gardens. I am certain my visit will be a lovely, comfortable one."

"I will ensure it," Tristian promised her. Before releasing her arm, he grabbed her hand and laid another kiss on her knuckles. "Rest well, Sabine."

She smiled and nodded then waited for him to retreat before she and Lisbeth stepped into the suite.

Only when the door was shut and they'd retreated into the room did she turn her astute gaze to the redhead. "I am appalled but completely unsurprised."

Lisbeth's eyes were wider than normal as she stared at Sabine. "I'm not sure he said a single thing without an insult of some kind, and he... He killed those soldiers! They were awful but to have them killed?"

"I know," Sabine said with a sigh. She looked around, taking in the frilliness of the room as though the mounds of bows and lace just popped into existence before her, her nose wrinkled in distaste. After locating a chair, she sank into it, finding the thing far too plush. "If I had to guess, those men were killed so he could demonstrate taking decisive action for their crimes against you and my estate. Death was unwarranted, though. We both know as much."

"Oh, I doubt I was even a passing thought when he ordered those men to be killed. He thought you'd be impressed if the way he's spoken to you this last half an hour means anything." Lisbeth took her own look around the room. "This room is disgusting. It's so pink and frilly, and why are there so many roses? This man knows nothing about women, let alone you. Thank the Spirits you aren't considering marriage to this man."

"I think marriage would be rather foolish, and not just because I'm certain his mother slept here before she passed," Sabine replied. She wanted to laugh at herself for the letter she wrote soon after Faron had broken her heart. Thank the Spirits she'd burned the thing.

"Have you noticed how bare the manor is? The only real decor I saw on our way to this wing were portraits, and even those were sparse." Sabine motioned around the room. "The finery here is more than a few generations old, but it's also not nearly as valuable as one would expect in an old noble state. Do you think he has a money problem?" Poor financial status might very well influence Tristian's stark support of Grégoire.

"It's possible, but Meri might know more. She was here a few times with your parents when they were forced to visit, judging by her grousing." Lisbeth looked around once more, her nose twitching, before heading to the wardrobe. Throwing it open, Lisbeth quickly stepped back in disgust as a cloud of dust came to greet her. "Spirits, he didn't even have the wardrobe emptied or cleaned before your arrival."

"Are you surprised?" Sabine asked, getting up to help dust off Lisbeth.

"Not really, but still. Does he expect you to wear these?" Lisbeth motioned toward the wardrobe which held dresses at least ten years out of fashion and likely meant for the deceased dowager comtesse.

"I highly doubt it," Sabine replied as she picked a dust ball from Lisbeth's hair. "No one just has clothes waiting around for a guest to pluck them out and show off."

"So, he just doesn't care to make sure his possible future wife has clean and decent accommodations." Lisbeth's face turned malicious. "Do you think there are merchants in the village who wouldn't mind taking these off our hands?"

Sabine raised an eyebrow in surprise. Surely, Lisbeth was joking. "I'm sure there are, but I wouldn't try to rid the estate of them. We don't want any accusations of my people behaving poorly, after all."

"Damn," Lisbeth said under her breath but nodded all the same. "May I at least shove them under the bed so I can make room for your clothes? I'll put them back before we go."

"If you would like," Sabine agreed. "Honestly, I'm tempted to tell you to shut those doors and my things will just remain packed."

"I would object, as your dresses will get wrinkled, but honestly, it's just the comte."

"Exactly, and we can do what we can to resolve anything too untidy looking."

"We can work around that with some help from Meri," Lisbeth said thoughtfully. "What's your plan from here?"

"I need to gather as much information as I can, both about what Tristian knows, or suspects, and how he plans to act. From there, I think Prince Louis needs to be consulted. I genuinely suspect a battle before long, and we need to know what we will be facing."

Lisbeth tilted her head to the side in a thoughtful manner. "I would write to him about what you were told today. But I wonder, if you could get into his study, maybe you'd find information that could be useful there. Or send Avana."

"Sending Avana would make the most sense," Sabine said. She was smaller, less noticeable, and had proven herself capable of sneaking into places without detection. "And she'd be least suspected of mischief if caught. I think I'll ask her."

"I'm glad you have a plan for things like this. I would make a terrible duchesse."

"The secret is to never let anyone know that you just make it up as you go along," Sabine replied with a shrug. "Genuinely, there are so many things I just have to react to and hope for the best."

"Well, you do a much better job than I ever would," Lisbeth said with a laugh.

"You never know. When you are called on to act, you'd be surprised how many people can rise to the occasion if it is required of them." Sabine sighed. "I suppose the others need to be let in on what we've heard thus far."

"Maybe let's not tell Faron all of it. He's still upset about the Merscale incident. Telling him of the plan to strip Fythias of all spiritual freedom might upset him enough to do something to the comte," Lisbeth warned.

Of all of them, Faron and Avana were the most at risk in the home of someone spouting the nonsense of the Mother. She'd have sent them back to her own estate if she thought either would listen. As much as they planned on watching after her, she felt both needed their own guards. She wondered if she could get Faron to agree.

"I know he's been upset, but I don't think it's fair to keep the information away from him. He needs to be able to look out for himself if need be. You heard Tristian, and you know the merchant selling Merscales in our village spoke of coming here as some reprieve from my judgments. Elves are not safe here. You probably aren't either."

"I know," Lisbeth said. "But if he goes on a rampage…" She gave Sabine a bright smile so she'd know Lisbeth was joking.

"I'll send Avana after him."

"I look forward to seeing that," Lisbeth replied.

Sabine chuckled even though she didn't feel up to it. It felt as though every passing moment presented her with the prospect of some new horror. She took a breath and pushed the thoughts away. "Would you like me to walk with you to the rooms you were allocated, or are you comfortable going there yourself?" Sabine asked. Her luggage had not yet been delivered, and there was no reason to keep Lisbeth here indefinitely.

"I don't want to go alone, but I also don't know where my rooms are, nor do I want you to walk back here alone. I think, if you're alright, I'll stay here until one of the others arrives. I can start a bath for you?" Lisbeth offered.

"You're welcome to stay. I'm going to try to relax, as much as one can in this room, while the time has been allotted."

"Of course. I hope you rest well."

"So do I," Sabine replied. She pushed herself out of the chair and walked farther into the suite, finding the bedroom. She closed the door, separating herself from Lisbeth, and settled in for a nap.

Chapter Nine

Faron looked around the room he was to reside in for the duration of their stay, and he was not impressed. He knew Sabine was very good to her people, giving them spacious bedrooms with washrooms. He'd been so astounded by his assigned space when first arriving at the Vassetre chateau, he'd asked around to make sure he hadn't received special treatment. And his space was quite remarkable, spacious, and filled with furniture and fixtures to accommodate his size. He'd grown used to the comfort, to the generosity she shared, but he'd forgotten most nobles were not so giving to their staff.

Here, the bare stone walls would do nothing to keep the cold out in the winter months, and though the room held a fireplace, the filth and poor condition made him wary of its use. The floor, covered in thin faded rugs, offered no support or shield from the night air. The room was small, maybe a bit larger than a jail cell, and the washroom... Well, at least he had a place to clean and relieve himself. He had stayed in worse places, Faron reminded himself. He'd just gotten soft while working with Sabine. He would have to figure out a way of combating that once they returned home.

Speaking of soft, when he sat on the small twin bed, his face twisted in displeasure as the wooden frame creaked ominously and the straw poked through the old mattress. The bed would break sometime in the middle of the night, he could already tell. He was simply too large for the bed to accommodate him.

Standing, he walked to the door and stepped out into the corridor, only to see Meri in the doorway of the room next to his, hands on her hips, glaring at the room she was assigned. Finn, across the hall from Meri, watched her with a raised eyebrow.

"She's displeased," Finn shared with Faron. He leaned against the doorframe, arms crossed, and wore an amused smirk.

Faron looked from Finn to Meri to ask why, only to have Meri say, "It's a twin. There is no way my wife and I can sleep together on a twin."

Faron had to admit she wasn't wrong. Neither woman was large. Meri kept with her guard training the best she could with her leg, while Lisbeth was softer and curvier but still on the small side. It would be a tight fit, but they would make it work if they tried.

"Oh, bed size isn't the real problem," Faron said, a slightly teasing note to his voice. "The mattresses are straw."

Meri let out a string of curses that would make the guards blush.

"Uncomfortable though it might be, the conditions are what one would expect to find in servants quarters at most estates," Finn said reasonably. "We've all been spoiled by working for the Vassetre family, and we've all remarked on the fact numerous times. Even though the allocated space isn't wonderful, we'll only be here a few days. Let's avoid embarrassing Her Grace."

Faron glanced around, thankful for the reminder that they could be under watch even now. They would need to be more guarded in what they said, even if he thought the complaints about their accommodations were far too kind.

"Thank you for the reminder, Finn. Here's hoping I won't need more," Meri grumped.

"I think we all know the strain on her shoulders," Finn replied. He pushed off the doorframe from where he'd been leaning and took the couple of steps required to join Meri and Faron. "We need to make sure anything we do helps to relieve her of the worst of it."

Both nodded in agreement. Faron looked around once more. "Finn, is it normal for there to be none of the comte's people around? I know we just arrived, but Sabine normally has someone watch over visiting servants in case they get lost or have questions." Also to prevent spying, but Faron wasn't going to say as much out loud. "I would have assumed it's a normal practice?" he asked. He gestured, emphasizing the empty corridor aside from himself, Finn, and Meri. "No one is hiding nearby. I'd hear them."

Finn shook his head. "No. At minimum, the entirety of the comte's household should have been waiting to greet us upon arrival. Notice the handful of guards, the lack of business from the staff." He gestured around them much in the way Faron had done only minutes before. "Note how most of the house was stripped of finery. I think the comte is hemorrhaging money."

"Weren't there rumors of his father's enjoyment of gambling?" Meri asked, even as she motioned the two closer in case anyone did come their way.

"There were, though when Tristian took over, he had enough in his coffers to do some damage control from what I understand," Finn confirmed after the three drew close. "He must have his own vice."

Faron was interested to know how Finn knew what was in the comte's coffers, but the man was resourceful. Finn had the ability to never give the appearance of line-crossing while blatantly doing whatever it took to gather needed information. "We should figure out his vices. Sabine might be able to leverage it against him."

"She probably could," Finn agreed with a nod. "And Tristian's stupid enough to divulge without a lot of prompting." The steward glanced around once more, confirming they were still alone.

"We'll have to talk to her about it, then," Meri said.

"With just what we've seen, Sabine will already know. It's just too obvious," Faron added.

"I would say becoming friendly with the staff might help, but the girl who led us here was jumpy to the point I wouldn't trust her with a plate of food," Meri murmured.

"We are not at the Vassetre Chateau," Finn reminded them with a shrug. "Expecting anything here to be the same would be foolish, and we know the comte doesn't hold the same values as Her Grace."

Meri raised an eyebrow. "I know we're treated better than the majority, but the girl was jumpy the way abuse victims are. I think things are worse than lost money and a difference in values."

Faron agreed with Meri. The girl hadn't even known how to accept their thanks.

"You might be right," Finn said. "But again, none of us have the liberty to do as we might in our home. The comte is going to be looking for reasons to lash out because of the way Her Grace responded to his guards destroying the gardens. I suspect he would be willing to do more."

"We shouldn't be here," Meri said with a sigh. Her hands, now at her sides, were balled up into impotent fists. She obviously wished to act, though she knew they had no recourse.

"But we are, and we will do everything we can to keep Sabine safe. Especially from Comte Tristian. If he is abusing his staff, it's just another weapon we can place in Sabine's hands." Faron nodded decisively, knowing he was right so long as the visit remained productive. With the little they'd gathered through observation alone, he could hold onto his hope a bit longer.

Finn nodded in agreement. "And we will need to have information to hand to her. I would bet every piece of gold I own she will be pressured about going to Coralia while we are here. I would bet the same on him bringing up marriage. We know both items come from above Tristian, but Tristian will likely be expected to act as enforcer while he has the opportunity to do so."

Faron did his best not to growl, but from the looks Meri and Finn shot him, he hadn't been successful. "Best suggestions for how to gather that information?" Faron asked. He wasn't the best for information-gathering missions.

Finn looked down the corridor. "Avana is small, and she managed to sneak into the chateau without getting spotted," he said. "Perhaps she can break into an office or two."

Faron nodded in agreement.

Meri looked thoughtful. "I can offer my services in the kitchen. It's possible I could learn more from servants coming and going," she offered. "And offering to help will make our household look good. We'd be helping to pull our weight while being hosted."

"You should do that, and I'll stay with Sabine. I worry I'll intimidate anyone I try to talk to," Faron said with snort.

"The comte also glares at you anytime you're in the room. You're actually safest when you stay close to Her Grace," said Finn.

Faron had noticed the looks. The comte wasn't very subtle. "I have no idea what I did to upset the man, but you're right."

Finn shrugged. "Maybe he doesn't like elves. Maybe he doesn't like the way you look at Her Grace. Maybe both."

"He could just not like her having a personal guard and he's no longer left alone with her," Meri pointed out, causing Finn to laugh.

"Wait, she was left alone with him before I was hired?" Faron asked. His brows knitted together in frustration. How stupid could they be to allow her alone in Tristian's presence?

"Rarely. One of us always made excuses to be there," Meri answered.

"It took the incident with the suitor to get her to agree to having a personal guard," Finn added. "There are probably dozens of examples of her meeting alone with people you would not approve of."

Faron hadn't met a suitor he'd approved of if he was being honest. "Did all of them make her as uncomfortable as the comte does?" Faron asked. It was something he'd wondered about for a while, though he supposed the degree of discomfort did not much matter.

"She meets with more people than suitors, you know," Finn said with a snort. "And some of those non-suitor meetings were ones she needed people present to keep others in line. But to answer your question, no. She's never felt at ease with the comte around."

"She doesn't complain about the guilds and the others like she does the suitors. Other than the Jewelers' Guild, I haven't seen any other problem," Faron said with a shrug.

"That's because most people look at you and think, 'If I piss off the duchesse, her elf is likely to squish my head like a grape,'" Meri said before glancing down the hallway again, her face concerned.

Finn seemed to understand. "Do you want one of us to go look for Lisbeth?"

Meri shook her head. "She may have decided to stay with Her Grace so she's not alone." Even with the declaration, Meri bit her lip, and worry lines remained throughout her face, dimpling between her brows and bracketing her lips.

"Well then, Faron and I will go in search of Her Grace and Lisbeth," Finn offered. "Once we find them and assure Her Grace is well, I will make sure to bring Lisbeth back to you."

Faron nodded his agreement, and Meri gave them both a grateful smile. "Thank you."

"Come on, then," Finn said to Faron, and the two men left in search of Sabine and Lisbeth.

Chapter Ten

Sabine,

It lightens my heart to hear that, while you have refused my order to travel to Coralia, you have finally decided to visit with my dearest friend, Tristian, the Comte du Ciel. I am certain you will enjoy his company and find his home warm and comfortable. I confess it is my sincerest hope you will finally put away silly notions of your ability to run your estate and surrounding lands without a more sensible male influence to dampen your more hysterical tendencies.

As I will be arriving in your area in a few weeks, I cannot wait to hear the good news of your engagement, and if you haven't reached an agreement by then, I will be more than happy to see you tied to the comte in wedded bliss myself. I had hoped to arrive sooner once the comte wrote to me of your visit, but I am delayed having to smooth things over with my friends from Coralia, something we will be discussing when I arrive.

Grégoire, King-to-be of Tythias

Despite Tristian's dislike of his gardens, he invited Sabine for another stroll the next morning. After a morning meal, she was thankful for the milder weather which accompanied their second stroll in the garden. Tristian's discomfort was less pronounced now, and he walked with an enthusiasm his usually benign expressions and mannerisms never hinted at. Like last time, Lisbeth walked several paces behind, serving as a chaperone.

"The weather is always so much nicer earlier in the day," Tristian observed. "After that, it is often much warmer, something I've noticed isn't often true of your lands with the beach nearby. I'm sure we can figure something out between the two of us, though."

Sabine cast a glance out of the corner of her eye. She'd received the letter from Prince Grégoire before breakfast, though she'd only commented so far as to pass it to Finn. She'd behaved as though she'd not been all but ordered to marry, but based on Tristian's behavior, she'd bet he'd received his own correspondence.

"Oh, I think you will continue to enjoy your estate and I will enjoy mine," she replied simply.

Tristian patted Sabine's hand and gave her a smile bordering on condescension. "Of course, though I have often wondered, when you do marry, would it be your estate as the primary household or would it be more of a holiday household? Closed down during the colder months and such."

"Even when I choose a spouse, I intend to live in my home, as my parents did before me and my grandparents before them."

"It is a very pretty house, and the estate is valuable," Tristian mused.

"All of those things are true," Sabine agreed, her gaze pointed forward. She didn't want to divulge anything, even neutrality, to the comte. "Of course, the people I care for are truly what I find important. Do you not think the same of your own?"

"Naturally, I do, though there has been a slight amount of upheaval lately. I've sent my soldiers out to handle the problem." Tristian scowled and let out a sigh. "I'll have to go to the village later today to oversee some of the people who were arrested."

"Really?" Sabine said, hoping her interest came out as a concern. She dared looking directly at Tristian now, wanting as much in the way of details as possible. "What sort of upheavals have you been facing?"

"We've seen an uptick in beggars and the like over the last year, and some of the villagers did not like the solutions I've implemented to handle the issue. They blame the rise in taxes when they honestly have no idea what they speak of." He shrugged. "My soldiers have thrown several in the stocks, and a few more are set to be hung from the gates as an example to others," he said casually, as if it were an everyday occurrence. Sabine suspected it likely was.

"How awful," Sabine said, alarmed by both the problems he described and the solutions. "Has there been any violence from the villagers?"

"They've been protesting and such, but there has been no violence as of yet. If I take action now, there won't be." He patted her hand once more. "Solutions like this have always worked. Hang a few outspoken villagers from the walls, behead the next group, and the larger population tends to calm down and accept their places."

He must have thought she looked frightened or alarmed, and Tristian smiled reassuringly. "Not to worry, my dear. There will be no violence while you're here. You are completely safe." He glanced around and picked a rose from one of the bushes then held it out for her. "The prince approves of such methods. Don't worry. I have his full support."

"I'm not worried about my safety," Sabine said, although it probably was not the response Tristian expected. She absently accepted the rose, not giving the effort much thought. She held it by the stem, using her thumb and two fingers, and somehow managed to avoid pricking herself on any of the thorns. "I just cannot comprehend having to execute people when violence has not erupted."

"It's to ensure violence doesn't happen, a preventive measure if you will," he said in a patronizing tone. "I'm glad you've never had to take such measures. I'd hate to think of you in over your head in such distress."

His eyes flicked over her, making Sabine feel as though he doubted her capable of making tough decisions when they were needed, but Sabine had grown accustomed to others underestimating her.

"I think I would worry over retaliation from the villagers," she said. "Small infractions resulting in deadly repercussions would spark some unhappiness, would it not?"

"I haven't found that to be true. Making examples of those who are the loudest, those who others might follow into violence, has led to peace."

Tristian changed the direction they were walking, leading them to what Sabine could see was the chateau entrance to the village. She hadn't seen the village yet. The large walls surrounding the estate blocked it from view. As they approached the gates, they spotted a large, broad figure standing just outside, his body not turned toward the village but to the wall itself.

"I see your ... guard was considering going to the village."

Sabine detected a hint of anger and disgust in his voice. "Faron is not an idle man," Sabine replied. "I'm not surprised he'd want to venture out."

"Yes, well, it would have been nice if he'd stayed inside and out of the way. You do not need a guard here." Tristian's voice had taken on its normal placid tone, but his eyes spoke volumes about his dislike of Faron, or maybe just Faron's position.

Hearing them coming, Faron turned toward Sabine and she saw his eyes widen slightly. Sabine's brows raised in question, though she couldn't outright ask him what he was doing without alerting Tristian. Faron's expression and posture told her something was terribly wrong.

She looked back and smiled at the comte. "I cannot complain when it comes to Faron. He takes his job seriously. Surely, you've heard the news that I was forced to defend myself from a suitor who decided to become forceful with me."

Tristian carried on, apparently not noticing the silent alarm. "I've heard about what happened, and I've also spoken with the lord. He says he never meant for his actions to be seen as an assault on your person. I advised him to apologize, and I assured him you are a kind and forgiving woman," Tristian said, as if he had cleared everything up for her with a single conversation.

Upon reaching the gate Tristian released Sabine's arm and took several large steps away, turning to look at the wall.

With the comte being wholly distracted, Faron moved closer to Sabine. "I wouldn't go out there. You don't need to see this," he warned in quick, hushed tones. Even in their respective positions, Sabine saw the storm of anger brewing in his eyes and felt the stiffness of his shoulders.

"He's been bragging about some of what he's done," she muttered so quietly she knew Tristian wouldn't hear her. "But I need to know what we are dealing with. I can't help otherwise."

"People have been hung from the walls," he warned her. "It's gruesome."

Sabine glanced back and saw a pale and shaken Lisbeth. She took a breath, knowing what she was about to witness would be horrific. She stepped forward so the bodies came into view, and her hand, which had until that moment been holding the rose Tristian plucked, went to her chest, just below her neck. She took in the horror of decaying bodies strung along the walls, eyes bulging, flesh swollen, and necks clearly broken. Birds she had not noticed until now pecked at the dead, cawing mirthfully as they feasted.

Tristian sighed as he took in her reaction. "I hate such measures had to be taken and that you're having to see this," he said as he took a few steps toward her. "But sometimes we have to do things we wish we did not, and if you look out on the village, you'll see all the disruptions have been handled."

Sabine could not hide her disgust. No amount of political gameplay could make her. She stepped back from Tristian, closer to Faron. "I'm afraid I've seen enough to put a damper on my morning. If you'll excuse me," she said. He could think her weak and hysterical for all she cared.

Tristian reached out as if to touch her before dropping his hand. "I apologize. I forgot how delicate of constitution ladies are. Your maid also does not look well. You should get her inside." Tristian sounded apologetic, but his apologies were thrown off by the way he looked at Faron.

"Yes," Sabine agreed. "Faron, will you help Lisbeth inside? She could use some rest and something to drink, I think."

"Of course, Your Grace." Faron gave a respectful bow and moved to Lisbeth's side, offering her his arm, the two waiting for Sabine.

Tristian, seeing this, gave Sabine a shallow bow. "I have to go check on the people in the stocks. I'll see you for dinner." He turned on his heels and started down the steps to the village.

Sabine waited until Tristian was well out of earshot. Even then, she kept her eyes on the comte as she spoke. "Inside."

They nodded, and the trio walked quickly into the chateau, along the corridors, and to Sabine's assigned suite of rooms. "Sit," Sabine directed Lisbeth once the door was shut. Lisbeth obeyed, sitting down in the large cushioned chair while Faron got her some water.

Sabine, meanwhile, paced the room, thinking through the conversation and the numerous bodies along the wall, placed by the gardens, presumably, to help conceal the stench of rotting flesh. "He did that over tax protests."

Faron ran a hand down his face while Lisbeth clutched the glass of water to her chest. "I was going to visit the village to see what it was like when I saw them. One of those bodies couldn't have been more than seventeen," Faron said.

The youth of one of the deceased had not escaped Sabine's notice, although many of the usual signs, like a smattering of freckles or residual baby fat, had been marred by the decay. She couldn't image what a child could possibly do to deserve death. "Grégoire has been here. Presumably, he knows and approves of Tristian's actions."

"Supposedly in Quenall, the king also displayed bodies of people he deemed his enemies. Having never been to the capitol, I don't know if it's true or not, but if it is and Grégoire has contact with King Sargarus in Coralia, I can see him following the example," Lisbeth said.

"My contacts in Coralia have told me about executions in every major city," Sabine confirmed with a tired nod. "Hangings are seen as useful because the bodies easily remain on display. Fythias, though… No one I regularly correspond with has reported the same."

"Spirits," Faron breathed out, collapsing onto the large sofa.

"Tristian made it sound like he's regularly executing people," Lisbeth added.

"Either way, I have to write to Louis," Sabine said, mostly to herself. "And not just about this."

"What else do you need to write to him about?" Faron asked.

"I received a letter from Grégoire this morning. He tells me I can either marry Tristian of my own free will, or he will enforce it when he next arrives in the area." Sabine rolled her eyes. "I'd like to see him fucking try."

"So would I." Faron's voice was dark with promise. If Sabine asked, Faron would kill both Tristian and Grégoire.

"Tristian also speaks as if it is a done deal," Sabine said, not at all surprised by Faron's response. He may not love her, but he cared about her, and he took his position seriously. She had no cause to doubt her safety in his presence. "I am not motivated to leave yet. Something must be done about the people in Tristian's village. We need to see what else he knows about Grégoire's plans. His financial troubles alone are worth investigating."

"Avana said she would break into Tristian's study tonight. She says the windows are badly secured, and he usually drinks himself into a stupor once you've retired in the evening. His steward has indicated the drinking is a normal occurrence," Faron informed Sabine.

"She's looking for his ledger and any letters, correct?" Lisbeth asked.

Faron nodded.

"I wonder if he's giving over the excess taxes to Grégoire," Sabine pondered. She took a seat beside Faron on the sofa, her brows knitted together in thought. For once, his closeness didn't quite enrapture her, as she was occupied with other thoughts. "It's one of the few reasons I can see Tristian being viewed as useful. He's not very bright, nor is he resourceful."

"It makes the most sense. Well, that and his excessive drinking," Lisbeth said softly.

Faron nodded, reminding Sabine of the times Tristian had visited her home only to drink enough to need an escort to his room. Considering he'd been there to show he'd make a good husband, it had been an off-putting choice.

"Go let the others know what we've heard and witnessed," Sabine said with a sigh. "I will write to Louis, and Finn can smuggle the note out when I'm done."

"I'll go," Lisbeth said. She placed her water glass on the table closest to the chair and stood, giving Faron a look before walking toward the door.

Faron rolled his eyes and turned to Sabine once it was just the two of them. "None of us want you alone here with us several wings away. I let the others know I would broach the subject. I assume you'll be happier with Lisbeth, Meri, or Avana staying with you if you approve. I know you wouldn't want it to be me."

Sabine raised an eyebrow. The first part of his request made sense. She didn't need to be alone and so far away from her people. The second only made sense in terms of the changed situation between the two of them but not in any protective context. "Lisbeth would be useless in an attack. Meri's leg would hinder her ability to do much for very long, and I took down Avana with very little effort."

"All points they made, and Finn apparently cannot handle the sight of blood." Faron shook his head with a laugh. "It's just, with everything going on, I wasn't sure you'd want me in the room you're currently sleeping in. Though this love seat is much more comfortable than the beds we are sleeping in."

Sabine sighed and rested her head on the back of the sofa. "If it would make you feel better, you can stay here. I suspect if I didn't let you, you'd forgo sleep and stand outside the door, and you'd be of no use to me in that condition."

"If you didn't want me here, then I wouldn't be here. If you asked me not to stand in front of your door, then I wouldn't. I would stay in my room as requested and get little to no sleep there instead," he admitted. "I don't like you so far away from me... From us. I know the comte has a key to this room, and I suspect he'd use it. There are numerous concerns, but if you said no, I would listen."

Sabine didn't respond at first, because the feelings she'd so carefully ignored so far that day flared in her chest. She wanted him there. She actually wanted to curl up in his lap and just allow herself some retreat from the horrors of the morning. She didn't have the option, but she could help alleviate some of Faron's worries. "Then stay."

"Alright," he said simply and settled in next to her, his shoulders seeming to relax with her allowance.

Chapter Eleven

Faron cursed internally as he stared up at the ceiling of the room he shared with Sabine. The last two days had been awful, seeing her upset and unable to comfort her, touch her, hold her. He understood why. He really did. He approved of the distance she'd put between them, but somehow, being in this room with her made things so much harder than they needed to be. His restraint hung by a thread with the want to climb into that oversized pink frilly monstrosity of a bed she'd been given and hold her close. Instead, he tightened the grip on himself and rolled over as best as he could since he really didn't fit on the small sofa. At least it was still more comfortable than the bed.

And it wasn't as though Sabine was sleeping. She said nothing, nor did she toss and turn in her bed, but Faron could hear the breathing of someone who was very much awake and likely stressed beyond words. He couldn't blame her. Her usual responsibilities coupled with all she'd learned since arriving at Tristian's estate weighed heavily on the duchesse. She wanted to prevent war. She wanted to prevent the country from being run over by the terrors spreading from Coralia. Anyone in her position would suffer as she did now.

Giving up on sleep entirely, Faron sat up. Leaning back against the chair, his head resting at an angle he wasn't quite comfortable with, he looked over at Sabine. He could see her well enough, even in the darkness. "Do you wish to talk about it?" he asked softly.

The soft sound of laughter came in response. "I feel like I've spent the whole day talking."

"I think you have," Faron joked, his voice soft. "We could play cards or drink?" he offered, looking over at the bag he'd brought once they determined he would be staying with Sabine. He was sure he had cards inside somewhere.

"You don't drink," she replied.

"I drink tea," he pointed out.

"And yet, tea is not the kind of drinking you were suggesting," Sabine replied.

"I was not, but I also didn't think you would complain if I drank tea while you had something stronger."

He heard her sit up and saw her long light caramel hair fall around her shoulders. Even in the darkness of the room, where he could only properly see her in beams of moonlight, Faron's pull toward her felt impossible to resist.

"Pour me a drink, then," she directed.

Faron nodded and stood, careful to use what little light there was not to run into anything. On a table close to the door sat several crystal decanters of liquid. Avana had checked each for poisons. She may have been a terrible assassin when it came to blades, but she knew her poisons better than Meri. "Do you have a preference?" he asked.

Sabine shook her head, throwing back the covers and swinging her legs to the floor. Her nightdress revealed her legs, smooth and pale. Faron quickly diverted his eyes from her legs, lest he decide touching them was a really good idea, and instead, focused on pouring amber liquid into a glass. He thought it might be some type of brandy, but he wasn't completely sure. Most alcohol smelled the same to him.

Sabine grabbed a robe before joining Faron on the sofa, although her nightdress wasn't as sheer as some she'd worn. Once covered in the second layer, she then took a seat next to him and brushed a length of her long hair from her shoulder before accepting the drink.

They sat closer now than they had at any point since before leaving the Vassetre Chateau, and Faron was determined to behave, to offer her comfort if needed without invading her space. "I'm sorry you're having to deal with all of this."

She shrugged. "It's my job."

"Monsters like Tristian, Grégoire, and Sargarus shouldn't be your problem. They should be your king's problem. I'm aware you currently lack a king," he said with a laugh at the look she shot him.

"I'm going to declare a king. There's nothing else to do at this point. I shouldn't have to flaunt my power like this." She looked defeated in making her confession, her shoulders slumped, her gaze on the glass of brandy.

"Is the younger prince strong enough to stand up to Grégoire and, if needed, King Sargarus if he decides to use Coralia's might against him?" Faron asked. He didn't know much about the younger prince other than he supported, and was there for, Sabine.

"I think he is," Sabine said after she finally took a drink. "But like me, he wished for matters to be resolved peacefully if possible."

"Do you think it can be resolved peacefully?" Faron doubted it could be, but there was always a chance.

She shook her head. "Not anymore. Tristian is stupid in thinking the villagers aren't going to call for his head, and he will not be where they stop."

"He doesn't have the manpower to quell a rebellion if it were to start, and it would spread to other villages because if he's doing it, other nobles who have sided with Grégoire are as well." Faron leaned his head back against the sofa, looking up at the ceiling. "I'm thinking of going to the village or sending Meri and Lisbeth. They can send any orphans they find to our village. My friend Phindel will take them in."

"I was thinking of something similar, and I had Finn send notice for relief efforts from our people," Sabine shared.

"It will have to be kept quiet, or Tristian will think you're moving on his land." Faron sighed. "I wrote to some people I know in Coralia and let them know you were considering hiring more guards. I'm hopeful they'll come to Fythias. Even if you don't hire them as guards, they are good, skilled people. I know they'll be good additions to the village. Having more people will also help should the worst happen."

She turned to look at him. "Anyone you know who needs refuge, have them come to our village. Work, food, and shelter can be found for them."

"Sadly, too many people I know won't leave. It's their home, and they'd rather stay and fight. There are also rumors of different Coralian provinces where Sargarus is less popular."

"I'm not surprised," Sabine said before drinking again.

"I'm just glad someone in Coralia doesn't support the king." Faron looked at Sabine. She looked exhausted and worn down but still beautiful. Faron was honored he was allowed to see her like this when so few were. There were other feelings there too, but as normal, he ignored them. "Things will be okay. I'm sure you will have no problem crushing anyone who would support Grégoire and these mad ideals under your heel."

Sabine shook her head. "I've no doubt we can deal with Tristian and Grégoire or that we can put Louis on the throne. But things will not be okay. Not for so many. I know how it feels to lose family. You never really recover. You just learn to live without them."

Faron nodded and, noting Sabine's glass was mostly empty, used the excuse of going to grab the decanter to give himself a moment to think about his own parents. He'd lost them decades ago, and the sting of their losses never truly left him. He imagined he would carry the feelings around for his whole life, along with so many other pains.

He returned to the sofa, decanter in hand. "You're right, but stability helps. Not worrying where your next meal is coming from or if you're going to be targeted for being different matters quite a bit. It sounds like since the death of the last king, things haven't been stable." He'd heard so many rumors about the death of Grégoire and Louis's older brother. Most believed Grégoire had caused the accident that took the king's life. Others wished the rumored hidden child of the king with an elf woman had been true so the chaos an empty throne caused hadn't happened. There were more tales, more rumors, but at the end of the day, the kingdom was under threat until they had a king.

"Things haven't always been as chaotic as they are now," Sabine replied. "But Fythias has been unstable."

"I've heard. The villagers gossip. Especially the older ones."

"I'm just thankful more people think like me than not, especially those who have money and influence. Going the way of Coralia, falling in line with Grégoire, would be the easier choice despite it being the wrong one." She leaned forward long enough to put her glass down before settling back on the sofa.

Without thinking, Faron wrapped his arm around Sabine. "You are going to set things right. I believe in you more than anything else."

She leaned her head against his shoulder and closed her eyes. "Keep reminding me."

"Of course," Faron said as he allowed his eyes to close as well.

Chapter Twelve

"Sabine," a voice whispered, prompting a sleepy sound to rumble in the duchesse's throat. She did not respond further.

"Sabine, you need to wake up," the voice insisted.

"Does she need to wake up?" asked a higher-pitched feminine voice. "We could quickly copy down the information, and she can get some rest." Sabine recognized Avana speaking as soon as the question was posed.

"True," Faron agreed.

Sabine felt him carefully start to remove his arm from behind her. She opened her eyes and realized they'd fallen asleep on the sofa. She sat up slowly and a little stiffly and narrowed her eyes to partially block out the early morning light streaming through the windows.

"You two look cute together," Avana observed, not a hint of teasing in her words.

"Thanks," Faron responded, glancing at Sabine.

"Why did you wake me?" she asked the two as she finger-combed her hair so it wasn't in her face. She needed to do something about the sheer amount of the caramel strands.

Avana held up parchment in one hand and a cowhide ledger book in the other. "We probably have just a couple of hours before Tristian wakes up and his steward gathers his items for the day. Possibly longer since he drank more than normal last night."

Sabine nodded, covering her mouth with a hand before she reached out to take the items from Avana. "Will one of you get me some water?" she requested as she opened the ledger. The tidy scrawl and precise organization on the cream colored pages surprised her. The condition of the estate and the surrounding village had her thinking she'd find something much less organized.

Faron rose to his feet and headed to get Sabine water. She noted he rotated the arm she'd slept on, trying to get feeling back into it, most likely.

"He's been funding the prince. There are other transactions marked I can't figure out." Avana placed the letters on the table between her chair and Sabine's. "It's also not his everyday ledger. It was in a hidden drawer in his desk."

Sabine quickly skimmed the pages, her fingers trailing down the rows of sums and the notation made by each. "Either Grégoire has very little money, or he doesn't want Tristian to have any," she murmured. "The question is, which is it?"

"You would think Grégoire would have enough money, being the prince and all. Unless he's funding something big enough to consume all his money," Faron mused, holding out a glass of water for Sabine.

"I didn't read the letters, but they don't all look to be from the prince," Avana said.

"Having a title doesn't mean having money," Sabine said. She looked up and took the water from Faron with a smile of thanks, then took a drink before setting it aside. Closing the ledger, she handed it off to Avana. "That needs to go to Finn for another skim," she said before reaching for the letters.

"I'll take it to him now while you read those," Avana said before she quickly but quietly left.

"She's a shit assassin but a damn good thief," Faron admitted.

"And you didn't want her to stay," Sabine joked without looking up.

"She's still a pain in the ass."

"You only think so because you didn't handpick her to live in the chateau with us," Sabine replied. She put a letter down and picked up another.

"Or because our introduction was her trying to kill you," Faron said, his tone nonchalant.

"Her attempt was rather poor, though," Sabine replied. The second letter she placed on top of the first. "Grégoire doesn't seem to have a lot of support so far," she said tentatively, picking up a third.

"Not even from the minor nobles?" Faron asked, his brows knitted in confusion.

"Not so far," Sabine said, shaking her head. "I know a handful of people who back him, but these letters... They are surprising."

"Anything I should write down?" Faron asked. He went to the desk and grabbed parchment, quill, and ink and returned to his seat beside Sabine on the sofa. "You can summarize for me while I take notes."

She nodded slowly as she skimmed a third letter. "There's definitely a problem with the prince's funds, and Tristian is sustaining him if these letters are to be believed," she began. "Vicomte Ancien, for example, alludes to payments to Coralia."

Faron's quill quickly moved across the parchment. "Why is he sending money to Coralia?" he asked.

"My assumption is to fund their wars," Sabine said. This letter she sat in a different spot and picked up a fourth. As her eyes skimmed the page, she made a disapproving sound. "Marquis Lior has pro-Grégoire leanings and limited funds."

"Did you believe he leaned the other way?" Faron asked. "I wonder what Grégoire is getting in return for his money."

"I actually didn't know one way or the other," Sabine replied. "He's always been a grubby little worm."

Faron snorted and said out loud as he wrote, "Marquis Lior is a grubby little worm."

Sabine laughed despite herself. "Very useful note-taking, Faron."

"It seemed like a helpful note."

She shot him a playful look and went back to the letters. By the time Avana returned with Finn in tow, they'd finished reading and taking notes.

"Discover anything fun?" Avana asked cheerfully as she plopped down into a seat.

"Depending on what Finn tells me about his ledger observations, I think I have a working theory about some things," Sabine replied.

"I only got to browse about half of it before Avana decided I was taking too long," Finn replied. "But it seems like most of Tristian's money ends up in Grégoire's pockets, which is likely why Grégoire is so eager to sell you to him. Your estate would reinvigorate the comte's, and your power would satiate his greed."

Silence followed Finn's announcement as everyone took that in before Avana finally broke it. "Can I poison him?"

"I'd rather not kill anyone unless we are left without a choice, Avana," Sabine replied. "But yes, I think the operating theory of why he's trying to marry me off to Tristian makes sense. Well, until you consider the parade of suitors."

"Most were thought to be Grégoire's supporters, right?" Faron motioned to the letters. "What if he thought they would make Tristian look appealing?"

"Faron makes a good point," Finn said.

"So then why does Tristian back Grégoire specifically?" Sabine asked. "Is it because he believes the same things Grégoire does? Because he's next in line for the throne? A combination of the two? Something else?"

Avana shrugged.

"From what you and Lisbeth have said, it sounds like he believes in Grégoire and his new ideals, but there could be more to it. Is there anything else in the letters?" Faron asked.

"You were here when I went through the letters," Sabine reminded him. "I suppose motivation doesn't matter. We know what's at stake now."

"We could have missed something," Faron said with a shrug.

Avana stood, stretching. "If you're done with these, I need to get them back. We probably don't have a lot of time before he's up."

"Then get them back to the proper place. Once you're done, everyone should go get ready for the day," Sabine said. She didn't feel better with the information she now had, but at least she had it. She could work with information.

Avana gathered up the letters and the ledger and, with a cheerful wave, was off once more.

"How long are we staying again?" Faron asked, looking between Sabine and Finn.

"A day or two more, I think," Sabine replied. "Now that we've gathered sufficient information, we can't just run off without raising alarm. You also said you wanted to go to the village to facilitate helping the orphaned children."

"I do, but you also mentioned Grégoire's intentions of coming here. With everything we know and suspect, I would rather you weren't here when he arrives," Faron admitted.

"We could send two of the guards we brought with us out to scout," Finn suggested. "They would be able to give us time to retreat if needed."

"I think we have a plan," Sabine agreed with a nod. "If one of you will send a couple of our people?"

"I'll go talk to the other guards and get them sent off," Faron said, standing. "I'll be back in a short while." Faron gave Sabine a soft smile and nodded his head to Finn before leaving.

Finn watched him go before turning back to Sabine. "I take it you two made up?" he asked.

"What do you mean?" Sabine replied. She'd leaned forward and gathered the notes Faron had taken for her. She rolled the parchment up and handed it to Finn for safekeeping.

"Frankly?"

"Yes," Sabine said, nodding.

"The two of you were very obviously engaging in a quite passionate physical affair, and then one day, not long ago and without explanation, there was suddenly a distance between you. That distance seems to be eroding." Finn spoke factually rather than questioning her, and Sabine appreciated his respect for her privacy. She suspected her steward, Meri, and Lisbeth had probably gossiped about the topic, but there wasn't much she could do about it.

Sabine sighed, deciding to be honest if only because she didn't want rumors floating around the chateau. "Faron indicated he did not feel for me what I thought he might. I did not want to be anyone's plaything, so it was best for certain lines to no longer be crossed."

"Ah," Finn said with a nod. "Of course. I'll let Lisbeth know you wish to get started on morning preparations." He bowed and left the room, leaving Sabine to her own devices. She rose from the sofa, stretching her arms above her head as she walked to the washroom.

Chapter Thirteen

"We didn't see many orphans, which was heartening, until one of the merchants informed Faron and me the children never come out in large groups after some of the comte's guards were ordered to round them up," Meri informed Finn after an afternoon in the village seeing the horrors of Tristian's estate management up close. Their findings confirmed what they already knew of Tristian, but it didn't make the reality any less horrid. Thankfully, Sabine had consented to help in any way she could, though Faron hadn't expected any less from her.

After returning, Faron and Meri decided to gather with the others in Faron's room to discuss the experience. As always, they kept their voices low in case one of Tristian's few servants came by.

"No one knows why the order was given or what's happened to the children who were caught," Faron added as he sunk into a chair he'd "borrowed" from a nearby storage pantry.

"Conscription might be an answer," Finn said. He stood near the door, back against the wall and arms crossed. "It's not unheard of for armies to have younger children run around picking up supplies after battles and older children serving as soldiers. Coralia would need soldiers."

"It's not," Faron agreed. Children being sent to Coralia or to fill the ranks of whatever military unit Grégoire managed to organize presented Faron with an upsetting picture. He would figure out how to look further into the children's location. "Some of the adults who have already lost their homes or are at risk are going to escort the remaining children to our village."

"We should write to Marcelle and let him know they are coming," Lisbeth said from where she sat on his old creaky bed. Lisbeth had been forced to exchange positions with Avana after the comte caught her yawning while he and Sabine read in the library. Meri walked over and sat beside her wife.

"I will make sure Marcelle gets the appropriate information," Finn assured the group.

Faron nodded, and the group sat in silence for a little while. Faron let his thoughts linger on the village and how much it reminded him of Myrefall in Coralia. How broke, upset, and disheartened the villagers were. The main difference, however, was the undertone of anger missing from his home. Sabine had been right to say the villagers would rise against Tristian before long.

Before he could mention his thoughts, Lisbeth spoke, breaking the silence. "I'm glad we're leaving soon. I hate it here, and I'm worried about Her Grace."

"Other than the obvious, what has you worried?" Finn asked.

"I just don't like the way he looks at her, and Tristian was so very eager to make me leave today. I know he can't force her to marry him, but I have a bad feeling I can't make go away." Lisbeth shrugged, having explained herself poorly.

It left Faron on edge. He hated that he couldn't be with Sabine while she was with the comte, if only because Sabine was trying to keep things civil. Tristian was anything but when he was around. He also just missed being around Sabine. The last few days had been very hard, and their evening together, where nothing but some talking and sleeping happened, hadn't nearly satiated his desire to be close. "Back at the estate, we talked about Sabine telling Tristian she was interested in another of her suitors. Did you ever broach that topic with her?" Faron asked Lisbeth, even as the words tasted like ash in his mouth.

Lisbeth exchanged a look with Meri before nodding. "I did, but she wasn't interested. Said she'd rather be honest about having no interest in marriage than lie and have the gentleman in question show up to the estate thinking he had a chance."

"After what Faron did to her, I don't know why anyone thought she'd be up for lying about her interest in someone," Finn said.

All the heads in the room turned to look at Finn.

"I knew you did something!" Meri hissed, turning back to look at Faron.

Simultaneously, Lisbeth asked, "What did he do?"

Faron pressed his lips together and looked at Finn, waiting to see what Sabine had told him, an uncomfortable feeling stirring in his gut. He'd known his admission of not loving Sabine had been the cause of their problems, but they hadn't broached the subject. Knowing he was about to hear the truth from Finn, he almost wanted to be sick.

"She wasn't exactly forthcoming on details, but from what I gathered between what she did say and how she sounded, he left her feeling quite used," Finn explained.

"That was not my intent," Faron said softly.

"What was your intent? What exactly happened?" Meri demanded.

Faron knew he would have to explain, even just briefly, what had happened. "I told Sabine I'm not in love with her. I tried to convey that I do feel a deep longing for her, a need to possess her, claim her, and keep her safe. But not love." Faron winced as he recalled the words he'd spoken for a second time, realization of his poor explanation settling over him.

Looking around the room as a shocked silence descended, Faron saw Lisbeth's eyes had widened dramatically as she blinked repeatedly. Meri's mouth hung open in shock before it snapped shut with a click of her teeth. Both women's heads turned slowly to look at Finn, who looked very unhappy.

Finn surveyed him with a pitying look. "I'm not saying your intentions were cruel, but you have to know how badly you've hurt Her Grace."

"I'm aware. It wasn't my intention. I knew right away what I'd said hurt her, even if I didn't and still do not understand why. She doesn't love me. She can't. It wouldn't work out for either of us." Faron spread his hands out in front of himself as if to say there was nothing he could do.

Finn shook his head, looking over to Lisbeth. "He's your friend. Please explain to him exactly how stupid he's being."

Lisbeth took a deep breath and moved from the bed to kneel in front of Faron, taking his larger hands into her smaller ones. Faron couldn't help but feel like a child about to get scolded.

"Faron, I love you, but you're an idiot. Sabine loves you very much. It's clear for all of us to see. She has for quite some time. It's one of the reasons she can't keep her hands off you and vice versa."

Faron narrowed his eyes at Lisbeth as he thought over her words. "Love isn't needed for two people to have sex."

"No it isn't, but Sabine has taken very few lovers, and each one she has taken, she cared for deeply," Lisbeth said gently.

Faron looked away from Lisbeth, unable to meet her gaze as his mind replayed the many conversations he'd had with Sabine, including the relationship she had with the Sirene from town. He couldn't deny that Lisbeth was right, which meant there was a very good chance Sabine did care for him deeply, maybe even loved him. "I'm not a noble," he said weakly.

"Neither was her mother," Finn said.

"What?" Faron asked. He had assumed both of Sabine's parents were noble.

"Her grandparents owned the old bakery in the village, the same bakery her mother grew up in. The Duc Vassetre met her at a village social, and for a year, he would ride into the village every evening once she was done working," Finn explained.

"And he didn't need the approval of the king? It didn't hurt his standing at all?" Faron asked almost breathlessly. The issue of outliving Sabine wasn't resolved, but if their stations didn't make a difference, maybe they had a chance.

"The king does not have the power to enforce or deny a marriage, even if they try to sway someone," Finn explained. "Even now, if Grégoire wore the crown, he could not compel Her Grace to marry Tristian."

Faron tried to remove his hands from Lisbeth, but she held on tight. "You care about Sabine. You probably love her.

Stop denying it, because you're hurting her and yourself for no reason," Lisbeth said before letting him go. She rose to go sit next to Meri, who looked like she wanted to flay Faron open with her eyes, when Avana burst in and dramatically threw herself face-first onto the empty bed.

"Why is the comte so dull, and why can't I stab him?" she said, seemingly not noticing or ignoring the tension in the room.

"You cannot stab him because then Her Grace would be compelled to let you be arrested, unless you had good reason," Finn replied with a chuckle. "Did you leave Her Grace alone with the comte, or has she returned to her suite?"

"She's in her room." Avana rolled onto her back and spoke to the ceiling. "We might be leaving earlier than intended. Tristian tried to get intimate with Her Grace when one of his servants approached me to ask questions. She handled the situation without me having to get involved, but she is very unhappy."

Faron rose to his feet. "He did what?" He took a step forward. He didn't feel right not being the one to guard her room. Not if the comte had tried to take liberties and certainly not after the conversation he'd just had. However, he found himself quickly sitting back down at Lisbeth's pointed stare.

"You heard me. I'm not repeating myself," Avana said, waving him off.

"Does she want someone there, or would she prefer a few minutes to herself?" Finn asked.

"She asked for a few minutes, but I still made sure there was a guard outside her room. The steward said he was going to have refreshments brought up, and I didn't want a stranger hanging around without someone we trust there," Avana replied. "Figured I should let everyone know what happened." She looked around from her chosen position on the bed, seeming to note the lingering tension. "What did I miss?"

"Faron being an idiot," Meri muttered.

"Oh, that's not news," Avana said and looked to Finn for more of an explanation.

"Faron said some unkind things to Her Grace before we came here," Finn replied, glancing at Faron again.

Avana shot Faron a look. "I know you're not the brightest, but why would you do that? Marcelle has told me when you do something to hurt someone you care about or love, you should apologize."

Lisbeth cut her off. "He says you should apologize to anyone you hurt, friend or stranger."

Avana rolled her eyes. "Not the point. You love Sabine, so go apologize and make it right."

"I never said I loved Sabine," Faron said, giving Avana a flat look.

"You don't have to. And if you think you don't, you're lying to yourself," Avana replied.

"Honestly, you probably shouldn't bring it up if you can't be honest about your own feelings, even if it is to apologize," Finn said. "She is very obviously hurt by your rejection and the implications of only wanting her for very specific reasons, and being obtuse about what you actually think and feel won't help matters."

Faron huffed and opened his mouth, a sharp reply on the tip of his tongue, when he stopped himself. Finn didn't deserve his ire, and he was right. Faron knew what his feelings for Sabine were and had from the beginning. He just didn't want to admit them, but slowly, every excuse, every reason was being chipped away. Leaving only one left.

"What is holding you back?" Lisbeth asked.

Faron couldn't stop himself from saying, "I'm an elf. She's a human. Our lifespans are drastically different. I don't think I could carry on for another hundred years without her."

Finn's expression softened. "You're going to have to do that anyway. Would you rather it be after enjoying the time you could have together, or would you rather be miserable regardless?"

"He's right, you know. Meri could have an accident in the kitchen. I could get sick tomorrow and pass in my sleep, yet we would treasure the time we did have together," Lisbeth said.

Meri nodded in agreement next to her.

"The next assassin could be a good one, and then you'd spend the rest of your life mourning her anyway. Stop being an idiot, and go tell her you love her." Avana made herself more comfortable on his bed and closed her eyes.

Faron threw his hands up in the air as he stood from the chair. "Yes, I'm in love with Sabine. I'm going to go see her." What else could he do? Denying his feelings grew more difficult every day, and knowing he'd hurt Sabine felt unforgivable. "Make sure she doesn't fall asleep in my bed, please," he requested as he went to the door.

"You're not sleeping here, so it's not a problem," Avana mumbled before yawning.

Chapter Fourteen

Faron had planned to dismiss the current person guarding Sabine's door and stand watch for a few hours until his head was clearer, and he was more at peace with the fact that he'd finally admitted to himself and those four busybodies that he was in love with Sabine. He'd been in love with her practically since the day they met. It wasn't an easy thing to come to grips with, not after months of fighting it, denying it, refusing to let it take shape in his mind. However, he'd said it out loud, and now, despite his very valid fears of outliving her, he could no longer keep his feelings to himself.

Upon reaching the correct corridor, he spotted the current guard about to admit the beady-eyed, nervous looking house steward into Sabine's room unattended, and the ignorance could not stand. Approaching the two men, he saw the steward holding a platter with several different covered plates on it. He quickly took the platter, dismissing both the steward and the guard. Once they were both out of sight, Faron raised his hand to knock, only to freeze and lower his hand again. He could do this, he could talk to Sabine and admit his feelings. With any luck, not everything was ruined and lost. With a deep breath, he raised his hand and knocked.

No answer came at first, though movement from inside the room told Faron she was there. He lifted his hand to knock again when the door crept open, revealing Sabine just inside. "I see Avana went running," she observed before backing up and opening the door to admit him.

Faron stepped into the room, making sure to close and lock the door once they were both inside. "She let us know you wanted time by yourself, and I'd planned to stand guard outside when I saw the steward with this." He motioned to the platter as he set it down on the small wooden table in front of the love seat he'd been sleeping on.

"Food is the last thing I want right now," Sabine said.

"From what Avana said, I can understand why," Faron said, his tone serious. "Are you okay?"

"He didn't end up doing anything," Sabine replied with a sigh. She took a seat on the sofa, her dress and hair pristine. Clearly, whatever Tristian tried had been ineffective. "And I will be fine."

"Avana made it sound worse," Faron admitted. "I am happy to guard your door if you want time alone."

Sabine shook her head. "You can stay if you want. There's food." She gestured toward the tray.

Faron wasn't hungry, but he wanted an excuse to stay, so he uncovered the dishes. It was a simple fare, well put together, featuring a white soup with what he thought were sausages and potatoes, a salad with walnuts on top, and several small sandwiches. "I'm not hungry at the moment, but the food looks delicious. For all his trouble, the comte seems to have kept a decent cook on staff." Nothing he said was what he wanted to talk about, but it was something.

"Regardless of anything else going on, food is always a source of comfort. I'm not at all surprised by the quality produced here," Sabine replied. She sounded tired and dejected.

Faron looked at Sabine, intending to ask her if they could leave tomorrow. Just forget all this and go. They had to have enough information that she no longer had to put herself through handling the comte. Instead, to his utter mortification, what came out of his mouth was, "Do you love me?"

She looked over at him, perhaps surprised by his question, though her expression didn't suggest it. She let out a sigh. "Of course I do."

The admission hit Faron like a punch to the gut. She could so easily say what he had been fighting against for months, what he had refused to admit or see in her. How stupid was he to have ignored all the signs? To have convinced himself she didn't love him and vice versa? He needed to make this right. He just didn't know how. So, he decided to start with the truth. "Until a few minutes ago, I had refused to see or acknowledge that you felt that way for me, and now, I look back at the last few months and can't help but curse myself for my stupidity and the pain I've caused you."

"It's not like you owe me anything, Faron. You said you didn't feel the same. I accept that."

Faron clasped his hands in front of him. "I do, though. Sabine, I owe you everything."

"Why?" she asked.

"Because I have wronged you greatly, and I wish, no, I *need* to make it right. Hopefully, in the end, you'll be willing to forgive me and take this fool of an elf back into your arms and your heart."

She turned to look at him, her expression exhausted, though her vivid green eyes met his darker ones. "You didn't leave my heart just because you said you didn't love me."

"Here's hoping you'll still feel that way when we're done talking. If you're up for a serious talk after everything with Tristian." Faron was willing to wait, to hold off on this conversation, as much as he knew they should have it now.

"We can talk," she said.

Faron took a deep breath then paused. He needed to communicate clearly the first time. There could be no misunderstanding here. "The night you asked me if I loved you, I had spent the day convincing myself I didn't and was sure you did not love me at all."

Her brows furrowed in thought, and her lips pressed together in thought before her eyes widened in what looked like comprehension. "You saw your friend earlier in the afternoon."

Faron nodded. "I had. My friend Phindel takes care of the children who have no place else to go. He tells me you visit them sometimes. I knew him and his wife Clara from Coralia. They helped me after... Well, they helped me." He sighed, thinking back to those long ago years. "They were so in love. They were each other's everything, but he's an elf and she was human. Even with her magic, she was never going to live as long as him. He still has a long life ahead of him, yet he looks closer to death than he should. He looks for her constantly. I lost count of how many times he turned to tell her something, eyes full of joy, only for his whole expression to turn empty when he remembered she wasn't there. The children help, but she was his entire life." Faron hoped he was explaining this well.

Sabine slowly nodded in what Faron hoped was understanding. "I take it the notion scares you."

"Very much so. I was also under the mistaken belief that since you're a member of nobility, we wouldn't have been able to marry. So, I thought I would save myself even more heartache when I was forced to let you go anyways."

She reached over and took one of his hands with her smaller, softer hand. "Why didn't you just talk to me?"

"Having convinced myself you didn't love me, I thought it would be easier to keep my concerns to myself. If you thought I didn't love you and you didn't love me, it would be easier to let you go when the time came," Faron admitted, looking down at how well her hand fit into his.

"And what has changed now? I am still human. Unless something terrible happens, I will die before you do. Spirits, I will look older than you before many years pass."

"It's been pointed out, in several different ways, that either of us could pass at any time. I asked myself, would I rather mourn what we could have had for the rest of my life or enjoy what time we do have? While I'm still not alright with our differing lifespans, I would rather take the second option." Faron sighed and looked back up at Sabine. "I love you. I think I've loved you since the moment I laid eyes on you."

She smiled, finally, though the expression was blunted by her clear exhaustion. "You are a fool of an elf," she said. "But I love you."

Faron brought his free hand up to cup Sabine's face. "I am very much a foolish elf, but I am a foolish elf who loves you with all his heart."

An arm went around his neck, drawing him close enough for Sabine to kiss. Faron let her lead the kiss for several long, beautiful seconds before pulling back enough to rest his forehead against her. "Does this mean I'm forgiven for being an idiot?"

"I love you, and I forgive you," Sabine said. "The hurt of what you did will fade in time, but I don't want to deny either of us what we want."

"I will spend the rest of my life making up for the hurt I've caused you." Faron gave her a wry smile. "And any hurt I cause in the future."

"You do like to monumentally mess up every few months," Sabine teased.

"Apparently. I'll try not to make it a habit."

"Okay," Sabine replied. She kissed him again, deeper this time, as her hand settled against his cheek. The kissing quickly deepened, as Faron felt like he'd been starving without her touch. His hand swept down her side before his arm went around her waist, pulling her closer. She used the opportunity to crawl into his lap, straddling him.

The kissing broke temporarily when the need to breathe could no longer be ignored, and she looked down at him, her green eyes boring into him. "I don't want to think. I don't want to make decisions. I just want you."

Faron wrapped an arm around her upper back and another under Sabine's ass to ensure he had a good grip before standing. "I am fairly certain I can make you forget anything outside of this room." He gave her a teasing grin and he strode toward her bed.

"I don't want to be aware of anything but you and me for the next several hours," she replied.

"As you wish, Your Grace," Faron said as he gently placed Sabine upon the bed before dropping to his knees. His hands trailed along her legs, starting at her ankles and moving up. Slowly, he lifted her skirt, inch by inch, revealing her stocking-covered calves, knees, before reaching her bare thighs. He kissed just inside her right knee. "I have missed you," he said before kissing farther up her thigh. "Your taste," he added before biting.

She sucked in a breath. "What else?"

"The sounds you make when I do this." He nipped at her upper thigh again before kissing away the sting.

"Make sure I can feel the mark later," she requested.

If she wanted to feel his marks later, Faron would comply. He bit down harder this time, sucking the skin into his mouth. Then, he moved to the other thigh, repeating the motion. He groaned at the thought of the beautiful picture her otherwise creamy thighs would make when dotted with purple love bites.

He slowly pulled free the laces holding up her stockings, and Faron rolled the fabric down, revealing her soft, smooth skin. As he rolled the stockings down, his mouth followed, deciding to make that beautiful picture a reality. As he reached her ankle, he pulled off the first stocking, tossing it across the room before repeating the motion on her other leg.

Small moans escaped her mouth as he made each mark, and her hand found its way into his hair, a sensation Faron thought he might never again experience, until now. Faron sighed against Sabine, letting himself enjoy the tingling sensation traveling down his spine. He finished removing the second stocking and left a trail of bruises from her upper thigh to her ankle, before he started making his way back up toward her center.

Nudging her thighs further apart, Faron's hands found her hips, and he pulled her forward. "Lay back," he instructed, and when she complied, he brought her legs to rest on his shoulders.

Faron took hold of her skirts, bunching them up around her waist and just taking her in. The pink of her sex, the soft caramel curls, and the bud at the center. He drank in the view for another moment before leaning in and taking her needy bud between his lips. He nearly groaned at the taste of her, the way her hips shifted encouragingly toward him, the soft, breathy way she moaned his name.

Her breathing grew rapid under his efforts, her hips shifting restlessly, encouraging him all the more. He spent several long minutes using his tongue, mouth, and fingers to tease and delight her, sucking and nibbling as soft moans and cries left her delectable mouth. Faron cast his gaze up, watching her fists curl into the frilly bedding just before she cried out in her first trembling orgasm.

He only backed away as her body began relaxing, though Faron was far from done with her. He rose to his feet then climbed onto the bed, hovering over her, careful of his weight upon her smaller frame. He leaned down, kissing her possessively, letting her taste herself on his lips.

He did not rise up when those heated kisses drew to a close. "You're mine," he said, his voice deep and husky with his own need. "I am the only one allowed to kiss these," he said as he ran a finger along her lips. "Nip them." He followed through on his words. "Devour them." He kissed her now, deeply, delving into her mouth with his tongue.

She moaned softly in response, kissing him desperately in return. An arm went around his broad shoulders, pulling him down closer. Not able to help himself, he thrust his tongue slowly in and out of her mouth as his hips followed the motion, grinding against her in a deliciously slow tease.

He ran a hand along her side, down and back up, before moving to cup one of her breasts through the layers of her dress. "These," he stated, pulling himself up so he was straddling her. "These are perfect." He cupped the other breast now, gently fondling them both. "They are just the right size for my hands, as if made only for me."

His hands left her breasts to grasp the top of her dress, which rested just above her cleavage. "May I?" Faron asked. He still didn't know what the comte had tried to do, but this dress would forever be part of that memory for Sabine, and he wanted to replace it with something better. He waited for her permission, which she granted with a wordless nod.

With both hands, he tore it apart, laces and eyelets breaking under the strain. He did the same with the corset, leaving her bare breasts on display for him. Faron took a moment to enjoy this view as well, before he raised his hands to cup her breasts. "Perfect," he said, brushing a thumb over a firm, rosy nipple. "Look how responsive they are." He leaned down, one hand moving to support his weight, and took a nipple into his mouth, licking and sucking it to a tight bud. The action was brief, teasing, and he pulled away almost as quickly, blowing cold air onto the wet bud. "They respond beautifully. You respond beautifully," he said softly before taking the nipple back to his mouth. His other hand mimicked the movements of his mouth with the other nipple.

She suppressed a moan, and Faron's head rose. "No," he said. "You will moan for me so everyone can hear you." He bit down again. His other hand pinched her rosy, stiff nipple before he resumed licking and sucking. She moaned, loud and unapologetically. They continued like this for several more minutes before he lifted his head and switched to the other breast.

"I need more," she breathed out.

Faron chuckled against her breast. "I will give you more. I'll give you anything you ask for so long as it is within my power." He slowly started kissing down to her stomach, his tongue delving into her navel.

Sabine's hand found one of her abandoned breasts and gently began kneading. He watched her intently, nodding approvingly as he sat back on his knees. "Lift your hips before I rip your dress from your body."

"I'm surprised you haven't already," Sabine replied as she complied with his directive.

He slid the rest of the dress out from under her and tossed it to the side. "Next time, I'll tear it all to shreds if you want." He moved to her ankle and started kissing back up to her inner thigh, where he once again bit down.

"What else?" Sabine asked.

Faron's mind had to scramble before he recalled their conversation. "One would think you like being possessed, my lady."

"By you, yes," she replied.

"Only by me," he repeated. Instead of continuing to kiss to her center, Faron stood and took Sabine in, eyes traveling from her feet to her eyes. "You are the most magnificent, most beautiful creature I have ever laid eyes on," Faron observed as he continued to drink her in. "You are marvelous to behold."

"You admire what is yours?"

His eyes darkened with sheer lust at her words. "I admire you. You are perfect in every way. You being mine is just a benefit." He moved his hands up to the laces on his leather vest and started to undo them, shrugging the garment off his shoulders and onto the floor before starting on his shirt.

She sat up and beckoned him closer. Faron closed the distance between them, letting his hands fall to his sides. Her fingers trailed down his chest, brushing against the dark hair as it was revealed. She looked up at him, gazes locked as she pushed the fabric of his shirt from his body. Faron held her gaze as his chest was bared to her, scars and all. She only broke eye contact when she leaned in to kiss along the hollow of his throat. A hand moved down lower to cup his erection through his trousers.

Faron gave a low moan and balled his hands into fists but did not stop her. "Enjoying what's yours?" he asked.

"Exceedingly," she replied, lips brushing against his skin. She undid the button at the top of his pants, letting her fingers trail along the path from his navel downward.

Faron's breath sped up, but he kept his eyes on her, watching everything she did, every expression that crossed her face, drinking her in. He'd never understand how she'd so thoroughly bewitched him, but he did not begrudge the spell.

With his pants now unfastened, she directed him to remove his boots, and he kicked those off without protest. Only then did she push his trousers from his hips and gently directed him to step out of them. She looked back up at him, meeting his gaze with her own. And while looking at him, she leaned forward a bit, taking him into her mouth.

"Sabine," Faron hissed out, gently grasping her hair in one hand while the other went to her shoulder. His eyes watched as his cock slowly disappeared into her mouth. "You're so beautiful with your lips wrapped around my cock."

Mischievous eyes looked up to him as her tongue swirled around the sensitive head. As her lips and tongue worked, she took his balls in hand, ever so gently kneading them. She groaned in satisfaction as they drew closer to his body.

"Spirits," he growled out again, his hand tightening slightly but not painfully on her shoulder as he fought not to thrust into her mouth. Faron's breathing grew ragged, her name falling from his lips like a prayer and unrestrained moans escaping from his lips. He fought to keep his hips still, but soon, he issued a warning. "Sabine, you should stop, lest I lose control." The words only prompted Sabine to do more as her focus returned to the head of his aching cock.

Faron grasped her hair tightly, stilling her movements, and began to thrust into her mouth, pulling out and thrusting as deep as she could take him. She made no protest and even groaned in delight as he fucked her throat. She put a hand on one of his, grasping it with no demand.

"Spirits, Sabine," he moaned and increased his pace, thrusting deeper, trusting her to stop him if needed. No such request came. She made sounds of affirmation and encouragement. As he felt himself grow closer to release, he picked up his pace, hitting the back of her throat.

He roared as he came, harsh and without warning, and he rocked his hips in jerky movements until he finished spilling. "Swallow," he ordered, his voice rough. Briefly, he wondered if he had pushed too far, but as he withdrew from her, she gazed up at him, licking her lips.

He dropped to his knees, pulling her in for a deep, bruising kiss. Her hands tangled in his hair as they kissed, hard and needy. He looked at her half dazed when she pulled away, her breathing heavy and her lips slightly swollen.

"Are you alright?" he asked, resting his forehead against her.

"Mmmhmm," she replied, and she laughed softly. "Just need a moment."

"Take as much time as you need," Faron said as he raised one hand to gently run it through her hair. "You are stunning," he told her softly.

"Am I? I think the same of you, you know," she whispered before kissing him again.

Faron just smiled, warm and content, though he did not reply. "If ever we repeat what just happened, if I am too rough, you will tap my hand."

"You did not go far enough," she replied, surprising him. "But I will remember all the same."

Faron raised an eyebrow. "Would you like me to truly choke you on my cock next time? To shove it so far down your throat you gag on it, struggling to breathe?" he asked her, his voice low and rough.

She nodded. "And if you insist on pulling my hair, you should commit to the task."

The hand stroking her hair stopped. Without warning, he grabbed a fistful, forcing her head back. "Like this?" he asked before using the angle to lean down and bite her neck.

"Yes," she breathed out. "Why do you like biting me?"

"Because you are mine, and these marks tell the rest of the world." He kissed up to her jaw then down the other side of her neck. "You also moan so loudly when I do it." He bit down, ensuring he left a matching mark.

"Do you enjoy seeing them on full display?"

"Oh, yes. I enjoy knowing you wear my marks, even in places others can't see." He felt himself stirring again against her hip.

"And where is your favorite place to leave one?"

"Here," he said, kissing the spot on her neck where one mark already bloomed. The hand wrapped around her waist moved down along her hip and between her legs to press down on the mark he had already left on her inner thigh. "And here. Though truly, there isn't a spot on your body I wouldn't enjoy marking. With my mouth or my hands." The hand on her inner thigh trailed along to her hot center, slowly caressing her. "Spirits, you are dripping." He groaned softly and dipped two fingers inside of Sabine, taking in the way her eyes closed and lips parted. He crooked his fingers up, slowly and carefully teasing her. His thumb pressed against her clit, rubbing gentle circles at first. As his hand worked, he lowered his mouth back to her breast.

He sucked the taut nipple into his mouth, biting down and twirling his tongue around it before pulling off and repeating the action on her other breast. The pace of his fingers increased, almost desperate to drive her to climax. He felt her tremble as waves of pleasure surged through her, and Faron continued thrusting into her with his fingers, only slowing as she came down from her climax. Pulling away from her breast, he kissed her deeply once again.

When the kiss broke, he lifted her from the edge of the bed and deposited her back in the middle of the bed. As he kissed down her body, he paused long enough to look up at her. "Place your hands above your head and do not move them. I am going to see how long I can enjoy what is mine before you break and push me away."

He growled with satisfaction as she obeyed, intoxicated by her willingness to explore and open herself up to him in ways she never had before. He moved so he was positioned between her legs, and after placing them over his shoulders, Faron leaned in, licking from her entrance to her clit before sucking the bud into his mouth.

A soft moan left her mouth at first, though the reaction grew the longer his mouth and tongue teased her. "Fuck," she breathed out as a third orgasm grew close. Faron grinned around Sabine's clit, nipping at it gently, before his tongue started long firm strokes against it.

The action was enough to trigger another orgasm, and he watched as she struggled to keep her hands where she'd been instructed to. "Good girl," he praised. Then he lowered his head and resumed his prior actions. Knowing she was still going to be sensitive, Faron gripped her hip in a near bruising hold.

"Oh," she breathed out in a near whimper, her body moving as though internally debating if she should pull away or not.

The hand grasping her hip let go long enough to give her a small slap as a reminder she was to stay put as he tongue-fucked her to climax. A short sound of surprise left her at the light slap, and Faron realized she had not liked it or, at least, wasn't sure if she did.

Faron broke away long enough to meet her eyes, an apology written in them before his mouth met her center again, then his fingers joined. She was close. The way her limbs twitched and her breathing grew more rapid and desperate, Faron knew it was only a matter of moments.

"I can't. I can't..." she insisted, her hips confirming and contradicting her words.

Faron's fingers didn't stop. He did, however, remove his mouth from her long enough to respond. "You can and you will." He resumed his actions, his tongue lapping at the abused bud with unmatched enthusiasm.

When she fell to pieces moments later, limbs trembling, he wasn't surprised to see her lower her arms and force herself back from him before simply collapsing on the bed.

Faron sat back on his heels and smiled at Sabine with a hungry, needy grin. His need stood prominent, though he gave her a few moments before he crawled over her. His arms bracketed her head as his erection brushed against her center. "I would ask if you are ready, but I can already tell you are." He shifted his hips until the head of his cock pressed forward. A soft, weak moan left her mouth as he entered her, and in their new, more intimate position, she put an arm around his shoulder.

He waited for her to settle. "Wrap your legs around me," he said before leaning in to kiss her as he began with slow, shallow thrusts, knowing the more intimate, softer moment was needed and appreciated. He pressed his forehead against hers when the kiss ended. "You're amazing," he said. "And feel amazing."

"Yeah?" she asked, the hand resting on his shoulder moving up to the nape of his neck.

"Yes," he said with a moan. "You always feel good."

"So do you, almost too much," she said with a shaky laugh. "How?"

"Like, I physically cannot stand more, but I might die if you stop."

Faron made a pleased sound in the back of his throat. "Then I will not stop anytime soon."

She let out another shaky laugh. "Try to go a little slower for me if you intend to continue."

"Whatever you need," Faron said. The slower pace had her clinging to him still, especially as her body threatened to be seized by another ruthless orgasm. "Come for me," he whispered against her lips, feeling her start to tighten but knowing she was fighting it.

She nodded and kissed him, and she held on to him as tightly as possible as she gave in to her body's demands. Faron kissed her deeply, swallowing any cries that passed her lips as he continued thrusting. He felt the familiar build of pressure precluding his own release, and when he came, it was accompanied by a roar of a moan. His hips moved in a jerky rhythm until his pleasure stuttered. He kissed her again, softly and lovingly, before pulling out.

Not wanting to hurt Sabine, he moved to lie on the other side of her and pulled her to him. "Are you alright?" he asked. His free hand began lightly stroking her light caramel hair.

Sabine nodded against him, and noting the exhausted trembling in her limbs, Faron just continued to run fingers through her hair.

Eventually, after several long minutes of silence and Sabine's breathing returning to normal, she laughed softly. "Are all elves this insatiable, or is it just you in particular?"

Faron chuckled. "I cannot speak for others, but even now, I want you." He pressed his lower half against her, already half hard again.

"You will have to wait," she murmured.

"And I shall." Faron kissed her forehead then slowly disentangled himself from Sabine. "I will be right back," he promised as he stood.

He walked into the washroom, and soon, the sound of running water could be heard. Lavender and mint wafted through the air as Faron rejoined Sabine. Without a word, he lifted her in his arms and carried her back to the washroom. He lowered her into the water of the large deep tub, then stepped in and settled back, pulling her against him.

"I see you have learned how a woman is to be carried," she couldn't help but tease.

Faron knew his low laughter could be felt by Sabine as it vibrated through his chest. "I don't know. Being able to carry you over my shoulder with your pert ass within biting reach does sound like fun."

She laughed as well. "You would think so," she replied.

"I would, yes." He reached for a cleaning cloth and soap, and wordlessly, he began gently washing her. She closed her eyes, relaxing more against him as his hands passed over different parts of her body, careful to avoid being too intimate.

"I love the way you touch me," Sabine shared. "I don't even care how."

"I love touching you," Faron replied, placing a soft kiss against her hair.

"I can feel just how much," Sabine jested, laughing softly. The physical manifestation of Faron's desire pressed against her. A rumble of affirmation sounded in Faron's throat at the acknowledgment. "I may have to do something about it."

"You are tired and likely sore," Faron argued.

"I am," Sabine replied. "But I want you." She looked over her shoulder, green eyes meeting his dark ones. Faron would deny her nothing.

Faron made a sound as he thought then nodded as he made a decision. "Turn around and straddle my hips."

She rose from her position and turned easily, thanks to the size of the tub. She straddled his hips, helping to anchor her position by putting her arms around his neck.

"Ride me," he instructed. "At your own pace and speed. Tell me where to touch you or if I should keep my hands to myself. But I want you to ride me."

"Do not keep your hands to yourself," she replied. "I want them wherever you think they need to be." She let an arm drop from him as she moved slightly, then took his erection in hand to guide him inside her. She adjusted the spread of her knees and slowly sank onto him.

A low moan left his lips, and Faron's head fell back against the edge of the tub as he took in the feeling of being buried deep in her. A hand went to her hip, fingers brushing along her smooth skin. For a long moment, they remained still and connected, and when she finally rose and fell, it was at a teasing pace.

She increased the pace in incremental amounts, moaning softly as the motions ignited her nerve endings again. She leaned in and kissed him deeply as she rode him. Faron's hand smoothed up her back and back down, this round entirely more gentle and intimate. He loved it just as much.

Sabine's breathing grew more rapid as she moved, and Faron noticed the signs of her impending climax.

He drew her into another heated kiss. "Close already?" he asked playfully, knowing he wasn't far behind.

"Yes," she replied breathily.

"Come for me," he commanded. "I'll take care of you after."

She nodded, her movements growing more erratic as she rode him. He could feel himself getting close as well, but he wanted her to fall apart again. He needed it. She leaned into him, grasping on as her body fell into delicious tremors.

Faron gave a low growl and made slight adjustments to their positions so he could pursue his own climax. He took hold of Sabine's hips and began thrusting into her. She moaned with increasing volume and depth as he fucked her, and Faron drank in the sight of her. The way she tilted her head back, her throat exposed, his bite marks available for all to see, the way her breast bounced up and down. "Perfect," he moaned and increased the pace.

Keeping one hand firmly on her hip, he reached with the other to her core, where he began rubbing her sensitive bud again. "Once more," he demanded roughly. "You're going to come for me at least once more."

The sounds she made at the renewed contact were nearly primal, and Faron didn't quite know how he managed to hold back. "Scream for me," he said. "Let the whole estate know how much you want me." He gritted his teeth, holding back, listening to the sounds leaving her mouth as she simultaneously sought and resisted his renewed efforts to bring her over the edge.

Only when she finally fell apart did Faron give in, roaring her name as bolts of pleasure shot through him. Even when his body relaxed and occasional aftershocks rocked him, having withdrawn from her, Faron held her close, in no rush to lose their connection. "You did so well," he whispered in her hair.

"I don't think I'll ever walk again," she murmured against his skin.

He laughed softly. "You will. Just maybe not tomorrow."

"How long until you'll want me again?" she retorted in a tired, but teasing tone.

His cock twitched. "Oh, not long, I suppose," he said casually, before wrapping an arm around her to hold her still while he drained and refilled the tub. He leaned back, gently pulling her with him. "Rest for a minute. Let the water relax your muscles. You'll be less sore in the morning if you do." He smiled as she nodded and remained draped over him, and he allowed himself to gently run fingers through her thick hair as he held her.

After some time had passed—Faron had no idea how much—he spoke. "Let's go to bed."

"Okay," Sabine replied, quiet and content. She sat up and eased off of his lap, allowing him to stand. He offered her a hand, helping her to her feet. Faron stepped out of the tub then helped her, careful in case she was unsteady after their evening. He pulled her against him, kissing her softly, and only released her long enough to grab one of the nearby towels. Wordlessly, he knelt before her, gently drying her.

"And why are you doing that?" Sabine asked.

"Because it pleases me to do so," Faron said as he slowly dried up one leg then down the other.

"It makes me feel adored."

"As you should." Her legs now dry, he started drying her torso, making sure to soak up every drop of water.

"And do you adore me?"

"With my entire being," he said, no hint of sarcasm in his voice.

"Then finish drying us off and take me to bed."

Faron nodded and continued to dry off her chest, then back, then arms, and gently wiping the wetness from her face before moving to her hair. Once satisfied, he quickly dried himself before asking her silently if he could pick her up. When she nodded, he lifted her, one arm under her legs and the other under her back as he cradled her to his chest. Striding to the bed, he laid her down gently.

Sabine looked up at him from her new position, spent and beautiful. "Join me," she requested, reaching out for him.

And Faron did. Laying down next to her, he moved the covers over them and pulled her against him, letting out a contented sigh.

"Good night," she said quietly. "Try to give me at least a couple of hours."

"So, you only wish for two hours, then?" Faron asked playfully. "I can grant you that."

"I might," she said with a gentle laugh. "I want you as badly as you want me. I just seem to have a longer recovery period."

"Then sleep, and you know I will seek to have you again before morning." He kissed her softly and rolled onto his back, pulling her mostly onto him.

Chapter Fifteen

Tristian sat behind his desk, head bowed, red hair lit up from the way the sun shone down on him from the windows behind him. The quill in his hand scratched quickly across the letter he wrote. He barely acknowledged Sabine as she entered the office after he'd invited her in. She paused only a moment to allow him to greet her, and when he did not, she spoke. "I see you are busy, so I shall not take much of your time," Sabine said, looking down at Tristian.

Tristian finally looked up at Sabine, his normal bland smile on his lips, but there was something off about it somehow. "Not at all, my dear. I was just finishing some correspondence, but I am done now. Please sit." He motioned to the seat on the other side of the desk.

She debated sitting, feeling as though compliance would be viewed as an invitation to linger. He might also view the action as happy obedience, a trait Sabine was not willing to provide him. Still, she sat on the edge of one of the chairs, poised beautifully but ready to rise as needed.

"Let me get you a drink. I know I'm parched," Tristian said, rising from his desk. He leisurely strolled over to one of the tables close to the door. On top sat several different types of liquor in pretty crystal decanters. "What would you like? Wine or something stronger?"

Sabine shook her head, the motion reminding her of the marks on her neck, now covered by the jewelry she wore. Her desire to impart news and be on her way was more than desirable. "I simply wish to speak with you," she said.

"Please, speak your mind," Tristian said, flashing another not-quite-right smile before turning his back to her as he made himself a drink.

Sabine nodded. "My staff and I have enjoyed our time at your beautiful estate. However, it is time for us to depart. I have asked my people to prepare for departure, so we will soon be out of your hair."

"Truly, I'm sorry to hear such news." He turned to face her but did not return to the desk. Instead, he casually walked past the door, stopping in front of it. "May I ask why? I thought you would stay until the prince arrived at the very least."

She watched him carefully, alert of some unseen danger, though she could not act. "I am afraid I am ready to return home, as is my staff. His highness is welcome to visit me at my estate if it pleases him."

Tristian nodded and studied Sabine. "I assume you've put no more thought to marriage? We could be very good together."

Sabine shook her head. "I am afraid I am not available to marry, nor is it an arrangement I think would benefit either of us."

Tristian let out a deep sigh before he once more turned his back on Sabine so he was facing the door. He made a move Sabine couldn't quite see, but the clicking of the lock sliding into place echoed loud enough in the silent room to let her know what had happened. "I think the marriage would benefit both of us, but my dear Sabine, do you think I'm stupid?' he asked as he turned back to face her. Leaning against the rather solid door, he took a sip of his drink from the crystal glass. His left eyebrow raised as he waited for her answer.

"I do not," Sabine replied. "But I think you believe me naïve."

Tristian gave a dark chuckle, a sneer forming on his normally bland face. "'Place your hands above your head, and do not move them.' I assume that has more to do with your refusal to marry me than any other objections," he said, the casual tone to his voice not matching his demeanor. "You can make up a pretty lie of course, but I think we both know better."

She stood then, meeting his shrewd gaze with her own. "I believe I said I was not available to marry, and I am not. Not that I am required to defend myself, but I have not lied."

The glass in his hand shattered as it hit the desk to the left of Sabine, and suddenly, Tristian was there in front of her, eyes burning with rage. "You are not turning down my suit for some lowborn elf. You will not disgrace me like this. I refuse to allow it," he growled out.

Sabine remained where she was, shoulders squared and expression unimpressed. "I am rejecting your suit for a great many reasons, not the least of which is a man who can make me writhe in absolute bliss."

The words barely left Sabine's mouth before Tristian's open palm collided with her cheek, the force of it might have sent her to the ground except for his other hand coming up to wrap around her throat.

She struggled against the hold on her throat, hands clawing at the fingers around her neck which prevented her from calling out or breathing. Tristian carried on as though he took no notice.

"My maid told me how you like to be fucked. She listened to your entire sordid evening, and you know what it tells me? I should have held you down and fucked you in the library like I wanted to. I should have shoved away your persistent rejections and your skirts and fucked you like the whore you are." Using the hand on her throat, he dragged her to one of the small tables against the wall then used his free hand to clear it with a quick sweep. Tightening the grip on her throat, he lifted her so she was perched on the table then slammed the back of her head into the wall.

"I think I will rectify my mistake of kindness now. Then when I'm done, I will call in the priestess. We will be married before the day is done, and your body and lands will be mine." With his free hand, he started to undo his belt. "I am going to enjoy owning you," he growled then forced his lips against hers.

The nails which had clawed at his fingers now struck at his face, leaving four long scratches going down the length of it. Sabine reached for something, anything, to better defend herself.

"You bitch," Tristian yelled as he was forced to pull away from the unwanted kiss, his hand tightened even more on her throat. "You don't have to be awake. I just thought your screams might be fun." His belt undone, he started working on the buttons of his trousers.

Sabine's fingers found and wrapped around something long and metallic. Her eyes darted to the side to see the small dagger she usually carried with her, still concealed in a hidden pocket of her dress. Her vision already swam, having had no proper breath for several long seconds. Without thinking or much thought to aim, she drove the thing into the closest fleshy part of Tristian with as much force as she could muster.

Tristian screamed and, in his surprise and pain, let go of Sabine, dropping to his knees as he saw the tiny dagger buried halfway into his side. He looked at it, then back to her, shock written on his features.

Gasping and dragging in air, Sabine barely noted a pounding from outside. As she took a third gulp of air, Tristian grabbed her by the ankle and pulled her off the table. She fell to the ground with a cry of pain, the back of her head bouncing off the stone floor with an audible smack. Her vision swam and her breathing felt more difficult than it should, and try as she might, she couldn't pull herself away from her attacker.

Tristian pulled the dagger from his side, dropped it on the ground, then scrambled up and onto Sabine, straddling her waist. "I was going to go easy on you. I was going to be gentle, but now? Now I'm going to make it hurt." Tristian backhanded Sabine again then wrapped both hands around her throat. "With enough money, the priestess will declare us wed. You won't even have to be there. I'm going to enjoy fucking you until the only name you know is mine."

Blackness swirled around the edges of Sabine's vision, slowly growing as Tristian continued to cut off her air supply. She felt him pull her skirts up her legs, the cooler air touching her skin somehow breaking through the fog. She felt her consciousness fading, and her hands, which had clawed at his own in feeble attempts of escape, fell to the ground with soft thuds. As blackness engulfed Sabine, she didn't much care what happened next.

Just before she fell unconscious, two things happened at once. The window behind Tristian exploded in a shower of wood and glass as a leather-clad figure broke through. Avana screamed out her rage as daggers flew. On the other side of the room, the large oak door shattered, and Faron strode in, covered in blood, his family sword held in a firm grip. Later, no one would know if the three daggers managed to kill Tristian before Faron severed the comte's head from his body in one strong sword swipe.

Tristian's grip on her throat released, and Sabine could suck in deep lungfuls of air. Blood spurted from Tristian's neck, and his body slumped forward, landing against Sabine with a *thump*.

"Get him off me," Sabine gasped out, parts of the words halted by her bruised throat.

Avana kicked the body off Sabine as Faron set his sword down and dropped to his knees beside her.

"I need you here to watch our backs," Faron said to Avana as he helped Sabine to sit up.

"They jumped you too, huh?" the blonde asked as she pulled her daggers from Tristian's body, wiping them off on him before going to guard the door.

"What can I do?" Faron asked Sabine, anger shining in his eyes as he took in the purple bruising on her throat and her swelling face.

She coughed again and shook her head. "Don't think there's much to do," she managed, hand gently touching the front of her neck. She pulled off the intricate necklace she wore, as though freeing her throat from the heavy jewelry would help her breathe. She looked up and noted his appearance. "Are you okay?"

Faron held out a hand for the necklace and tucked it away in a pocket for safekeeping. "Yes. I heard glass shatter, and when I went to investigate, the guards attacked me. Tristian planned out the attack."

"I was attacked too, and for once, I was minding my own business," Avana said, shooting worried glances at Sabine.

The sound of footsteps had both elves looking at the door. Avana took her daggers out, sneering, while Faron rose in a smooth motion, picking up his sword and standing guard over Sabine.

Finn came into view, pausing in the doorway as he spotted Avana first, then Faron. "What's happened?" he asked, eyes wide.

"Tristian attacked Sabine. His guards attacked Avana and me. You were safe? Are the others safe?" Faron asked as he knelt beside Sabine again.

"I am safe, but I haven't seen Meri and Lisbeth," Finn said. "I will go look for them and fetch a healer." He disappeared from the doorway without further discussion.

Faron turned his attention back to Sabine. "Where else are you injured?"

Sabine reached up and gingerly touched the back of her head. "He slammed my head against the wall. I hit it again when he pulled me off the table."

Faron reached out and gently ran his fingertips along the back of her head. His eyes never left hers.

"What the shit even happened? Why did he attack you?" Avana asked from her position near the door.

Sabine winced as Faron's fingers hit a particularly sensitive spot on the back of her head. "He had a maid report hearing Faron and me last night. He quoted very specific things." She swallowed, hoping it would relieve some of the pain.

Faron's hand paused, rage and guilt flooding his expression.

"I'm okay," Sabine quietly promised, helping to calm his strong emotions.

Faron nodded. "May I pick you up?" he asked.

"Can you with your injuries?" she asked, though she nodded her consent all the same.

"They are barely flesh wounds. You have a head wound," he pointed out before gathering her into his arms and standing. "Avana, please guard our way."

"With pleasure," she said as they left the office. With Avana in the lead, they moved as quickly as possible to Sabine's rooms, where Lisbeth and Meri waited outside. The redhead paced in front of the door while Meri leaned against the wall just watching.

"Your Grace!" Lisbeth moved to rush to Sabine's side, only for Meri to stop her.

"Love, open the door, and let's get her somewhere safe," she said.

Lisbeth quickly did as instructed, making sure to secure the door as soon as everyone was inside.

Faron gently set Sabine down on her bed. "Where is Finn?" Faron asked.

"He said he was going to see if the estate had any healing potions. He also wanted to make sure no one is in trouble for what happened to the comte. He was concerned he might have to go to the village," Meri said.

Despite the headache she would inevitably suffer for days and the swelling of bruises on her face and neck, Sabine was mostly doing well, which allowed her to think quickly. "We are going to have to answer for his death."

"Considering how beaten up you are, I think we will be just fine," Meri replied. She pushed Faron out of the way, no small feat with the way he hovered over Sabine. The older woman blew on her hands, and they began to shimmer as her stifled ice powers emerged. She rested them on the sides of Sabine's aching, swelling face. Sabine could just make out the magical gold bracelets on each of Meri's wrists that kept her magic subdued.

The duchesse shivered a little at the initial touch, though laughed softly at herself before wincing from the pain in her throat. "I'm never quite prepared for the cold."

"No one ever is, but at least I'm useful in a pinch. You'll have to show me where the lump on the back of your head is so I can get that next."

"Will Finn be able to find a healer?" Faron asked Lisbeth.

She shrugged. "I hope so."

Sabine cleared her throat before speaking, though she immediately realized it had been a poor decision. "I think it's safest to assume we won't find a healer on the estate. Not with how he's treated the villagers," she rasped before pointing out a tender spot on her head for Meri.

"You should make sure the swelling doesn't go down too much," Avana said from the other side of the bed. "If Finn went to get someone official, they'll want to see what he did to her."

"I know, but thank you, Avana," Meri said as she moved one hand to Sabine's throat and the other to the back of her head.

"What happened?" Lisbeth asked quietly.

"Tristian tried to force himself on me. He slammed my head into a wall and choked me, and after I fought back and stabbed him, he told me he planned to hurt me. Badly," Sabine replied.

Meri let out a low growl. "And you said he's dead?" she demanded of Faron.

"He took three of Avana's knives to the back, and I removed his head from his shoulders. So yes, he is dead."

A knock sounded at the door before Finn let himself inside. "Tristian has been discovered," he reported to the group.

"What is the initial reaction, and by whom?" Faron asked.

"The maid bringing him breakfast," Finn shared. "And when she reported it to his steward, the few staff who are here had already reported hearing distressed female screams and fighting." He looked at Sabine. "I believe they know you were his intended victim, and the village authorities have arrived to validate the accusation with the staff. From what I overheard, no one is blaming you or any of your staff."

Avana scoffed. "I bet he told his handful of soldiers to take care of me and Faron and planned for no other questions or trouble."

"It's possible. None of the staff seems to know what happened, but they are willingly telling the honest version of events," Finn said. "With you and Faron detained, or worse, he could have gotten away with much more than he managed."

"He didn't think things through very well," Sabine rasped. Lisbeth walked to the side table where a pitcher and glasses waited, and she poured the duchesse a glass before bringing it to her. Sabine took small, tentative sips. "I outrank him in title and assets. My lands are larger and produce better goods. I'm also well-liked by my people. Had he gotten further in his efforts, he'd still have much to explain." She glanced over at Faron, wishing she could offer some comfort. He fidgeted as though he craved something physical he could do.

Faron reached out and took Sabine's hand, and in his eyes, she could see he wished he hadn't killed Tristian quite so quickly. "You should demand payment for what has happened to you."

Sabine squeezed his hand gently, letting her thumb gently caress the top in a soothing pattern. "I will have to demand quite a lot in restitution," she agreed. "In more stable times, the ruler would have to intervene on Tristian's behalf as he is not here to speak for his actions. We have no ruler, just two feuding princes."

"We should send a request asking for Prince Louis's aid. He does owe you for your continued support," Meri pointed out.

"I will write to him," Sabine confirmed.

"Why don't I pour you some wine, and Lisbeth can write as you dictate to her?" Finn suggested. "The wine might soothe your throat a little better." A nod from Sabine had him crossing the room to the decanter display while Lisbeth gathered parchment, pen, and ink.

Once the new drink was in her hand and Lisbeth was ready to write, Sabine began speaking, explaining with great detail what she had experienced at Tristian's hands and how she'd been forced to defend herself.

As she wrote, tears ran down Lisbeth's cheeks while the others listened in silent horror and fury. Lisbeth handed over the parchment, and Sabine quickly skimmed it.

"Make a copy for both princes, and I will sign them," she said, her raspy voice a little stronger than it had been. Her throat hurt. Everything hurt, but she could not resolve those complaints.

"I will, and I'll get them both sent off as soon as you sign," Lisbeth promised.

"I'll take them. No one will fuck with me on the road," Avana volunteered.

"Be safe all the same, Avana," Sabine replied. "And thank you."

Avana nodded and went to stand beside Lisbeth as she copied over the letter.

"What should we do now?" Faron asked both Sabine and Finn.

"The wisest course would be to wait until one of his people requests to check on Her Grace," Finn replied. "We can start packing to leave for when the interview ends."

"I would appreciate being ready to leave," Sabine confirmed.

Another knock sounded at the door. "Your Grace?" a voice, one belonging to Tristian's steward, could be heard at the door.

Finn walked to answer as Faron stood, drawing his sword but keeping the point down, while Meri palmed a dagger. Sabine chose to remain seated, a decision based on what made her seem most vulnerable and best displayed the extent of her injuries. She took a breath and nodded to Finn.

"How can we be of assistance?" Finn asked after he opened the door.

The steward made to step in, but he paused as he took in the expressions of everyone in the room. "I, uh." he began, and spotting Sabine in the distance, he quickly bowed. "Your Grace, we have been made aware of the comte's attack and his subsequent death. The local magistrate is interviewing the staff now, but she would like to speak with you as well. Assuming you are amenable."

"Of course," Sabine replied.

The steward nodded. "Thank you, Your Grace. I will let her know." He looked down, shamefaced. "I cannot apologize—"

"It is not for you to apologize for Tristian's actions," Sabine replied. "Based on his aggression, not only did he intend to violate me, but I can safely conclude he wished to kill members of my staff. His death occurred in my defense, and his actions will be reported to the royal family."

"Of course, Your Grace," the steward said. "As is your right. I would be happy to provide additional guards for you while you wait for the magistrate. Anything at all you need, I can provide."

Sabine motioned to Faron. "He is in charge of my security, and given the use of the guards to apprehend my own during the attack, I think I must decline the offer."

The steward grew pale. "This estate, this house, could never condone an attack on a guest such as Your Grace—"

"The bruises around my neck suggest it does," Sabine snapped. "Whoever ends up overseeing the estate in the future should make sure the people in its employ are trustworthy. Safe."

"Lord Tristian's father would be appalled by your attack. I assure you, we shall let no further harm come to you and your party while you await to speak with the magistrate." He bowed once more to Sabine. "Please, if we can be of assistance, let one of the members of the household know." The steward saw himself out.

Sabine, meanwhile, finished her glass of wine.

Faron looked at the others in the room. "Out," he demanded of them.

Meri gave Faron an unimpressed look, but she grabbed Lisbeth, who was shooting worried looks at Sabine. "We will be right next door packing," she said as they left.

Avana walked over to the letters Lisbeth had finished, scrawled a signature which vaguely resembled Sabine's, then scooped up the parchment before leaving as well. Finn nodded to Sabine before doing the same.

The moment the door was closed, Faron moved to lock it before prowling back to where Sabine sat, his knees hitting the ground hard in front of her. He gazed at her, taking in the bruises and the swelling, compassion and love in his eyes, which were tinged with guilt. He raised a hand and gently caressed her cheek, careful of the bruising.

Sabine closed her eyes, leaning into his touch.

"I hate what happened to you, and I swear on my life it will be the only time," he vowed. "I will kill every living person, every living thing on the planet before I let someone hurt you again."

She didn't respond at first, just focused on the feel of his hand on her skin and his voice. "I was not prepared for his violent response. I thought he was going to kill me." She shook her head. "I think he was going to strike, no matter what else might have occurred."

"There is a chance he would have held off until he thought you were trapped in an engagement." He moved onto the bed, his arms open for her. "I would never have let that happen."

"Both Grégoire and Tristian thought the matter was settled," Sabine pointed out after she went to him without hesitation.

"There's nothing I would not have done to prevent a marriage between you and Tristian," Faron replied. His gaze drew dark and distant before finally returning to her.

"Your words suspiciously sound like a plan," she said before requesting more to drink.

Faron rose, refilled her wine, and resettled beside her. "If I had to run off with you to prevent a coerced wedding, I would have done it. I'd have married you myself if necessary. I know a priestess who owes me a favor."

"You'd have married me like that?" she asked after a couple of sips of wine.

"I would have asked you properly once we were away and safe," Faron conceded. "But I would never have allowed you to marry Tristian. I'm not rational about you, and I grow less so by the day."

She nodded and allowed herself to rest her head against his chest. "You should reach out to the priestess who owes you a favor."

"Should I?" he asked, hope ringing in his voice.

"You should," she confirmed. "I told you. I am yours."

A sound rumbled deep in Faron's throat. "And I am yours." His eyes darted away from Sabine for a moment and then back. "I don't have a ring or any of the other traditional items."

Sabine shrugged. "Such things can be acquired. My desire to marry you isn't marred because you don't have a token to exchange."

"Still, had I not been such an ass and acknowledged my feelings before last night, maybe I'd have had something for this moment." Faron reached out and took Sabine's hands in his. "I can at least do this part right." He gave her a soft smile from where he now rested on his knees. "Sabine Vassetre, will you marry me?"

She smiled despite her aching head, throat, and face. "Of course. I am yours, and I want to be in every possible way."

Faron rose up to kiss Sabine gently before settling back down onto his knees. "I think I can fix the ring issue," he said, and he raised his hands to his hair and began making a small braid.

Sabine watched as Faron's large hands created the delicate braid, smooth and detailed in a way a man of his size usually could not manage. Once the braid was complete, Faron reached down with one hand and pulled a knife from his boot. He made a careful cut at the top part of the braid before putting the knife away.

"A braid?" Sabine asked, curious.

Faron reached out for Sabine's hand again, and he wrapped the braided strand of hair around her wrist. "It's a very old elven tradition. In place of rope or token, one would give the other their hair to wear as a bracelet to show they are taken and that it's a love match." He tied off the end, giving it a little tug to make sure it was secure and wouldn't slip off. "Until we find a suitable ring or other token."

"Oh," Sabine said as she turned her wrist to look at it. She smiled, finding it a suitable symbol. "Then I shall wear it."

Faron's face took on a reddish tint as he looked at the lock of hair around her wrist before raising her wrist to his lips and laying a kiss on Sabine's pulse point. "When you are feeling better, we will celebrate property. But I think it may be best if we rest now. What do you think?"

"I agree," Sabine said. "And we need to wash the blood from you, either way."

"I will prepare us a bath after you've spoken with the magistrate," Faron promised.

"Okay," she agreed with a nod.

Thankfully, they did not have to wait for long for the magistrate to visit. Sabine's rank and obvious injuries endeared her to the older woman. They quickly ran through the events, with Faron standing close the entire time.

"You poor thing," the magistrate said as she gathered her notes a half hour later. "I suggest a good pain tonic and some sleep. I shall make sure Comte Tristian's people treat you well until you are ready to leave. I shall also notify the princes of my findings. They will both be alarmed at how poorly you were treated."

"Thank you," Sabine said with a nod.

The magistrate saw herself out soon after, leaving Sabine and Faron alone again.

He leaned down and gently kissed her. "I'll be right back," he said before heading into the washroom to prepare a hot bath.

Sabine took a breath, willing herself to calm, especially when she longed to leave these walls. Somehow, she knew she would remember every horrific moment of Tristian's attack for some time to come. After a moment, she rose to her feet, ignoring how the back of her head throbbed with the effort, and walked to the washroom to watch Faron.

Faron turned, concern etched into every line of his face as he moved to her side. "I was hoping you would wait for me. Are you dizzy?" he asked.

She shook her head. "Not dizzy. Just achy," she replied. "Besides, I do not wish to be alone."

Faron nodded and held out a hand.

"I am okay," she reassured him again as she took it.

"I know you will be," Faron said and gestured to the bathtub. "May I help you undress?"

"Yes," she agreed.

Faron ushered her further into the large washroom and stepped behind her, carefully pushing her hair over her shoulder so he didn't pull on it while undoing her laces. Slowly, he began to undo the laces. He wasn't even halfway done when Sabine heard his intake of breath.

She glanced over her shoulder to look at him. "What?"

"Your back is bruised as well," he told her softly.

"Ah," she replied then thought back to what had happened. "I am not surprised."

"From when he pulled you off the table?"

"I think so. Nothing else happened to bruise my back."

Faron leaned down and pressed a gentle kiss to her shoulders before continuing to unlace her dress. Finishing the laces, Faron helped peel down the top of the dress before setting to work on the corset. "I may send Finn or one of the ladies to the market. Someone there should sell at least a mild pain-relieving tonic."

"That would be appreciated," she said.

Faron nodded as he started to work the skirt down her hips. When she was undressed, he held out a hand to help her step into the full tub. She took his hand, thankful for the contact, and stepped into the warm water. Already, she knew it was what she had most needed.

"May I join you?" Faron asked.

"You'd better," Sabine replied.

Faron quickly stripped down. He soon settled behind her then pulled her gently against his chest. She relaxed against him, closing her eyes and ignoring the persistent ache in her body. "Rest," he whispered. "I have you."

Chapter Sixteen

Hours later, Sabine and Faron lay in bed, blood washed away, dressed in clean clothes. The pain of Sabine's assault lingered as she'd known it would, but a regular dose of a tonic kept the worst of it at bay. Her head rested on Faron's chest, eyes closed, as she focused on his fingers running through her loose hair. The repeated light tug of her caramel strands comforted her, and Sabine wondered if she would ever feel well enough to separate from him. His presence, the relative safety of the bedroom, and their relaxed positions still left Sabine feeling dazed, and she could practically feel Faron fuming.

Faron had a right to be angry. Tristian had felt threatened by Faron's presence, and he'd done nothing to hide it. He'd also hated Faron because he was an elf. Tristian represented all of the horrors which led to Faron fleeing his country of origin, and all of those things existed before accounting for Tristian's attack on Sabine.

"You're allowed to rage, you know," she said, her quiet, strained voice echoing in the otherwise silent room. "You can rage in front of me if you need to, and I will cheer you on. You can even break things."

Faron glanced down at her, the rage in his expression softening as he took her in. "What would raging accomplish other than making a mess? I'd rather injure someone. Severely."

"As you don't have the option of causing injury, breaking things is the next best choice," Sabine replied. She had no doubt he'd find a way to further work out his frustrations, though the person responsible for his anger no longer lived.

"Oh, I believe I could convince some of the guards to fight with me, and there is always Avana." His faint smile suggested jest on Faron's part, though Sabine gathered he'd be easily swayed into fighting most anyone.

"Go pick a fight with Avana. Let me know how she responds," she encouraged.

Faron carefully pulled Sabine closer. "No, I do not want to leave you, even if I am angry enough to do some very real damage."

"I understand the anger. I am angry," Sabine assured him. The persistent stinging ache in her throat remained one of numerous reasons. His anger and the attack against members of her household were others.

"You know, there is something I wouldn't mind breaking, but I would rather you come with me," Faron admitted after a moment.

"And what is it you want to break?"

"Everything in that damned office."

Sabine couldn't fathom wanting to step foot in the place where she'd been attacked, especially so soon after. Still, she gave a tiny nod, understanding, in part, why the idea appealed to Faron. "They'll have removed his body by now. You should go in there and do it if you need to."

"Are you okay going anywhere near there?" he asked, his voice tinged with concern. "I wouldn't want to leave you here alone."

"I suppose we'll find out," Sabine said, despite her reservations to go. She sat up so Faron could rise, although her movements were slow and careful. She wanted to avoid anything strenuous enough to cause pain.

Faron rolled off the bed and held a hand out for Sabine. "Would you like to change?"

"No," she said, taking his hand and standing from the bed. "I am suitably dressed, and changing would only delay us going." She wasn't sure what time it was, though the dark night sky which she viewed from the window suggested most in the manor would be sleeping by now.

Faron nodded and, with a hand on the center of her back, well below the more bruised section, escorted Sabine from the room, unsheathing his sword for the short distance.

Sabine was thankful for the very physical reminder of Faron's presence, although nothing on her face showed distress. She'd faced many difficult things in her life. An attack where no lasting damage had occurred was easy enough to embrace.

When they reached the office, the empty space helped Sabine to relax a little, though she took in the broken door with a detailed observation she hadn't managed before. Stepping inside, she saw no other cleanup had been attempted. Splinters from the door littered the ground, as did window glass.

Faron looked down at her, concern marring his handsome features. "Are you sure you can be here?"

Sabine took in the scene once more, lips pressed together as she recalled the events leading to the current state of the place. "You are here, so I can be."

Faron nodded and glanced around before his eyes landed on something out of place. Most of the small tables in the room had items meticulously placed except for one. Its contents were scattered on the floor and Sabine's bloody dagger lay nearby. Faron picked it up, cleaned it off on the fabric of a chair, and handed it back to her for safe keeping. She stored it in a pocket.

"Is that where he tried to...?" Faron trailed off, nodding at the table.

"It is," she confirmed.

Faron nodded, his gaze moving from her to the table in a long stretch of silence. Sabine wasn't certain of his intent until he sheathed his sword. With a deep breath, Faron picked up the small table.

Sabine realized his intention quickly enough to protest. "Wait!" The shout had her wincing in renewed pain, but to her relief, Faron stopped, not throwing the small table at the desk, but instead, he shot her a confused glance. "We should take any important documents first. Then you can destroy the room."

Faron stood there motionless for a moment before he set the table down. "Not like Tristian will miss anything," he muttered.

The two moved to the back of the desk and quickly opened the drawers, removing anything that looked important before Sabine motioned to where Avana had said the secret drawer was. "Go ahead and break it open," she told Faron who, after working to get a good hold, ripped the drawer from the desk. Sabine gave a small pained laugh and gathered up the papers, including both sets of financial ledgers, before moving back to the doorway. "You may continue your destruction," she said, causing Faron to laugh.

Again, he picked up the table and threw it as hard as he could at the desk, breaking it in half. Small pieces of wood showered the area. Then with a feral roar, Faron's sword was in his hands again, and he hacked at not only what remained of the small table, but the large desk too.

When little remained of the first victims of his anger, he moved to the bookcase and pulled it down from the wall. Another small table, which he threw one-handed, crashed on the other side of the room. Quickly and efficiently, he destroyed every item in the office except one, an ornate side table with decanters of alcohol on it. Now satiated in his rage, Faron stood in the middle of the space, his body coated with sweat, his long hair disheveled, breathing hard. He glanced toward Sabine. "How do you feel?"

"Oddly satisfied," Sabine replied, surprising herself.

"Good," he said, holding out a hand for her. When she took it, he gently pulled her closer and kissed her. "I want you to do one thing for me," he said to her softly.

"What?" she asked him.

"Go pick out a decanter for us to share."

She laughed gently and nodded, feeling a little lighter for having done so. After pulling away from Faron, she crossed the room, stepping over broken furniture and glass. When the decanters were in reach, she picked one up at random, her fingers gingerly handling the crystal, minimizing the expected sloshing of the liquid it held. Expensive, delicate, and no doubt filled with equally expensive drink, Sabine guessed Tristian's family had long owned the decanter. She felt no guilt when she threw it across the room. It smashed against a stone wall, liquor and glass spilling to the floor. She stared at the new mess for several long moments before selecting another decanter, this one just as full, and walked over to join Faron.

"Feel a little better?" he asked her, an arm going around her waist.

"Yes," she replied after taking a couple of seconds to measure her mood. She couldn't deny feeling a little better. "Let's go back to our room. We're leaving early tomorrow."

Chapter Seventeen

The Vassetre Chateau welcomed the group home the following afternoon, and as Sabine stepped out of her carriage, she pretended to miss the shocked faces of the staff who stood by to greet them. Swollen purple blotches appeared on Sabine's face and neck, angry and more prominent than they had been in the aftermath of her attack. Every movement reminded the duchesse of their presence, and the pain tonic Faron had insisted upon barely touched the discomfort.

Thankfully, Sabine did not have to address the staff. Finn stepped down from the seat up front and approached the waiting household. "Her Grace is unwell. Please make sure her bed is ready for her, her fire lit, and food and drink waiting." A group of workers who usually reported to Meri gave slight bows and hurried inside. The coach and footman moved to the carriages to unload luggage. Once inside, the items therein would be unpacked, cleaned, and returned to the appropriate people.

"Thank you," Sabine said as she passed Finn. Finn nodded in response and quickly returned to overseeing their arrival.

Sabine gave a brief smile to those who met her gaze as she walked into the estate. Despite her bruised face and back, she gave no sign of worry or weakness in front of her household. Her current condition confirmed the validity of worry. She held the responsibility of quelling anxiety, and she intended to honor her duties.

Faron followed along behind Sabine, his face set in stone as they went, obviously still upset about what had almost happened. Once they were away from the staff, she felt a large hand settle on her midback, an offer of comfort and more. Leaving the entryway, they turned into a corridor where they stopped to talk. "Grégoire will come here," she said quietly. "Despite the justification, he will come to question what happened."

"I assumed as much," Faron said, his voice low and words deliberate. Faron simmered with lingering anger, and Sabine could see it in every action he took. "You have more guards, people who love and support you, and you have me. We will stand united against him when he does come. And if he gives you too much trouble, I can always lop his head off too." Though Faron's tone was jovial enough, his eyes told Sabine he would follow through if needed. She would not subject Faron to the prospect of regicide, even if he currently craved it.

"We'll be more than ready for it," Sabine confirmed. They began walking again, with Sabine leading the way toward her quarters. They soon found themselves outside the doors leading into her suite. She pushed them open and stepped inside. Faron followed along behind her, securing the door after he shut them.

"Do you need more pain tonic? Tea? Anything?" he asked Sabine.

"Finn ordered food and drink brought up," Sabine reminded him. She saw the fire had already been lit and her bedding drawn back, both welcome comforts. "Given how I look, I'd be very surprised if pain tonic is left off the trays."

She walked further back into the bedroom of her suite, carefully undoing the tie at the end of her simple braid. Sabine moved slower than normal in the task given her bruised back.

Faron's boots thudded behind her. "Let me, please," he requested, reaching for her hair. His hands twitched, showing how anxious he was to do something to help her, to make her feel better.

"Okay," Sabine agreed. She took a seat at her dressing table and waited as Faron carefully unwound the braid, careful not to catch a single strand. When he finished, he set the pins aside and started running his fingers through her hair as he normally did.

Sabine appreciated the soothing gesture and his careful avoidance of the back of her skull where her head had met stone the day prior. "You're quiet," she observed.

"Just thinking about everything that happened," he admitted.

Sabine glanced down, unable to blame him. Her face, throat, and back ached from the assault, and even in the early afternoon with beautiful sunlight streaming through the window, she wanted to go unconscious for a bit.

A knock sounded at her door, echoing from the sitting area back to where she and Faron were. "That should be food."

"I'll get it," Faron offered. He withdrew his hands from her hair before he quickly headed to her main room. Less than a minute passed before he came back, carrying a tray with several covered dishes on it. Faron carefully set the tray down on her vanity before uncovering them to show two steaming bowls of soup and other easy-to-swallow foods. A vial of pain tonic sat in one corner, a light orange color made paler than usual by the lingering bubbles from a very recent mixing.

Sabine selected the tonic first and drank it before setting it aside. She didn't much care for the taste, but it was easy to swallow, so the flavor bothered her very little now. "You need to eat as well," she instructed Faron, motioning toward one of the bowls.

"I admit, I'm not very hungry. I doubt you are either." He picked up Sabine's bowl and handed it to her.

"I'm not, but I will regret not eating after drinking the tonic," she said as she took the bowl in her hands. The warmth of the soup radiated into her hands.

"Well, if you're willing to eat, then so shall I." Faron lifted his bowl as if in a toast.

She gave a huff of laughter at Faron's response, though she did not return the gesture. Too tired and sore to act overly playful, she went to drink the soup, appreciating how the warmth provided a little relief as it ran down her throat. She couldn't identify the flavor, having paid it no mind.

Faron finished sooner than Sabine. Setting his bowl down, he reached for a plate, this one with soft finger sandwiches. "Would you like to try one? They should be soft enough not to bother your throat."

As appetizing as she was certain they'd be, she shook her head and put her soup aside. "I think I am going to undress and nap for a bit. Travel is already exhausting enough when I'm not purple and achy all over."

Faron nodded and put the sandwich aside. "Would you like help undressing?"

"Yes," Sabine replied.

Silently, Faron held out a hand to help Sabine to her feet so he could start undoing the laces of her gown.

She remained quiet as he helped her undress, the process going slower than usual. Movement still caused pain, but going slower made the process easier. "You should move your things in here when you have time," she commented.

She felt Faron freeze for all of a second before he said, "Alright."

"Unless you prefer to sleep on another floor," she joked lightly. His surprised reaction, no matter how temporary, amused her. "Some married couples do have separate quarters."

"No, no," Faron quickly replied. "I would like to share space with you. Moving in with you just hadn't occurred to me." He kissed her shoulder as he continued to help Sabine undress. "It has been a long time since I shared a room with someone."

"When was the last time?"

"Before Mother died," he admitted. "While I have had other relationships, none were serious enough for me to consider living with them. Most of my prior jobs allowed me my own private space."

"I could kick you out from time to time if you would like the space," she offered, still teasing. Finally down to her chemise, Sabine stepped out of her skirts and knelt long enough to pick it up and toss it over the back of a chair.

"Only if you feel the need. Spirits know I'll probably infuriate you from time to time. Or you'll be so sore you'll want me gone for fear I'll lay hands on you again," he joked back.

"I don't think I've complained about your hands being on me before," she pointed out. Her bedding had been pulled back, so crawling in and settling back took little effort.

Faron laughed. "No, I don't think you have, but one never knows." Faron pulled up the covers for her. "I'm going to stand guard. Rest," he said before leaning down and kissing her gently.

"You need to rest as well, you know," Sabine reminded him.

"And I will. I promise. Right now, I just want to make sure everything's okay here."

"Okay," she said before kissing him again. "Go look out for trouble."

Chapter Eighteen

Exhaustion threatened to overrule Faron's decision to walk through the chateau, checking in on those who had remained behind and making note of any possible security threats. He felt like he hadn't slept in weeks thanks to his rage over Sabine's attack. The hypervigilance he had felt since wasn't helping either, though he was trying to keep that under control. Sabine would not be happy with his sudden need to keep her with him at all hours just to ensure her safety. He was certain she'd toss him from the chateau if he tried to always monitor her.

It was for that reason he found himself in the kitchen instead of with Sabine in her rooms while she rested, watching over her to ensure no one could touch her again. The guards he'd stationed outside of her door and window gave him little peace, and he could not wait to be back by her side. He took in Meri, Lisbeth, Finn, and Marcelle. They all looked tired, except for Marcelle, whose furrowed brows and thin-set mouth told Faron the guard knew of the comte's actions.

Finn stood near the stove, warming a kettle so he could make tea. He looked over his shoulder as Faron made his way further into the kitchen. "Her Grace resting?" he asked, sounding more energized than anyone could possibly feel.

"Yes," was Faron's simple reply.

"She needed the sleep. Healing takes a lot out of a person," Lisbeth said. She spoke softly, keeping her eyes fixed on her clasped hands resting on the island in front of her. Faron suspected she felt as powerless as he did, as none of them had a way of healing Sabine. Meri ran a hand down her wife's back, prompting a small smile from Lisbeth.

"Traveling alone can exhaust a person," Marcelle said. He leaned against a counter close to Finn, his arms crossed as he watched the others. "What happened to her would only make it worse."

"The entirety of the visit was stressful. Lisbeth had to overhear everything that madman said to Her Grace while the rest of us had to be elsewhere," Meri said to Marcelle. She took a deep breath to calm herself, something Meri had to do with increasing regularity.

"She shouldn't have been left alone with the comte," Marcelle said, shaking his head. A couple of blond locks swung loosely around his face as he started speaking again. "I don't understand why precautions were taken at every other opportunity, but not when she went to see him."

"I was planning on entering the room with her when one of the guards at the door halted me to ask a question about a tactic he had seen me use on one of Lord Tristian's visits," Faron explained, still ashamed of the choice to stay behind, even for a few minutes. "Sabine nodded for me to answer. I was outside the door for less than five minutes and was making excuses to go into the office when I heard glass shatter and the men attacked me," Faron admitted, guilt and rage on his face. How could he have been so stupid?

"We're lucky they only went after you and Avana," Finn said, striking a tone of rationality Faron didn't think himself capable of when it came to anything to do with Sabine. Finn judged the kettle hot enough and poured water into cups where infusers filled with loose tea leaves sat in waiting. "But, I think we do not leave her alone in enemy territory going forward."

"We are very lucky the comte's whole plan was desperate and badly thought out," Meri muttered from her spot next to Lisbeth. She'd abandoned comforting Lisbeth long enough to pull out a bottle of alcohol, but she had yet to open it.

"Of course it was," Finn said. He sipped from his tea before continuing. "Grégoire may be a vicious man, but he does not underestimate Her Grace. Tristian thought very little of her and her abilities simply because she is a woman. He simply thought she was property which could be handed over by the prince without concern. He never considered the possibility of facing potential difficulties in removing her main support and forcing her hand."

"That he didn't realize he and his soldiers were dead men the moment he decided to put his hands on Sabine is very telling of his intelligence, and he made that plan before she agreed to marry me," Faron said casually. They needed something a little more positive to focus on. Well, he did at the very least, and his pending nuptials seemed up to the task.

Finn's gaze lifted from his teacup. "Really?" he asked, brows raised.

Faron glanced around. Lisbeth gaped at him, mouth hanging open and eyes wide. Meri's skepticism showed in her cross gaze and raised brow. Marcelle he couldn't quite read. "Yes. I asked her after the attack. Admittedly, it wasn't the best timing, but she said yes, so…" He found himself suddenly dodging Lisbeth's hands as she tried to smack him.

"Why are we just finding out now?" she demanded, thrill and exasperation all jumbled into a ball of ginger energy.

"I would assume it was because of everything following the attack," Finn said before he sipped more of his tea. "You know, the cleanup. The interrogation. The travel home." He grinned playfully at Lisbeth before shooting his gaze over to Faron. "I will say, I'm not sure if I am grateful you finally got your shit together concerning Her Grace or curious how she will ever get anything done again."

"Nothing will ever get done again," Meri said. Faron knew she was only half joking. She pointed a finger in his direction, her glare growing serious. "And until she's ready, you're going to keep drinking that tea."

Faron nodded, knowing better than to argue.

"I suspect she won't be ready for a while, given the more than certain fallout from killing Tristian," Marcelle said. His black eyes danced with amusement over Meri's warning. "Either way, a love match ending in marriage is something to celebrate."

"Hear, hear," Meri said, finally opening the bottle in front of her. Once done, she reached out and grabbed Lisbeth, stopping her from her excited assault on Faron, and motioned for her to get some glasses.

Faron just shook his head at Lisbeth's antics, too used to them after years of friendship to ever be upset. "It will be years before we have children, I think. There is too much to do without taking Tristian's death into account."

"Makes sense, but when do you think you will marry?" Finn asked.

"She asked me to reach out to a priestess I know the moment we arrived here." Faron titled his head. "So, while Sabine rests, I will send word to the priestess."

"Given the state of Her Grace and the travel, I suspect your earliest opportunity will come later in the week," Finn said.

"I would like for her to take some time to recover for a few days before I contact my friend," Faron confirmed. Although Sabine was well enough to move around, he knew the pain from bruises and attempted strangulation more than bothered her. He would wait however long she needed. She deserved to enjoy their wedding. "There is, however, a part of me that wonders if it wouldn't be better to be married before the prince arrives," Faron added.

"Given how he tried to push Her Grace into a relationship with Tristian, I think a solidified marriage would likely be safest," Marcelle said as he recrossed his arms. The amusement left his face again. "But then, she's not afraid of the prince, no matter what he thinks."

"He wishes Sabine were afraid of him," Lisbeth muttered as she passed around glasses of alcohol to everyone but Faron. Instead, she handed him a glass of water, which he greatly appreciated.

"She's more powerful than he is, and from the letters Tristain had, he may not have the support to push his agenda onto Fythias," Faron reminded the group.

"Which leads me to suspect his intended visit will come with subdued desperation. He will try to throw his weight around," said Finn. His tea now exchanged for liquor, he sipped from the glass without making an expression to show a recognized difference. "And we have gathered enough information to know what he wants isn't acceptable."

"We'll be more than ready for whatever desperate act he tries. We have to be," said Faron.

"Of course," Marcelle replied. He finished his glass with a couple of deep gulps then set it down with a clunk. "I am going to go inform the Sirene that Her Grace has returned and let them know how the newly deceased comte treated her."

Faron nodded. As much as he wanted Marcelle not to go because the man was one of the best soldiers they had, he understood why. Their allies knowing about what happened, and the high probability of Grégoire arriving any day, was best. "I know it's not far, but safe travels anyways."

"It's just down to the beach," Marcelle replied, finally grinning. "I'll be back in a few hours unless I slip on the rocks and hurt myself. I can't think of any other possible unsafe scenario," he added, this time directed both to Faron and Finn, who nodded. Marcelle made his exit without additional commentary.

Faron looked down at his cup of water. "I want to get back to Sabine. She's handling the attack well, but..." He shrugged, unsure of how else to express how he was feeling. He wanted to be there in case she had any need. To dote on her. To make sure she lifted no unnecessary finger.

"Then go back to her," Finn suggested. "We're just settling back in, and everything looks fine for now."

"I agree," Meri added. "Her Grace will have enough to deal with in the coming weeks. Let her have a restful time, and be with her since we all know she'd prefer it."

Faron nodded and finished his water.

Before he could go, Lisbeth stopped him by grabbing his arm. "Congratulations on the engagement," she said, excitement in her eyes.

"Thank you." He gave her a soft smile and left to go check on Sabine.

Chapter
Nineteen

Faron lay propped up on his elbow, watching a sleeping Sabine as the morning sunlight streamed through the window. The sun highlighted her fair skin and caramel hair, and had she been in better health, she'd have been radiant. Even now, Faron couldn't deny how beautiful his future wife remained.

Sabine had slept through the previous afternoon and evening without stirring, though Faron hadn't been surprised. Sabine's bruised condition left her exhausted before they'd traveled home the day before, and Faron suspected her pain tonic, which she'd taken without fuss once home, had been laced with a sleeping aid. It was just as well. Even with her perfectly serene expression, the discomfort in her eyes the prior day had been more than enough to tell him she was better off in bed.

Faron did what he could to keep her comfortable. Currently, Sabine laid on her side with a pillow behind her to keep her from rolling onto her back and aggravating her bruises. Remaining still seemed to help as she made no indication of pain, nor did she toss and turn from discomfort. The position also allowed Faron to carefully observe Sabine's numerous injuries. The bruising on her neck looked worse now than it had the day before, having transformed from vivid red finger imprints to bluish black marks, each a reminder of how close to death she'd been. No doubt, injuries covered by her nightdress would have followed the same path. He'd expected the change, had told himself he was prepared for her injuries to look worse before they were better. In truth, though, Faron only felt more outrage and shame.

It could be worse, Faron frequently told himself. As bad as her injuries were, and as sluggish as she'd been since her attack, she'd otherwise behaved as normally as she could.

When Faron first arrived on that terrible scene and lopped off Tristian's head, he'd been concerned by the extent of her injuries. Even with the pain, though, she'd had no real problems eating, drinking, or breathing, though she found the first two activities a little uncomfortable. The healer Finn had brought from the village—not a magical healer, sadly—had said she would be sore for days and bruised for longer. So, despite the purple outlines of Tristian's fingers and the way Sabine grimaced when she spoke for too long, she needed time and rest, and she would be okay. Faron intended to ensure she received plenty of both, but he did wonder how long it would take for Sabine to get tired of being doted on.

Sabine shifted in her sleep, and Faron knew she would wake, as her expression grew strained. She'd hurt herself in moving if the pain lines bracketing her mouth were any indication. Her vivid green eyes fluttered open, and she looked up at him and blinked a few times as consciousness settled in.

"Hi," Faron said softly, running his free hand down her cheek. He hoped his touch was light enough to avoid causing pain, but he had big hands and sometimes couldn't remain as gentle as he might have liked. "I have a pain tonic if you need it."

"I do," she confirmed softly, her voice rough from both injury and sleep. Sabine slowly moved into a seated position, grimacing when she did anything too quickly or moved in a direction her body did not like. Faron silently promised himself he'd make sure Lisbeth brought him several additional vials of pain tonic to keep on him during the day and on his side table at night for quick access.

Rolling over, he grabbed one of the few orange vials they had on hand and gave it to Sabine. "Lisbeth snuck in early. She said she cleared your schedule so you could just rest today. I know you don't like her unilaterally deciding what your schedule will be like, but I thought you'd understand her doing so for at least today."

Sabine removed the vial's stopper, drank the concoction, then handed the empty container back to Faron. "Good," Sabine replied. "I am not up to doing much else today, even though she has no business just deciding those sorts of things. I may have to have Finn talk to her."

"I can mention it if you want," Faron offered. He didn't disagree with Sabine on the larger point of Lisbeth overstepping, but like her, he could appreciate the thoughtfulness given how unwell Sabine felt.

"I'll think about it," Sabine decided before looking up at Faron. "How long were you gone yesterday?"

"Not long," he said with a shrug. He was content to leave the answer there until Sabine raised an unimpressed eyebrow at him. Apparently, she wasn't alright with such a sparse answer. He had no problem doing exactly as she demanded. "I let Marcelle know what happened at the comte's and advised him we need to station people further from the village so we have advanced warning for when the prince decides to show up. He's done one better and sent two people back to Tristian's, another set of people a day's ride beyond the Villa du Ciel, and a final set between your estate and there. We'll have advanced notice of the prince's arrival, and we'll be able to have the information arrive much more quickly as a result. And as soon as we know, the Sirene will know as well."

Faron thought about anything else she may need to know, and given her response to Lisbeth clearing her schedule without permission, he briefly debated the wisdom in detailing more of Lisbeth's antics. He decided to gloss over them. "I convinced Lisbeth she cannot burn the correspondence which arrived while you were gone, and other than that, everything else is okay. The staff are content and working as they always do. The village seems in order as well, and there have been no major tragedies or problems in need of immediate attention."

"That makes me feel like I should get up and read my correspondence," Sabine replied after letting out a long, annoyed breath. "But thank you for preventing Lisbeth from acting. She tends to want to just do things without stopping to consider consequences. She wanted to sell all of the clothing in my room when we were visiting the comte, and I had to explain why it was a bad idea."

Faron nodded in agreement. Lisbeth had a kind heart, and most of the time, her actions were meant to be helpful or kind, but she made rash decisions occasionally, and compounded with her clearing Sabine's schedule, he could understand Sabine's irritation. "From what Meri said, Lisbeth didn't even bother looking at who the letters were from. She just said Her Grace needs her rest, so these should be set on fire immediately." He said the second part in a higher voice.

Sabine let out a huff of laughter, though she still appeared cross. "Someone should go through the letters to see if there is anything from Prince Louis at the very least. And maybe prevent her from doing anything else quite so drastic while I am recovering. I don't want Finn to have to reprimand her, but I will have him do so if she doesn't calm down."

"I will try to reason with her," Faron promised, though he predicted anything he said would go largely ignored. Perhaps if he tried with Meri present... "Would you like me to go get your letters or send someone?" Faron asked. He was content to stay in bed with Sabine, but he knew she did need to sort through them to make sure they weren't ignoring pressing news.

"Either way," she decided. "I'm going to bathe, and I need to eat before I decide to do anything else. You probably need to eat as well, knowing you."

"Would you like me to start the bath for you or call Lisbeth to do so? I'm pretty sure she's pacing the hall outside still," Faron said with a small chuckle. Lisbeth was having trouble with Sabine being injured, more so since they had returned. Faron studied Sabine for a second, and he realized what decision should be made. "I should get Lisbeth. Seeing you naked right now might not be the best thing."

"No, I imagine the bruises look worse than they did two nights ago," Sabine agreed. Carefully, she got out of bed and walked to the stand where a pitcher of water and glasses waited. She poured herself some and drank deeply from it.

"Oh, it's less about that and more I don't trust myself to keep my hands to myself," Faron said, his tone teasing, though his eyes were serious. He wanted to replace Tristian's touch with his own, but she was still in pain, so now was not the right time. "I'll get Lisbeth."

"Okay," she replied, giving him a small smile. "Somehow, I think once I feel better, I might not ever sleep again."

"I'll let you get at least two hours a night."

"Collectively or consecutively?" she quipped.

"Let me think about it, but collectively sounds best." Faron strolled from Sabine's bedroom to her sitting room, and as he got closer to the main door, his ears could pick up Lisbeth outside the door debating if she should come in or not. Faron thought about startling her by throwing the door open, but he decided against it. He'd played similar pranks a few times when they were younger, and while Lisbeth's powers generally couldn't be used to hurt people, when startled, she threw flowers, like roses, and injuries could happen.

Opening the door slowly, he waved a hand to catch her attention.

"Oh, is she up?" Lisbeth asked.

"Yes, and she'd like to bathe and eat. You should go help."

Lisbeth moved to rush past him, and he gently caught her arm.

"Where did you leave her correspondence?"

"Kitchen," she said with a bright but strained smile.

"Thanks," Faron said, letting her go. He watched as Lisbeth sprinted through the sitting room to the bedroom.

Not wanting to be gone from Sabine's side for long, Faron walked as quickly as he could without breaking into a jog, though it was close.

Arriving at the kitchen, he could hear pots and pans banging and laughter coming from Finn. After entering, Faron was about to ask what was going on, only to stop in the doorway at the sheer amount of food covering almost every available surface. "What?" he found himself saying.

"Stress cooking," was Meri's sharp reply.

Faron looked to Finn, who leaned against a counter far away from Meri's efforts, for confirmation. Finn nodded. "This is the most convenient way for Meri to let off some steam," he confirmed.

"Either my efforts are spent cooking, or I go beat up some of our soldiers, and we're going to need them," Meri muttered, her shoulders tense with suppressed rage. Faron thought he probably looked the same. He wondered where all this rage was when they talked the day prior, though. Meri had seemed rather calm considering. It hit Faron then: she had been trying to stay calm for Lisbeth's sake, and now that Lisbeth was busy with other things, Meri was allowing herself to be angry.

"Yes, we are," Faron agreed as he cautiously stepped further into the kitchen. "What are we planning to do with all of the extra food?" he asked as he looked around. Bowls holding different salads, various seafood dishes, pies, and a lot of baked goods sat around perfectly crafted, all looking delicious.

"Usually, when Meri cooks so vigorously, she figures out who will eat after the fact." Finn said as he pointed to a pot bubbling over the fire. "She is making Her Grace some hot chocolate, so we can account for one dish."

"Sabine sent me for her letters, which Lisbeth said were here, and food. So, another dish accounted for," Faron offered.

Finn brightened. "I'm pleased to hear she's awake and wanting to eat."

"And she's taken the pain tonic, so she should be alright for a few hours." Faron looked around for a soup or something soft and simple Sabine could eat, only for Meri's hand to shoot out, pointing to a tray with several covered dishes.

"There's her breakfast. Her Grace should have no problems with it," Meri said before going back to what looked like a cake, but given the shape, Faron wasn't sure. Was the cake supposed to be oblong?

"She likes it," Finn said, taking in the confusion on Faron's face.

"It's just an interesting shape," said Faron. "Anything change since last night?" he asked, though he'd be surprised if there'd been any news. Someone would have reported new information.

Finn shook his head. "It's been quiet, but we expected as much. The whole of Tristian's estate and the surrounding village knows what kind of man he was, and everyone in the estate saw the evidence of what happened to Her Grace. When Grégoire appears, he's going to find it difficult to retaliate."

"He sounds like the type of person who will still try and find a way," Faron said.

"He is," Meri said. "He'll arrive here with a new story in mind, trying to pin the blame on an innocent person."

"He still hasn't figured out one important thing, though," Finn said.

"What's that?" Meri asked, moving the cake into the oven.

"She's not afraid of him," Finn said simply. "She could take over if she wanted, and everyone knows it. I think he probably knows it, too, deep down. But, he'll still try to bully her because he doesn't know what else to do."

"I asked her why she doesn't take over, or at least officially declare Louis as king. Sabine said she doesn't want to assume that sort of power, but I think the kingdom would be better for it. Or if Grégoire was dead," Faron said.

"Ruling is a great responsibility, and not wanting it is a sign of her capability in my opinion," Finn said with a shrug.

"But she knows how she wants to spend her life. You can't make her do any more."

"I agree. We shouldn't stage a coup and put Her Grace in charge. Louis wouldn't mind, though," Meri chimed in.

"I'll let Sabine know she's now the ruling monarch," Faron half joked as he gathered the tray with the food and the letters.

"When she kills you for suggesting it, we'll pick a nice spot on the grounds to bury you," Finn offered.

"Oh no. I'm telling her it was your idea," Faron said before also pocketing the letters and making a hasty retreat to Sabine's rooms.

Chapter Twenty

My dear friend Sabine,

I am saddened to hear of how you have been treated, both by my brother and his underlings. You do not deserbe his ire, nor his threats. My guilt in knowing I am at fault for your suffering plagues me, and I am not going to allow more of my brother's antics. Do what you must to protect and defend yourself and know whatever measures you must take will have my unwavering support.

I will arrive soon with additional protections for you and your people. I have left my estate and am traveling East. Hopefully, I will be with you in a few weeks, assuming good weather and safe conditions, of course. Please let me know of any news in the meantime. I look forward to seeing you soon.

Yours,
Louis, Prince of Pythias

The following week passed with an unexpected peacefulness, though Sabine never lost sight of the unspoken tension in the air. The whole of the Vassetre estate lay in waiting for the arrival of Prince Grégoire, who they knew would inevitably arrive. Word had gotten back from Tristian's estate two days prior. The prince had arrived expecting a marriage, only to discover the violent end of the comte's life.

Prince Louis's letter arrived the same day, though his words told her he had not received word of the attack against her when he'd last written. The knowledge of his intent to arrive at some point soon offered Sabine some relief. Although she could end the question of who would rule with little effort—and she was at the point of deciding for Fythias—she still held on to the hope of a resolution between the brothers.

She sat in the library that afternoon, continuing to relax as she recovered with Faron beside her. The purple bruises were slowly fading to greenish yellows, and so, she felt a little less sore every passing day.

Lisbeth stood at the large bay windows of the library that overlooked her garden, a scowl on her normally smiling face. "I wish Avana was back," she said.

"So do I," Sabine replied. "I knew the trip would take some time, but I grow concerned the longer she is away."

"As do I. The news of Grégoire's reaction to Tristian's death tells me Avana wasn't able to deliver the letter to him before he left his estate. I wonder if she's with the younger prince. They could be traveling together," Faron said from his place on the lounge chair next to Sabine.

"Perhaps," Sabine said. "If she is not back soon, however, I'm sending people out to track her whereabouts."

"Marcelle has been very worried about her. I think he'd like to go," Lisbeth said, moving back to where Sabine and

Faron sat. She started gathering up their now empty tea cups. Much as how Meri seemed to be cooking enough to feed the village, Lisbeth had taken to cleaning everything in sight.

"Those two have grown close," Faron mused.

"Well she knew how much you already liked her, Faron, so she had to make friends with everyone else," Sabine joked, looking up at him.

"And she did that," Faron said.

Sabine knew he still found it hard to believe how quickly the people at the estate had adopted Avana. Still, even his very strong opinions had changed over time. "She did," Sabine agreed. "Her experiences from before she came to us don't suggest she could not find something more fulfilling with us, after all."

"See, I would have thought her experiences suggest she was kept in a windowless area with very little food or outside contact other than the person who bought her and her trainers. That she's as sound of mind as she is suggests some of her trainers had to be halfway decent," Faron said, tipping his head back to look at the ceiling, his book set down next to him.

"When did I say her previous experiences were anything but horrible?" Sabine asked, eyebrows raised. "Her ability to create happiness here does not dismiss any experience she had before she arrived."

"Sorry," Faron apologized. "I'm just very surprised by her progress."

"Apparently," Sabine replied.

Lisbeth laughed. "He mutters about it sometimes when we have lunch while you're busy with your work."

"Well he wouldn't be Faron if he didn't find something to be grumpy about, now would he?" Sabine asked.

Faron rolled his eyes before his face slipped into an overly exaggerated, not-quite scowl.

Sabine laughed and leaned over to kiss him. "Good thing I adore your grumpy ass."

"And I am glad for that," Faron responded before kissing her again.

They both ignored Lisbeth's laughter, at least until Lisbeth said, "Does this mean you're going to tell Thaumas not to drown him?" She batted her eyes innocently even with the grin she still wore.

Sabine chuckled. "In fairness, he offered to drown Faron. I don't think I told him to."

Faron looked at Sabine in alarm while Lisbeth managed to laugh even harder.

"You haven't told Thaumas you two are together, so the next time Faron goes to the beach without you, Thaumas and his friends will live up to their myths," Lisbeth joked.

"I haven't been allowed to do much of anything since returning," Sabine reminded them both. "But if we think it's urgent, send Marcelle."

Lisbeth's tongue clicked. "Marcelle told Meri he thinks Thaumas should drown Faron a little bit. Even with you two together now, so..."

Faron's brows raised in alarm, and Sabine laughed again.

"You knew I was beloved when you did what you did," she teased.

"Yes," Faron agreed. "But drowning?"

"Not my request or suggestion," Sabine replied.

"I completely understand, but maybe you should tell Thaumas instead of Marcelle. Even being a little drowned sounds unpleasant," Faron said.

"I will talk to him even though I don't think he was serious," Sabine promised.

"But what if he was?" Lisbeth asked with a devious smile. "Faron could be walking along the beach one moment, and the next, dragged underwater. It'd be so fast, he wouldn't even be able to defend himself."

"I think Thaumas would be nice enough to wait until after we married," Sabine said.

"Is there some benefit to making you a widow?" Faron asked, confused for a second before rolling his eyes. "Never mind."

"I'd like to not be a widow, all the same. Do not worry," Sabine said, patting his knee.

"Then I'll just avoid the beach for the rest of our lives," Faron said.

Though he was smiling, Sabine had a feeling it wasn't a joke. "What about when I go swimming?" Sabine asked. "You were awfully concerned about my swimming habits the day you arrived."

"And I still am, so I will stay a respectful distance from the water," was Faron's easy response.

Lisbeth said, "That's definitely not going to help."

"No," Sabine agreed. She looked up as the library door opened and Finn strolled in, his expression serious. "What is it?" she asked.

"Grégoire has left Tristian's estate," he reported. "We received word not long ago. He may be here before the day is out."

The room silently took in the news before Faron stood in one fluid motion. He held out a hand for Sabine to take. "We've prepared for his arrival. We all know what to do," Faron said.

"Yes," Sabine agreed after taking Faron's hand and rising. "Please alert the rest of the household."

Finn nodded. "Marcelle has already gone to let the Sirene know. They will be on standby."

"Perfect," Sabine replied with a nod. "I doubt any violent outbreak will occur, but I'd rather we be overprepared."

Finn nodded and left without dismissal, while Lisbeth fled from the room to presumably prepare the staff she managed.

Sabine looked up at Faron now that they were alone again. "Do not worry. Grégoire isn't nearly as intimidating as he thinks he is."

"I'm more worried about the type of power he thinks he wields," Faron explained. "And what his opening move may be now that we've taken away one of his biggest supporters."

"He's going to find out what power I wield," Sabine said simply. "I'm tired of his attempts to bully me into submission. He thinks he's going to come here and tell me what I will do. He may be dealing the first blow, but he is not prepared for the retaliation."

"I can't wait to see what you do," Faron said, leaning down to kiss her.

She pulled him closer as they kissed. Even with the lingering pain of her injuries, nothing ever felt quite so right as when he was against her, touching her. The distraction it gave her, even for a few seconds, was needed.

When the kiss broke, Faron reached up and gently trailed his fingers down her cheek. "I'm going to make sure the guards have their orders and are ready if they are needed. It won't take me long."

"Then go see to it," Sabine replied softly. "There is much to do before his arrival."

Faron nodded and stepped away from Sabine with an obvious reluctance. "I'll be back soon."

"I know," she replied.

Grégoire arrived just before sunset, his travel party smaller than Sabine had expected, though she did not allow the small numbers to diminish her wariness. As the middle prince stepped down from his carriage, Sabine noted he looked much the same as he always did. Grégoire stood a few inches shorter than Faron, broad-shouldered and athletic, though he'd put on some weight in the months since she'd last laid eyes on the prince. His dark blond hair looked brown in the late afternoon light, and his neatly trimmed beard suggested he'd kept himself well looked after in his travels.

"Sabine," Grégoire said in a tone far too sharp to be pleasant. "How nice to see you." His eyes scanned her face and neck, taking in the slowly fading bruises.

"Your Highness," Sabine acknowledged with only a slight nod of her head rather than a bow, earning herself Grégoire's narrow-eyed stare. "I trust your travels were uneventful." Finn and Faron stood directly behind her, a line of her household, including Marcelle and Meri, waiting behind them. The diverse line presented a united state without emphasizing the threat they could pose.

Grégoire's smile now showed a lot more teeth. "Oh, it was very eventful, as I'm sure you already know." His eyes moved to Faron and back again.

"I imagine so," she replied. She kept her eyes forward, feeding as little information to the prince as possible. She doubted her connection to Faron was much of a secret, but she was confirming nothing unless directly asked.

Grégoire made an affirmative noise and glanced around once more, taking in what he could see of the grounds and the people who had come to meet him with Sabine. It came off as a very casual glance, but it seemed to Sabine like he was looking for something.

"I've always thought you had such a pretty home," he finally said, attention slipping back to Sabine. "I think my people and I would like to refresh before dinner. It's been such a hectic two days after all. Escort me," he directed Sabine.

"It would be my honor," Sabine replied, but she remained in place. Try as he might, Grégoire failed to intimidate her. "Finn, would you and Marcelle please assist in seeing to His Highness's party?" she asked. Finn nodded.

"Of course, Your Grace. We will give the matter our full attention."

"Well, come along, then," Grégoire said impatiently as he offered Sabine his arm. She took it as he added, "You can leave your elf behind. My guards are enough."

She felt Faron bristle beside her, prompting two of Grégoire's men to move their hands to their weapons.

"Faron is my personal guard," Sabine replied. "I do not wander without him, especially after recent events," Sabine replied, giving no leeway for argument as her copious bruises remained on full display.

Grégoire gave a careless shrug and motioned for Sabine to lead them on. "Yes, I talked with several members of Tristian's household. They mentioned the incident that left you looking worse for wear and my dear friend Tristian deceased." He sighed. "I'll miss Tristian. He was a good man, and he ran his estate and surrounding lands well. I'll be sad to gift them to Baron Cyrille, but I know he'll handle them well."

"Oh, I look forward to your proposal when you submit it for parliamentary review," Sabine said. "Certainly Cyrille would make an interesting replacement."

"I've already written to him telling him of my decision. He should move in soon. Parliament has other things to worry about." He waved her off as if the decision was already made, and in his mind, it was.

"Then let us hope Parliament agrees with you," Sabine said.

Grégoire just gave Sabine a smile that said he truly didn't care if they did. "Of course."

They walked, with Sabine choosing the shortest possible route without making it seem intentional. She never glanced back at Faron, but she could hear and feel his closeness, which provided some security. "Your correspondence makes it sound as though you've been traveling quite frequently," she prompted as they stepped inside the chateau.

"I have been visiting some friends," he said. "Both nobles from Fythias and some visitors from Coralia."

She nodded, knowing he was being vague on purpose. "Your interest in the atrocities Coralia has involved itself with suggested as much," she said.

Grégoire laughed. "You do assume to know much about my interests, but you've always been like that," he said in a patronizing tone. "There are a few nobles from Coralia who are interested in meeting you. They like women with… spirit in them."

Sabine caught the barely hidden threat. "I know you've written of your support of King Sargarus, and he is committing atrocities across our world, not just in his own country. I know his people are fleeing in droves. I know his cruelty is spreading to Azmarin." She also knew her words were blunt, but Sabine had no interest in game-playing. "And I can just imagine the sort of people who you'd like me to meet."

Grégoire raised an eyebrow at Sabine. "If his people were fleeing in droves, his economy would collapse and his kingdom would be in ruin. Since that's not happening, I would say you're drastically misinformed." His eyes darted to Faron and back. "Though considering you've taken in a handful of said refugees, all with their own awful stories, I'm sure nothing I can say would sway you from your opinions, as incorrect as they may be."

"I base my opinions on official reports from Coralia, including my own contacts through noble families residing there," Sabine replied. "But, of course, we all base our understandings and opinions on information made available to us."

"Of course," Grégoire said. "If I may, which Coralian noble families do you hold in high enough regard to write to?" he asked with a tone of genuine interest.

"Oh, I am well acquainted and friendly with many. Some in Branlin and Galel, to name a few." She could be just as vague as Grégoire, and she would not implicate anyone in their discussion.

"Branlin and Galel. Thank you. I haven't made friends there, yet."

"Unless you are willing to speak out against the cruelty shown by Sargarus, you may find it difficult," Sabine replied. "They harvest Nereid Merscales along the coast of Galel, from what I understand. And, of course, there was the massacre of the elven village."

"The elven massacre remained barely more than a rumor. There was no one to see it, and no one survived, so we don't know what happened or who was responsible. For all we know, another group of elves is responsible. Besides, it's not as if our past kings haven't done worse," Grégoire pointed out.

"As for the Merscale trade, Coralia has been partaking in the practice for generations. The only changes has been moving from waiting for the Nereid to shed their scales before collection to a much faster process." Grégoire's expression grew momentarily thoughtful. "The Sirene live nearby, do they not? They have the most beautiful feathers."

They stopped as they arrived at the room he normally stayed in, though Sabine found herself surprised by the appearance of the guest suite. She'd been too preoccupied with the discussion to pay attention to their surroundings. "As always, I enjoy our time together. It's so … informative."

"I find our meetings to be the same," Sabine replied. She could hear her irritation in her voice, and her hand rested against the hidden pocket of her skirt where she stored her knife. She wanted to plunge it into the prince's neck. "Do let us know if you need anything."

"I will," Grégoire said, his smile friendly, but his eyes knowing. "I'll see you in a few hours." He quickly disappeared behind his door, shutting it with a forceful thud.

Sabine felt Faron's hand on her back the moment the prince was gone. "I'm going to kill him," she said in a nearly inaudible voice.

"I'll help you do it," he responded, close enough to whisper it into her ear.

She nodded, took a calming breath, and turned to look at Faron. "Let's go."

Chapter Twenty-One

The rest of the day had not been as awful as Faron expected, while simultaneously feeling ten times worse. During dinner, the prince deftly avoided talking about Tristian and the events leading to his death, something Faron had expected him to bring up almost immediately given how close the two had been. Or pretended to be. In truth, Grégoire skillfully avoided any topic which could lead to friction or conflict. He'd been insulting, of course, but never outright, and since Sabine had been equally, and rightfully, patronizing, challenging, and dismissive, she'd not be in a position to call Grégoire out on his rudeness.

Before and after dinner, Grégoire stayed in his room, citing exhaustion from all of his travel and delicate constitution. He'd promised he'd be a better companion the next day after a good rest.

Faron didn't believe it for a second, but other than the feeling the prince was biding his time—for what, Faron did not know—there was nothing for him to act on. So, he'd doubled security and taken Sabine to their rooms the moment he was able.

Knowing how much Sabine enjoyed a long soak in a hot bath after a stressful day, Faron had the foresight to have Lisbeth run a bath before they arrived. He'd also asked for Meri to send some wine and an assortment of desserts up as well.

As they walked inside, he delighted in Sabine's pleasure over the presence of the items.

"My irritation must be incredibly evident," Sabine remarked as she looked at the items awaiting her.

"Not at all," Faron said lightly as he guided her further into the room. "I just thought you'd enjoy a relaxing evening."

"So, yes, and you decided I need to be pampered," she surmised. She put an arm around his neck and pulled him down so she could kiss him. "Thank you."

"It's my pleasure. I'm only forced to listen to him. You're forced to converse. I know which is worse. Food or a soak first?" he asked.

"Soak," Sabine decided. "The food and drink will be there later."

Faron nodded and motioned for Sabine to turn around so he could help her with her dress and hair. "You have handled yourself beautifully today."

"I'm still going to kill him," she replied, the certainty of her words no less diminished than they had been after his thinly veiled threat to the Sirene, even if she did sound less heated. Making her desire known without the immediate anger only solidified her certainty in her decision as far as Faron was concerned.

"Let me know how I can help," Faron requested. "Lisbeth could probably turn his body into fertilizer before anyone figures out what we did." He turned over several plans in his mind, ways to murder the prince and not get caught.

"If what we do is obvious, we'd have to do something about the entire party and their belongings," Sabine replied as Faron's fingers undid the lacing on the back of her dress. "If it is not obvious, it cannot be traced back to something we did or didn't do."

"We could take the entire group," Faron said after a moment. They could contend with the small party, though the size still surprised him. Faron wondered if Grégoire left some of his people at Tristian's estate. He made a mental note to have someone check. "Two of them are potentially magic users, so they might give us some issues, but honestly, making the entire group disappear wouldn't be hard. Nor would making it look like they've left here intact and had an accident hours down the road from us."

"If we can accomplish it after Grégoire has left, I think we will be safest." Sabine looked over her shoulder. "I saw the way he looks at you. He wants to strike against you."

"I'll talk to Marcelle and Avana. She should be back soon." Faron finished with the laces on her dress, then started working on Sabine's corset. "Between the three of us, we should be able to come up with a fairly solid plan."

"Just be careful when discussing anything. You don't know who might be listening, and I'm certain Grégoire is waiting for something."

"He is. I just can't figure out what. Do you think there could be more soldiers?" Faron asked as he finished with the corset. He helped her out of the dress and the corset, leaving her in stockings and a chemise. Faron could see the yellowed bruises on her back just above the neckline, and he forced himself to take a calming breath before starting on her hair.

"Perhaps," Sabine replied. "Again, though, he keeps looking at you, and I don't think it's because he can't seem to shake you when I'm around."

"I've noticed as well," Faron agreed. "Especially when he's avoiding the subject of Tristian. He has the full story, but he referred to your injuries as though you were in an accident when he first arrived. He has another narrative he's going to push, I think." He pulled the last pin out of Sabine's hair, freeing it to fall down her back in thick waves.

"He can't admit to what Tristian did without making himself look bad," Sabine said. She took Faron's hand and pulled him further into the room. She sat on the edge of the bed and lifted her leg so he could remove her stocking.

Faron complied with a smile. Kneeling so she could rest her foot on his shoulder, he slowly rolled the stocking down her leg. If his lips just happened to trail behind, he wasn't hearing any complaints. Once the stocking was removed, Faron tossed it aside and attended to her other leg. Faron's lips followed the second stocking before it too was tossed aside.

He smiled at Sabine as he stepped back, gently removing her legs from his shoulders as he did so. He held out a hand to help her off the bed. When she took it, Faron used a little more strength than necessary to help Sabine up, ensuring she ended up on her feet but pressed against his chest. Wrapping an arm around her waist, he kissed her deeply. Her arms went around him as they kissed, though her hand soon found his hair.

Faron broke the kiss, his forehead resting against Sabine's. "We should get you into the bath before it gets cold."

"Probably," she agreed. "You're distracting, though."

"I think you have that backward. Between the two of us, you are the distracting one." He pressed a kiss gently to her lips before pulling away completely. If he didn't, Faron knew there would be no bath for Sabine for several hours, if at all, and she needed to relax more than he needed to be inside of her.

"Fine," she replied in a playful tease. She strolled into the washroom, removing her chemise and tossing it at him in the process.

Faron shook his head, a laugh rumbling in his chest as he watched her go. He wondered if the need he felt for her, the desire, would cool as they aged. As he watched the sway of her hips, he knew the answer was no. He followed her into the washroom.

Sabine's fingers skimmed the water in the tub once she reached it. She must have found the temperature acceptable, as she soon stepped in and settled in the water, though she was careful to keep her long, thick hair from getting wet. Faron helped to gather it, and once she settled back, the long sheet of silky hair hung across the edge of the tub.

"I feel like I should have left it up until your bath was done," Faron said with a raised eyebrow. "You just looked like you needed it down."

"I did," she replied.

"Do you want me to brush it out while you relax, or would you rather have a glass of wine?"

"I'm fine right now," she replied. "Just keep me company."

"Of course," Faron said easily as he began to play with Sabine's hair. His mind went over the events of the day and how well Sabine had handled herself with the prince. Every day, she amazed Faron with something new, and he felt his respect and love for her grow even more.

They existed in a comfortable silence while Sabine relaxed. When the water grew cool, the tub was drained, and Sabine stepped out and dried off. Faron helped to towel dry

Sabine, careful of the fading bruising. Once done, he hung the towel back up and walked with her back into the bedroom, where he immediately went for the wine while she dressed in her robe, the same one she'd worn the day they met as she and Lisbeth had returned from swimming.

Faron uncorked the bottle and poured her a glass of wine. He held the glass out to Sabine before pouring himself a glass of water. "You should know, you won't be wearing that robe for much longer."

"Oh?" Sabine asked after she sipped from her glass. "And why is that?"

"Because I'm going to strip you down, tie you up, and have my way with you until you can barely remember your name," Faron said casually. He strolled over to the dressing table and withdrew the rope he'd purchased in the village just before the first time he'd been permitted to taste her.

"Interesting plan," Sabine replied after taking another sip of wine. "How long do you anticipate it will take until my name slips my mind?"

"A couple of hours. Then a few more just to help you relearn it."

"I think the way you moan my name might make it difficult. What do you think?"

"True." He made a thoughtful face. "Maybe we'll have to wait till tomorrow before you relearn your name."

"Oh, we can't have that, my love. You will not deprive me of the delightful way my name escapes your lips."

Faron laughed. "I would deny you nothing. Finish your wine, have some sweets, and I am at your command."

"I could never have any doubt over that," Sabine replied.

As prompted, she did finish her wine and have a bite to eat, though she did neither in a rush. Faron settled back in a chair, his eyes never leaving Sabine, his hands absently playing with the rope in his hands. They had all night. He wouldn't rush her now if he could help it.

Eventually, she sat her empty glass aside. "You are taking your time," she teased.

"You'll need your energy." Faron motioned to the chocolates. "And the wine will help you relax." He gave her a grin as he settled in more. "Take your time. We have all night."

"Indeed we do," Sabine replied, and she picked up her empty wine glass. "Surely, since you insist on me taking my time, you won't mind refilling this."

Faron reached out and grabbed the bottle of wine, refilling her glass with a steady hand. "I just want you to be as relaxed as possible after the day you had." He gave her a playful smile.

"Oh, of course," Sabine said as she brought the glass closer once it was filled. "I wouldn't dare accuse you otherwise."

Faron laughed softly. He wanted nothing more than to touch Sabine, to put his hands and mouth on her. But not yet. Well, maybe he could touch her, so long as he didn't give in and just ravish her. "I could offer to rub your shoulders. They do look a bit tense still."

"Do they?" Sabine asked. "Maybe you should see to them, then."

Faron stood and moved behind Sabine, doing his best to not appear overeager. Placing his hands on her robe-covered shoulders, Faron was surprised to feel just how tense Sabine truly was. Saying her shoulders looked tense had been a ruse to put his hands on Sabine, but feeling the knots in her shoulders, Faron gently started to work them out, making sure not to cause Sabine any undue pain due to her lingering bruises.

Sabine's glass was placed down again, and she sighed contentedly as his hands carefully massaged away her stress.

Faron's hands went to her shoulders, slowly massaging his way up to work out the knot at the base of her neck before working down to her upper arms. "How are the knots in your lower back?"

"Probably about the same," Sabine replied, her voice less teasing now.

"If you wish to lay down, I can help with that," Faron offered sincerely.

"Sure," Sabine replied. She waited until he removed his hands, stood, and went over to the bed. She removed her robe before lying on her stomach, resting her head on her arm.

Faron removed a jar from the bedside table then put a knee on the bed and leaned over Sabine. The hand not holding the jar gently touched along her back, pinpointing the knots, before he poured some oil on his hand. Placing the jar down, he rubbed his hands together before he got to work. Starting with her lower back, Faron began to massage the tension from Sabine.

Sabine let out a soft sigh of contentment as he worked, and thankfully, no touch aggravated the healing bruises.

Needing a bit more leverage for a knot in her middle back, Faron straddled Sabine's hips while ignoring the part of him that took great interest in his new position. He continued massaging Sabine's back, pleased to see physical signs of deep relaxation settling in.

"I feel that," she teased.

"I would hope so," he said with a laugh, shifting his hips for fun. He had to suppress a moan.

"I would think you could put it to better use than grinding, fully clothed, against me."

"I could, but then I'd never finish your massage." He dug his fingers into a particularly bad knot, still being careful of the amount of pressure he used.

"True," she replied. "And clearly, I needed a massage."

"You did. I don't think you've had a moment to relax since everything with Tristian happened," Faron said, his hands moving to her upper back.

"The past few weeks have been taxing, but my responsibilities can be taxing on occasion," Sabine replied. She sucked in a breath as his hands went over one of the more deeply bruised parts of her back.

Faron made a noise of agreement as he leaned down and laid a kiss on the painful spot in apology. He would need to be more careful until she was fully healed.

"You keep going, and I might fall asleep," she warned after a while longer.

"As much as I want you, if you need to sleep, I can always wait a few hours before I ravish you," Faron said before laying a kiss on her other shoulder.

"I don't need to sleep, but rubbing my back makes it easier to."

"Then I will keep this in mind for nights where sleep is elusive." Faron sat up fully, his hands working their way down Sabine's back from her shoulders to her hips, looking for any knots he might have missed.

"I'll take any reason to have your hands on me."

Faron just smiled as he moved back a bit, one hand resting on her hip while the other slipped between her legs. "Do you like my hands here?" he asked.

"I do," Sabine said, her voice taking on a breathier sound.

"I don't know if I believe you," Faron said, his voice playful as his index finger circled her entrance.

"Oh, you don't?" she replied, her breathing a little heavier now. "Why is that?"

"I don't know. Maybe you're not needy enough yet," he said, continuing to tease Sabine.

"Perhaps you should make me needy."

"I think I can do that," Faron said and slipped a finger inside. In response, Sabine took a breath and let out the smallest moan. Faron let out a small chuckle. "You can do better than that." He slipped a second finger inside, twisting his wrist so he could brush his thumb across her clit. A louder moan left her lips this time as his thumb brushed against the sensitive bud again.

"Not loud enough." He increased his pace, trying to drive her into a panting mess.

"Then you should earn it," Sabine managed.

Faron pulled his hand from Sabine and growled, "On your knees," as he moved back.

She shifted so she was no longer on her stomach, though she leaned back on her elbows, looking up at him. "You should show me exactly which 'on my knees' position you want."

Faron raised an eyebrow and pulled her up so she was on her knees. He then placed a hand on her upper back and gently pushed her down onto the bed. "I want you resting on your forearms and knees with your legs spread and ass in the air."

She looked up at him, her bright green eyes sparkling with delighted promise. She kept her gaze locked on his, inviting and challenging all at once.

Faron stood so he could go to the other end of the bed. Once there, he climbed back on top. Placing his hands on her ass, Faron leaned down and ran his tongue along her slit.

Again, she made sounds of pleasure, though they were more restrained than he liked.

Faron pulled away. "Are you not having fun?" he asked, his voice full of teasing lust.

"If it wasn't fun, I wouldn't be allowing it," Sabine replied.

Faron ran his hands along her smooth skin, his hands lingering on her delicious hips. Every part of him ached for more of her, but he was enjoying their current game. "And yet, you are so quiet."

"You're usually gifted enough to make me louder."

"Oh, so I'm not performing to your standards, then?"

"At the moment, you're barely touching me at all," Sabine replied. "But I think you know that."

Faron considered Sabine and the position he had put her in. Looking at the still healing bruises on her back and where the majority of the knots in her back had been, Faron didn't want to tie her up yet and certainly not tie her hands behind her back as he'd been considering. Coming to a decision, Faron said, "Sit up and move over." As Sabine did what he asked, he moved up the bed and laid on his back. "Come here." He reached for her hips. "I want you on my face." Sabine soon settled as he requested, her hands resting on the headboard for balance.

Faron thought about telling Sabine her grip on the headboard was too loose but decided against it. Instead, he grabbed her hips and pulled her down onto his mouth. He soon had her moaning loudly and her breathing coming in quick, shallow draws. Faron almost smiled as he played with and lapped at Sabine's core. These were the noises he'd wanted to hear.

He caressed her thighs, feeling the way her muscles flexed and relaxed as he teased her. His hands smoothed up to her hips, which now shifted, seeking more of his mouth.

Faron gave a low chuckle against her clit, causing Sabine to moan again. He felt her body growing rigid and knew her climax was imminent, so he sucked the bud into his mouth. He half expected her to topple over when she came, her body trembling with an unprecedented intensity. Thankfully, her hold on the headboard kept her upright.

For a moment, Faron considered stopping, the sound and taste and feel of Sabine clouded his senses, and he simply continued, swirling his tongue against her in all the ways he knew most thrilled her. When she jumped, an arm ensnared her thigh while a hand went to her hip, holding her in place and offering her no option of simply pulling away from him. He continued to absently play with Sabine's swollen clit for several long minutes, enjoying the way his name sounded as it passed through her lips. Not wanting to rush himself, his tongue abandoned the little bundle of nerves and, instead, teased at her entrance before slowly tongue-fucking her.

Again, she tried to jump but to no avail, and as one of her hands left the headboard to touch his hair, he knew she wanted more. So, he gave her more, focusing on every-thing she knew she liked while mixing in efforts he had not yet tried. He held her steady when she came again, get-ting little warning before she cried out his name as her very limbs shook.

Again, Faron considered stopping, but he knew it wouldn't take much to have her come a third and fourth time, so he continued. Sabine would let him know if she wanted him to stop. And she did after another couple of rounds.

Faron released his grip on her and gently helped her down his body and onto the bed. He removed a hand-kerchief from his vest and cleaned his face, then tucked it away. Residual tremors moved through her limbs, and she breathed heavily as she rested her palm against the flushed skin of her chest.

"You did so well," Faron said, his fingertips running up and down her side.

"You did seem quite pleased with yourself," she said with a breathy chuckle.

"More pleased with how much you seemed to enjoy yourself."

She reached up and ran a hand down his chest. "How could I not enjoy you?"

Faron knew there wasn't an answer that wouldn't make him look overly smug, so he just leaned down and kissed Sabine instead. "Rest. If you fall asleep, I'll wake you in a few hours."

"Good, because I'm still not done with you."

Chapter Twenty-Two

The sunroom, though rarely used before summer months, waited for Sabine and the prince come morning. Light poured through the windows, twinkling on the chandelier and room decor. Side tables ran along the wall on the far end of the room, and settled next to them sat a small round table surrounded by a couple of chairs.

With the tables festively adorned with flowers and large spreads of food, Sabine knew their visitor could compare the splendor of the space to many ballrooms and not be left lacking. She waited for the prince to join her, smiling as he strolled the space, his shoes clacking gruffly against the colorful tile.

"Your estate is rather beautiful," Grégoire said, his voice laced with unrestrained reluctance as he joined her.

"Thank you," Sabine replied. She waited for him to take a seat before she did. "My parents thought it important to protect all under our care. It was a good lesson, one I hold dearly."

"Your parents were idealistic, weren't they?" he said with a thoughtful look on his face.

Sabine shook her head. "No, I think they were often quite practical about the realities of life. Still, being realistic and knowing where to devote their attentions always worked well for them."

"Until it didn't," he said in a near flippant tone. "My older brother was the same way. Always trying to devote his attention to those in need and the betterment of everyone."

"And if one does not concern themselves with the betterment of those in their care, what possible other purpose do they find for themselves?" Sabine asked, her expression giving off subtle, curious interest rather than the irritation the casual insult toward her parents had inspired. Getting outwardly angry with Grégoire would serve no one.

Members of staff began serving both prince and duchesse, filling plates with delights cooked by Meri and her team and filling glasses with a pale, bubbly wine. Sabine thanked each person with a smile and a nod.

"One should concern themselves with those in their care. It's just there are some who deserve it and some for whom our efforts are wasted." Grégoire said, ignoring the staff completely.

"And what would you consider a wasted effort?"

Grégoire made eye contact with Sabine for a moment before looking down at his plate. "You know what my thoughts and opinions are on those who are and are not worthy. I am not up for a debate on who we should consider worthy of help and who we shouldn't." He paused to take a bite of lobster. "Instead, tell me your version of what happened at Tristian's."

"Oh, I do not mean to debate you," Sabine replied. "But I would point out every one of the people under my care would shed blood for me if needed." She knew he could accuse her of no threat, but her words held an undeniable threat. "As for what happened, Tristian sent his guards to attack my people, and while they were defending themselves, he attacked me." She motioned to the bruises on her neck.

Grégoire didn't react to her threat. Instead, he brushed a crumb off his vest.

Sabine couldn't help but feel he wasn't taking her seriously. He would learn how serious she could be if his decisions led him down a dangerous path.

"Explain the attack, please," Grégoire directed.

Sabine nodded, and she meticulously walked Grégoire through each part of the attack, the threats, and the injuries. She did not downplay the responses to the attack, including the actions resulting in Tristian's death. She felt like downplaying or denying them would make her, Faron, and Avana sound guilty of something sinister, and they weren't. "Given the circumstances and the multiple planned attacks, Tristian left little room for anything else."

Grégoire made a thoughtful noise. "Actions such as that, if true, would allow for no other response. You're right." He sighed and picked up his wine glass, sipping from it instead of saying anything else.

His doubt, whether genuine or not, didn't escape Sabine, but his actions barely concerned her. Sabine didn't need his beliefs or support, though Grégoire was foolish enough to think otherwise. She took a sip of her own wine, her gaze lingering on Grégoire. "Tristian seemed to be under the impression he could have access to my estate and my wealth."

"Only if you were married, seeing as he would be your husband," Grégoire said as if she should know this. "He truly was the best match for you, considering his own status." He looked off to the side, something catching his attention for a moment before he drawled, "I wonder if you've just been waiting for someone of higher status to show interest. Though, I hadn't thought you so greedy."

"I am a duchesse," Sabine reminded him, "and much higher ranked than a comte. Though, status does not worry me much. My mother, as you recall, was not born into nobility."

"She wasn't, and it was a waste your father didn't marry Lady Alméras. She was a much better match. Your mother, rest her soul, never fit in at court. Not truly." Grégoire picked up his wine glass again, taking another sip. "You're a duchesse, yes, but that doesn't mean you don't want for more. Though, I would assume Louis and his weak spine would be more your type."

"I'm afraid I have no desire for the throne."

"A lot of people say that. All of them are lying, but that's okay."

"If I wanted the throne, I would take it, Your Highness," Sabine replied. She sipped from her wine as she observed some fruit before picking up a berry between her thumb and forefinger. "There is a rather large contingent who believe I should have stepped in and resolved the feud between you and your brother by making myself queen. You will note I have not done so."

"I guess that's good information to have." Again he didn't seem as concerned about this as he should be.

A noise from behind them caught their attention, and both turned to see Faron, who'd silently stood by the door the entire time, helping a serving girl, who was coming in to check on them and seemed to have tripped, back on her feet. Sabine grew more aware of the braided locks of dark hair still tied to her wrist, a pride-filled thought. She couldn't wait to marry him, though their engagement had not been shared with Grégoire, as doing so seemed foolish.

"I don't know why you decided on such an ostentatious guard."

"I think Faron is rather useful," Sabine replied. "And he's quite good at his job."

"I'm sure he is," Grégoire said. "I just think one would want a more discreet personal guard."

"I've had some," Sabine replied. "Which is not to say they were not effective in their responsibilities. However, I find Faron to be a much better deterrent. I'm so much less stressed with him around."

Grégoire looked back at Faron once more. He studied the elf for a moment before turning back to Sabine. She was positive he was holding back a sneer. "I guess I can see how someone of his…size…would make someone think twice."

"I did notice he is rather taller and broader than the men you brought with you," Sabine said with a nod.

"I don't think there are many people, human or otherwise, built as large as your elf."

"No, I don't think there are," she agreed. "Aren't I lucky to have him?"

"I wouldn't say lucky, but I can understand the appeal." Grégoire gave a one-shouldered shrug.

Sabine nodded and continued eating. Although she didn't trust the prince as far as she could throw him, she was amused by the effort he made to keep his thoughts buried. After a few minutes of silence, the two finished their meals.

Grégoire said, "I was told there was a female elf on your staff. Are you letting go of your non-human staff?"

A moment of panic rose in Sabine, though she covered it by reaching for her glass and drinking. Why was he asking about Avana? "There is a female elf who resides in my home," Sabine corrected. "But I have not released any of my people."

"I wasn't trying to offend. I was just curious," Grégoire said, a slight chuckle to his voice and a hand raised as if in surrender.

"No offense taken," Sabine replied.

"I haven't seen her," Grégoire continued. "I have met many other members of your staff and would love to meet her too. Find out how she likes working here." He took a sip of his wine. "I'd convince your cook to leave with me if I thought I could."

"She is traveling," Sabine said simply, revealing nothing else. Avana had been present at Tristian's, and reports would confirm as much. She was also willing to bet Grégoire connected her to the elf he spoke of, but Sabine would not give him even that much information.

Grégoire nodded in acknowledgment with a thoughtful look on his face. "Well, if she arrives when I—" He was cut off by one of his own people entering the room, a letter in his hand.

"Your Highness, a rider arrived with this in hand." He held out a cream colored envelope, which Grégoire greedily snatched.

Sabine could just make out the Coralian crest pressed into the seal.

Grégoire lit up. "I am sorry, my dear. I must respond to this. I'll see you later." He rose from the table, barely looking at her as he hurried from the sunroom, the man who'd delivered the letter practically sprinting behind him.

Faron waited for them to pass before he closed the door, locked it, and crossed the space to Sabine in long strides. "Should we be concerned?" he asked.

"Very," Sabine said as she stood. "And his prying about Avana."

"He's trying to create his own narrative surrounding your attack, with Avana at the center," said Faron with certainty.

Sabine agreed with his assertion. "She's who he's been looking for. All the glancing around, the careful observations now have an explanation. I wonder why he now felt comfortable enough to ask directly."

"I don't know, but I would like to double your guard if, for some reason, I'm not able to be by your side," Faron said.

"More guards won't be a bad thing given where I think Grégoire's mind is going," Sabine easily agreed. "See if Marcelle can round up some of the Sirene to help."

Faron gave a sharp nod. "I'll send a runner and write up new orders for the guards. I would love to see the look on Grégoire's face if he realizes the recruits are from Coralia."

"Thank you," Sabine replied. She took a breath and led him out.

Chapter Twenty-Three

Faron had been lying in bed, Sabine's head resting on his chest as he pulled his fingers through her thick, silky hair, when news arrived of riders bearing royal colors in the village. Despite his annoyance at the interruption, both had risen and dressed, and Faron quickly assigned several guards to Sabine before he and a handful of trusted soldiers left the chateau and made their way into the village. Although the Fythian royal colors hopefully belonged to Prince Louis, Faron had yet to confirm it, so he and his men moved cautiously.

He had his hopes, of course, and one of those hopes would be the presence of Avana. He had no reason to assume she'd joined up with the youngest prince, but her appointed task of delivering Sabine's letter and disappearance after that were hopefully connected. If she did travel with Louis, she could be warned about Grégoire. They still didn't know what the elder prince wanted with Avana, but his interest could not be positive.

Making their way through the village, Faron and his guards quickly happened upon the intended group. Even at a distance, Faron could make out the youngest prince with little effort. Tall and lean, Prince Louis possessed a dark tan and golden hair that drew the attention of those he passed. Younger than Faron imagined, the prince still held the slightly rounded face of youth, and Faron had to wonder how such a man had won over so many. Louis had to be the complete opposite of his older brother. The young heir he'd produced with his wife probably didn't hurt.

The prince moved on foot, though he held the reins of a black horse, his soft words of praise just detectable to Faron from a distance. Guards flanked the prince, each glancing around the village with keen, curious eyes. When a dark haired woman with a ruddy complexion, dressed from head to toe in leather and armor, locked eyes with him, Faron debated approaching until he spotted Avana just behind the prince and his immediate guards. He grinned, despite himself.

"Well met," he called out as he approached the group, followed by his own guards.

Avana waved as she brought her horse to a halt and the dark-haired woman stepped forward, just putting herself in front of Louis. Avana rolled her eyes and ignored the woman. "Prince Louis, this is Faron, Sabine's personal guard." She gave him a wide smile.

"Step aside, Brielle. Avana knows him," Louis told the female guard, who listened without hesitation, retreating to line up with the next group of soldiers.

Prince Louis took his time observing Faron. His eyes, a dark green, traveled up Faron's height before the prince finally nodded to himself. "Sabine was smart in hiring you," he said in greeting. "I can imagine your very existence drives my brother mad."

Faron couldn't help his sharp grin. Louis's appeal made sense now that he'd spoken. Charisma carried a person far, and combined with the beliefs Sabine shared with him, Faron could see a possible source of relief in the young prince. "Considering his glare anytime he even glances in my general direction, I would say you're correct."

Louis laughed, his soft voice going deeper than expected. "Are you here to serve as escort or to warn us of what we will find?"

"I'm here to ensure Grégoire doesn't see Avana, but I am more than happy to serve as escort once she's safely on her way."

"Wait? What?" Avana asked, turning her head with such speed, her loose near white-blonde locks flinging through the air.

Faron turned his attention to Avana and her upset and confusion. He had a feeling the anger wasn't at him. "Grégoire has been asking after you, and we don't know why. Sabine thought it might be wise if you snuck in and stayed out of sight until we're ready," Faron explained.

"Sneaking her inside will only prove useful until my brother, or one of his ilk, spots her," Louis pointed out. "He won't be able to do anything to Avana if she walks in with us. Not with my protection and that offered by Sabine."

"True," Faron admitted, even if he didn't truly feel ready for a conflict with the elder prince. "I think Sabine wanted to wait until we were more prepared, but the best way to deal with an issue is to confront it head-on."

"Then let us be on our way. I haven't seen my brother in ages." Louis motioned in the direction of the chateau, a clear sign of having been there before, and the group began their trek in that direction.

Faron led the way, listening with one ear as Avana pointed out places in the village she took interest in as they went. Louis indulged the unrequested tour with good humor, and Faron shook his head in amusement.

Even with their leisurely pace, it didn't take long for the gates of the estate to come into view. Faron was unsurprised to see Sabine waiting for them, her guards in attendance. Grégoire surprisingly didn't wait with them.

Louis grinned upon seeing the duchesse. Passing off his horse's rein to one of his people, he approached her and honored her by kneeling before she had the chance to bow. "It is so good to see you, Your Grace," he said before placing a kiss on her hand.

Sabine smiled and inclined her head. "Far too much time passes between our visits."

"Indeed," Louis replied. He squeezed her hand then motioned behind him. "Your delightful friend found me."

Sabine beamed as she took in Avana. Her body moved as though she wanted to hug the young half-elf, but she paused, remembering herself and the circumstances that brought them all there. "It's about time you came home."

Avana gave Sabine a wide smile. "I got distracted," she said with a shrug and a laugh.

"Where's Grégoire?" Faron asked softly as he moved to Sabine's side.

"He has been locked up in his suite," Sabine replied. "I think one of his people spotted Prince Louis's party when they arrived in the village."

"Did they think he'd make a scene?" Faron asked, only half joking. With the way Grégoire behaved, Faron would have been more prepared for a child's tantrum rather than the prince's sulking in his bedroom. "Well then, we should enjoy our problem-free moments while we have them."

"I think he was uncertain of how to proceed," Sabine said. She looked at Avana again. "I was a day from sending Faron out to find you."

Avana handed her own horse off to one of the stable hands who had arrived to handle the horses. "He wouldn't have," she declared. "I'm so happy to be home."

"I imagine you would be," Louis said as his horse and those of his party were taken by Sabine's stable hands. "The Vassetre Chateau has always been a refuge from the tedium of the world."

"You flatter as though it will prevent you from dealing with Grégoire," Sabine said with a mirthful laugh.

"One can hope." Louis sighed. "Well, let us be in. I'm sure my brother will slink out at some point."

"If we're lucky, we might get an hour before he slinks out of his room." Faron offered his arm to Sabine.

"Has it been as awful as the visit to the comte's or worse?" Avana asked with a cringe.

"He hasn't repeatedly told me I'm a silly, stupid woman," Sabine said as she took Faron's arm. "But I would not call the visit an improvement."

"So, you mean he's not telling you all of his evil plans because he thinks you'll be so impressed as to marry him?" Avana said, her tone bright but very unimpressed.

"No, but Grégoire has implied Sabine has been waiting for him to offer marriage," Faron threw out, and Avana made gagging noises.

"That is escalation," Louis said with a hum to himself. "Last I heard from Grégoire, he thought you should marry one of his supporters. The Comte du Ciel, for example."

"He has something in mind," Sabine said as they crossed into the entry of the chateau. "But I think he's been scrambling since he thought I'd be bullied into marrying Tristian. Instead, he lost a supporter and still has me to contend with."

Faron shook his head, having nothing to add because he completely agreed with Sabine. The elder prince had a clear plan in mind that had more than fallen apart. "I fear he may grow more desperate. More dangerous," Faron said.

"He probably will," Louis agreed. "Which is why I suggested the duchesse stay close to those who will watch over her while he is here."

"Trust my fiancé has to be warned off from time to time," Sabine replied.

Louis grinned and glanced over to Faron and back at Sabine. "Oh, very good choice, and not just because it will drive Grégoire mad."

Avana cheered. "I knew this was coming. I just thought we'd have to wait a few more months." To Louis, she said, "He can be really thickheaded."

Faron rolled his eyes but didn't deny the truth. "I'm hopeful we can wed once everything with Grégoire is handled."

"You might be waiting a while if he proves as stubborn as he usually does," Louis said. The prince glanced around the entryway where they now stood. "I think I should like to rest a bit before possibly facing my brother."

"We have a few rooms made up," Faron said, looking to Sabine in confirmation.

"Yes, Finn had rooms prepared for you and your people," Sabine confirmed, though so far, the party traveling with Prince Louis had remained outside. "I also made sure to have you placed far from Prince Grégoire." She turned and saw one of Finn's people waiting to serve as an escort.

"Perfect. Let me know when you are ready to dine this evening," Louis decided. "Or if my brother leaves his quarters."

"I have guards stationed in his wing and at the doors leading to the wing, for his protection, of course. When he leaves, we will know immediately, and I'll make sure you know shortly after," Faron promised.

"Good," Louis replied. He turned his warm smile to the housekeeper, offering his arm before he allowed himself to be escorted away.

Faron watched the younger prince go. "He seems nicer than Grégoire or Tristian," he observed.

"He's very nice," Avana said. "A bit too trusting, I think, but still nice."

"He has always been so," Sabine replied.

Faron let out a harsh breath through his teeth. "I'm surprised he's still alive with a brother like that."

"He wants to believe Grégoire can be better, but thankfully, he knows not to put a lot of faith into that belief," Avana added.

Faron sighed and shook his head. "That's at least something. He needs more guards though."

"He does," Sabine replied. "But we can supply them while he's here. No doubt, our dear middle prince is going to have quite the tantrum."

"That might be an understatement," Faron said with a smile.

"I'll let Meri know there are more mouths to feed and that I'm back. Go enjoy your time together, lovebirds." Avana waved and headed off, a bounce in her step.

"She is very delighted about our engagement," Sabine noted, looking up at Faron. "You should scowl at her less."

"I don't know. It's more fun, and she thinks it's how I show her I care."

"I feel like you should be concerned with other types of fun."

Faron raised an eyebrow, his gaze running down Sabine's body and up again. Many of their sexual exploits began due to her desire for distraction and relaxation. His need for her was in no way diminished by her desires. He craved her more than he craved food or air, and he took advantage of any opportunity to show her his devotion. "I am always concerned with our type of fun."

"Oh really?" she asked with a teasing smile. "And we're just standing around by ourselves with all of your concern?"

Faron's eyes darkened, and he had to forcibly stop himself from throwing Sabine over his shoulder and marching to their bedroom. Instead, he offered her his arm. "Let's go do something more productive with our time."

Sabine took his arm. "Lead the way."

Chapter Twenty-Four

Faron leaned against the wall next to Sabine's desk, surveying Avana, who had asked for a moment to gather her thoughts. She now paced the length of the office, her index finger in her mouth as she worried the nail. Faron couldn't tell if she was nervous or excited, and he wouldn't know until she was ready.

Sabine sat in her desk chair, her thick tresses hanging loosely since she hadn't bothered having it put back up after their long, and very naked, afternoon. Faron thought the action intentional, especially since his fiancée knew how much he loved her hair. Even as they waited for Avana to speak, he contemplated what it might be like to wrap those long locks around his hand. Sabine knew where his thoughts drifted as she began playing with the ends. Maybe, if nothing came up, he could bend Sabine over the desk and—

"Grégoire is definitely the man who bought me from my mom," Avana said suddenly, and all thoughts of what Faron wanted to do to Sabine fled his mind.

Sabine leaned forward, her expression and posture much less alarmed than Faron expected or personally felt. "How do you know?"

Avana looked down, her cheeks growing pink. She didn't speak for a long time, though her jaw worked as though she silently debated what she wanted to say. Becoming concerned, Faron considered pushing himself off the wall to comfort her, no matter how shitty he knew he would be at the task. Thankfully, she started talking again.

"I had been more than prepared to head all the way to the princes' estates when I met Prince Louis on the road. I handed him your letter and explained my assignment, but he informed me Grégoire was on his way to Tristian's. So, Prince Louis asked me to ride with his group, and I didn't feel right turning him down."

Faron nodded, finding the story plausible given what they knew and how quickly she had returned. He said nothing as Avana looked up at Sabine, her hands fidgeting.

"While riding here, we talked about his home and the people under his care. Somehow, that branched out to Grégoire's estate and the awful conditions of the people he's supposed to care for. There were things he said, about the state of the town square and marketplace. How the fountain still wasn't fixed and the general feel of poverty and sorrow that reminded me of what little I was allowed to see of the town."

Avana paused long enough to flop down in one of the seats in front of Sabine's desk. "One night, when we'd stopped at an inn for food and sleep, I asked him to show me Grégoire's estate on a map, and I realized I'd been there. I'd lived there."

Sabine folded her hands on her desk. "How did you not know before?"

"I was never allowed a full map before I came to you. Or taught proper geography. Any map I was shown was incomplete and had no names. I was only shown one so I could memorize the path from one point to the next, so I knew landmarks in case I got lost. So my knowledge of those days and the map in front of me combine to create a pretty good idea of the man who sent me to kill you."

"You realize if you're right, we now know Grégoire first tried to kill me then tried to arrange a marriage with Tristian, and both plans failed. With Louis in residence, Grégoire is going to feel cornered. Desperate," Sabine said, though the distraction in her voice sounded more as though she was speaking to herself. She leaned back in her seat, and her fingers tapped against her chair arms. She let out a snort of laughter after several seconds of silence. "At least he recognizes how dangerous I am to him."

Faron's head snapped to Sabine. "Your amusement worries me," he informed her. Though, he completely understood Sabine finding humor in the midst of the threats. The prince's fear and threats could be viewed as complementary. Of course, now he worried if there were any assassination attempts they were unaware of and what Grégoire might do now.

"I will admit, I'm not completely sure, just sure enough to voice my thoughts. I feel I'll know for certain once I meet Prince Grégoire. I don't really want to, but I know I should," Avana said.

"You don't have to," Sabine replied. "His asking about you gives me pause in encouraging a meeting, even if there might be some benefit."

"I know I don't have to," Avana admitted.

Faron's heart went out to her at how small her voice sounded, if only for a second. She'd suffered more than any person needed to, even if she annoyed him.

"But if it's him, I would recognize his voice. It's the only way to be completely sure," Avana countered.

"If you're certain you want to be close enough to him to confirm your suspicions, I will not instruct you otherwise," Sabine said. She stood from her desk and walked over to Avana, placing a hand on her shoulder. "I will make sure you remain safe, regardless."

Avana nodded, her expression a mix of determined reluctance. "I need to do this, but thank you."

"Then why don't you join us for dinner this evening?" Sabine suggested. She squeezed Avana's shoulder and returned to her desk. "You will not appear by yourself. You should arrive with me, and of course, Faron will be near as well."

"I like that idea," Avana said after a moment's thought.

Faron made a mental note to have more guards stationed outside the dining hall tonight. He couldn't have them inside or Prince Grégoire could view their presence as a threat. He had a feeling something was going to go wrong, maybe not at dinner but soon.

"We have a plan, then," Sabine replied. "Grégoire might try to provoke upon seeing you, so be careful in how you respond if you choose to respond."

"I might just stay quiet. However..." Avana took another deep breath. "Can I stab him if he tries to hurt me?"

Faron wanted to nod yes, to give her the permission, but knew it was best to let Sabine make that call. Any consequences would fall on her head, after all.

"If you have no other option, you may defend yourself. I'm hoping Louis will deter Grégoire from doing anything too drastic."

"Thank you," Avana said, relief in her voice, before her eyes narrowed. "Do I have to dress up for dinner?"

Faron couldn't contain his laughter at her quickly changing mood.

"I think that is a question you should take up with Lisbeth," Sabine replied with an amused grin.

"Shit," Avana cursed under her breath. "I should get that done, then, unless you need me for something else?"

Sabine shook her head, her long hair once again catching Faron's attention. "Just be careful wandering about."

"Of course," Avana said and was out the door a second later.

Faron let out a low chuckle. "I think tonight is going to be fun," he said dryly, his eyes on the hand in her hair.

"I think we'll be lucky if there is no bloodshed," Sabine replied, looking up at Faron.

"Unless it's Grégoire's blood being shed. I think that would be a boon."

He pulled Sabine from the chair so she was pressed against him, then he cupped Sabine's cheek and leaned down to kiss her. She tilted her head up to meet the kiss, her lips inviting him for more. Faron brought his other hand up and wrapped it in her hair as he deepened the kiss. He coaxed her lips apart, nipping at the lower one as she softly moaned.

The hand on Sabine's cheek dropped to her hip. He let the kiss continue for another minute before he broke it. He couldn't help himself.

Faron stared down at Sabine, just taking her in before finally speaking. "Turn around, bend over the desk, and place your hands so that you're comfortable. Do not move them once you're ready." He had no doubt she would comply, and he smirked as she turned from him, shoved her chair out of the way, then placed her hands on the desk.

Faron took in the view, appraising her form. Sabine was gorgeous, sensual, and she listened so well. Stepping up behind her, he ran one hand down her back slowly. "You played with your hair the entire meeting with Avana. You know how much I love your hair, so I can only think you were doing it on purpose. Should I punish you?" he mused. He watched as the proud smirk formed on her lovely face, and he couldn't help but grin, knowing she was going to play along.

"Isn't that up to you?" she asked.

For just a second, Faron considered a slight slap to her ass cheek. He then remembered she hadn't much cared for the light slap to her thigh the night they'd gotten together. The night before her assault. So, he decided instead to go another route. He placed his hands on the skirt of her dress and slowly dragged it up her legs until Sabine was bare before him.

She gasped softly, though she made no protest, so Faron felt comfortable continuing. After securing her skirt, he ran his hands up the back of her thigh, and as his palms met her ass, he squeezed appreciatively.

"You like to tease," he said before leaning down to kiss her neck. He had to be careful, because as much as his mind wanted to go down his newly designated path, she could so easily turn his head, encouraging him to pursue something quicker, more desperate.

"I do," she breathed out, her head tilting back against him. Faron lifted his head and buried his nose in her hair, inhaling her intoxicating scent. Spirits, how did this woman hold such control over him?

He allowed one of his hands to travel to her hip, his fingers trailing her smooth skin. "If you like teasing, perhaps I should give you more of it," he whispered. His hand slid along her pelvic bone then down. His hand dipped lower, brushing along her center in featherlight touches. Each movement grew more obvious, and he could hear the subtle changes in her breathing, see the excited tensing in her shoulders. He was patient. He could wait for her to beg.

He smiled to himself as her knuckles finally rose into points, a physical sign of her frustration. She kept her palms in place, this a sign of her enjoyment. He would have to keep that in mind going forward. Pleasing his fiancée would always be a top priority for Faron. Finally, he slipped a finger inside of her, giving her enough stimulation to have her panting with need without giving in to her desire.

Sabine softly moaned as Faron kept his movements languid. His eyes switched from watching the way she drew him in to the rolling of her hips and the way her hands flexed on the desk. He knew what she wanted, and he loved denying her.

"Faron," she breathed out finally as he dragged his thumb across the little bundle of nerves.

"Hmm?" he replied. He repeated the swipe of his thumb and chuckled to himself as she practically jumped.

"You know what I want," she said.

"I do, but that doesn't mean you get it. Not yet." Faron continued, though his own patience started to unravel as Sabine's breathy little noises grew more ragged. "You still haven't asked." He could tell she grew close, and a devious smile crossed his face as he drove her to the edge before withdrawing his fingers. He caressed her thighs as she groaned in frustration.

"You're evil," Sabine said. Her fingers flattened back on the desk.

"You enjoy it," Faron said simply as he continued to caress her. "You enjoy not having to think. Not having to make decisions. Turning it all over to me." His fingers dipped back into her, causing her to gasp out again. Again, he carefully touched and teased her closer to climax, only to withdraw before she could get there. His kissed her neck as she voiced her frustration.

"Do you still like teasing?" he asked as his hand returned to her center, finding it hot and slick, her need refusing to be denied. She nodded her head, her breathing heavy. "Answer me," he commanded, needing to hear her desperation.

"Yes, Faron," she exclaimed.

"Then I shall just keep at it, then." His index finger ghosted across her clit, once, twice, a third time, before pulling away.

"Good," Sabine replied. "Don't stop. Not yet."

Faron gave a nod even though he knew she couldn't see it. He'd happily give her anything she demanded of him. His eyes raked up her back and down to her hands, watching her intently. They shared several more rounds of this dynamic, each time leaving Sabine near breathless. Faron thought he delightfully suffered just as much, his desire for her a needy ache, and finally, thankfully, she uttered the most beautiful word in existence.

"Please."

"Please, what?" he asked, drawing the words out.

"Don't tease me anymore," she replied. "Fuck me."

"Ask nicely," Faron growled, even as he started to undo his pants.

"Spirits, please, Faron. I need you to fuck me," Sabine begged.

Faron made a considering noise, as if her pleas weren't good enough. He considered taunting her further, making her beg more, but he'd be hurting himself as much as her. So he let out a chuckle. "Well, since you asked so nicely." One hand moved to her hair, grasping the thick locks before rotating his wrist so it wrapped around his hand. He gave one slight tug, relishing the pleased response from Sabine, before lining himself up and, without warning, thrusting to the hilt. Giving neither any time to adapt to the new position, Faron set a quick and brutal pace, one hand resting on Sabine's hip, the other still wrapped in her hair.

Her responding moan, the way her hips shifted to meet him, and her stubborn refusal to remove her hands from the desk all coupled with their overstimulated need for one another. Faron knew he wouldn't last long. Sabine wouldn't either. Using the hand on her hip, he guided her to take a step back, making for a small adjustment that had her groaning and sliding forward so her forearms rested on the desk.

Faron let out a moan of his own, not holding himself back as Sabine's hands slipped and letting his own climax take him. He continued moving his hips until he was completely spent. He finally released her hair and let his hands rest on either side of her waist. When she straightened up, he laid a gentle kiss on her neck.

"I think we may need to do that again in better positions," Sabine shared, tilting her head to the side so Faron could kiss her more.

"I think I like the idea of your hands tied behind your back, your chest pressed against the desk, and you unable to get away from me. That sounds like a good few hours spent," Faron purred in her ear.

"Mmm, whatever you like," she replied with undeniable enthusiasm.

"I want whatever makes you happy. Whatever makes you writhe in pleasure." He kissed her neck again. "Would you rather tie me up?"

"I would like that also," Sabine replied. "I have no complaints with your previous suggestion."

"Good to know." Faron felt himself start to harden again but he fought the urge. They'd spent most of the afternoon fucking, and she needed to recover. He backed away, cleaning himself off with a handkerchief, tucking himself away, then helping to straighten her skirts.

"I need to wash and rest before dinner," Sabine announced. "It promises to be an explosive evening, and I'd rather not be half asleep."

"Does that mean I should find somewhere else to be for a little while so you can get some rest? Or may I join you and pamper you until it's dinner time if I promise to leave you unviolated until after dinner?"

"I'd prefer you be with me, even if it sounds as though you wish to be elsewhere."

"I want nothing more than to be by your side always. You just have this uncanny ability to make me lose my self-control."

"I don't do it on purpose, my love."

Faron laughed and tucked a strand of hair behind her ear. "I believe that about half the time."

"And the other half?"

"The other half, you are most certainly tempting me."

"Only a little," she said with a playful grin. "Now, come along. I am tired."

Chapter Twenty-Five

The atmosphere in the formal dining room pulsed with tension. The usual long table had been replaced with a smaller one, allowing for no more than eight diners at one time, making it easier to converse while maintaining the safety of each person. Sabine thought a possible stabbing was a poor way to end the night. She sat at the table, patiently waiting for the evening attendees to arrive.

Louis was the first to show, looking rested and cheerful, both of which his boyish good looks and golden hair emphasized. Not one to stand on ceremony with an old friend, he'd insisted Sabine remain seated when he joined her at the table. They chatted and laughed for several moments, waiting for Grégoire before he finally joined them.

"Good evening," Grégoire greeted, pausing at the chair. In many households, even Sabine's during more formal occasions, a servant would approach and pull out a chair. As none appeared, Grégoire settled himself into the chair without assistance, looking as though he wanted to complain.

He smiled at each, though his lips twisted into a grimace. Sabine would swear everyone in the room might fall dead if Grégoire's displeasure had the power to cause it.

Noting that Avana hadn't arrived, Sabine discreetly motioned for Faron to send someone to find her and for Meri to send up some wine. As wine was poured for the three, a bread filled with cranberries and pecans was placed on the table alongside a container of jam and some butter mixed with honey.

"I'm surprised you came all this way, Brother," Grégoire remarked. "What with your wife being in delicate health."

"My wife and son are quite well," Louis replied before sipping from his glass of wine. "Alaoin is nearly a year old."

"Has it truly been a year? Astounding. One would think rumors of your wife's health would have improved instead of getting worse," Grégoire quipped. He selected some of the bread and added a generous helping of jam to the top.

"I am pleased to hear of Eloise's health," Sabine added as she picked up her wine glass. "She sounded quite delighted by motherhood in her last letter."

Eloise, a kind, caring woman, had been the daughter of a lower-level noble. Considered a moderate beauty and sharp wit, she was assumed to be ill-suited for court life by many nobles. Sabine had been told by Eloise, on more than one occasion, that she agreed. The princess used her pregnancy as an excuse to stay away from courtly presence and, in doing so, had provided some leverage to Grégoire when it came to rumors of her alleged poor health.

"It's funny how we naturally come across little rumors," Louis said flippantly. Louis enjoyed teasing his brother, even though the light jabs came from dislike rather than fondness. There was no need to pretend any affection existed between the brothers.

Grégoire pressed his lips together and sipped from his wine glass before turning to Sabine. "I see several extra chairs. Do you have other guests?"

"Just one more, but I am afraid my smallest table remains too large for our dining party this evening," she replied. She kept her tone light and friendly despite being well aware of Grégoire's agitation.

"It's not your elven bodyguard, is it? It seems like he's always at your side." Grégoire looked around. "Except for today, it seems."

Sabine shook her head, amused by his preoccupation regarding Faron and irritated at the othering in the reference. Never could she forget the sort of person Grégoire was or what a reign under him might look like. "I'm afraid Faron does not enjoy formal dinners. Otherwise, I'd have invited him to join."

"I can understand that, him being who he is and all," Grégoire said with a wave of his free hand, as if it was of no matter.

Louis sipped his wine again. "I quite like Faron," he said as he sat his glass aside. "He's observant and bright, and he has done a remarkable job of keeping our lovely hostess safe after she's been attacked. First by an assassin, then by the former lord of the neighboring estate."

Grégoire sat back in his chair, adopting a more relaxed pose that seemed forced to Sabine. "I don't know. What I've been told is that Sabine defended herself in both attacks. The elf was barely needed."

"Really?" Louis challenged, his demeanor unbothered. He fixed his gaze on his older brother. "I've received completely different accounts of what happened. I wonder over the discrepancies."

Grégoire gave a careless shrug. "I know where my reports come from." He looked about to say something else when the doors opened and Faron entered.

"Sorry we were late," he said as he stepped aside.

Behind him appeared a perfectly at ease Avana. Dressed in black pants and a blood-red blouse with a black vest over it, she looked quite smart, her blonde hair pulled back and braided. She gave Sabine a wave as she entered.

"I'm glad you two finally made it," Sabine said, smiling slyly to herself. She motioned for Avana to take a seat then looked to Faron. "Prince Grégoire was concerned about your dining this evening, and I believe he felt I should invite you to join us as well."

Faron bowed deeply, the motion hiding a broad, humored smile. "I would be honored to join you for dinner tonight."

From the side, Sabine watched as Grégoire ignored them, though he kept his eyes on Avana as she took her seat next to Louis. She would have to monitor him very closely since his attentiveness to Avana all but proved his intention to do something involving her.

"Then please join us, and I shall call for another glass of wine," Sabine replied.

As Sabine caught the attention of one of the servants, she saw the slight movement of Grégoire's hand as it tapped the table three times in a deliberate pattern. Two of Grégoire's guards appeared in the doorway and stood at full attention. One of them went so far as to place his hand on his sword.

Her gaze slid to Louis, whose own eyes watched the guards with some interest.

"Tell your brutes to stand down, Brother," Louis commanded. He didn't shout, nor did his posture stiffen, but something about the way Louis stared at his brother made the command come across as that much more authoritative.

Grégoire chuckled. "I have never understood why you think you have any control over what I do or am able to try and give me orders." He shook his head and casually stood. "I also doubt you understand the situation we've found ourselves in. You see, the woman sitting next to you is the assassin who tried to kill Sabine." He looked at Sabine. "Some of your guards really do like to talk when they've been in their cups," he said, his voice oozing with infantilizing sweetness. "She's also the person who killed Tristian after making another attempt on Sabine's life. I have statements from the members of Tristian's household. I don't understand why Sabine keeps trying to rehabilitate her, but she's always been soft." Grégoire's smile turned sharp. "However, I am not that soft. The murderer needs to be arrested and held accountable for her crimes."

"Perhaps, then, we should start with the person who gave the alleged orders to come to Her Grace's home to kill her," Louis replied in an equally casual tone. Unlike Grégoire, Louis did not rise from his seat. His demeanor radiated the sort of legitimate authority someone like Grégoire could only dream of possessing.

"As to your second accusation, I do not think Avana, nor Faron for that matter, has denied killing Tristian. They had a right to fight and kill in the defense of their mistress. Given her rank, she'd have the power to order his execution had he not died while she was being rescued from his assault." Louis looked at his wine glass, rolling the stem between his thumb and index finger. "You should also know that every member of this household sits under my protection, Grégoire. Her Grace's defenses outnumber your own without my aid, but rest assured, she has my backing."

Grégoire shook his head, a sardonic smile on his face. "It matters not if they are under your protection. Per the laws of our land, there is reasonable suspicion the elf," he jabbed a finger at Avana, who was openly glaring at him, "attempted to murder Sabine and did murder Tristian. The witnesses say it wasn't in defense of Sabine. This means her arrest, and the subsequent trial, are lawful, and there is nothing you can do about it. Or does the law you so love to talk about only apply when it's someone you don't like?" He motioned his men forward. It was noted he did not touch on the subject of who sent Avana in the first place.

Louis laughed dismissively at his brother as he stood, as did Faron. The guards might feel bold enough to go after a young elf, but attacking a member of the royal household gave them pause. "Your insistence on being right, on being the only person with power amuses me, Brother."

Louis's hand settled on the hilt of his sword. "Her Grace testifies that the death of Tristian Anouilh was the result of his attack on her. An attack, I might add, that has been verified by his household and the magistrate. Regardless of whatever changes to the story you proclaim to have secured after the fact, none but my own, and yours, of course, could possibly outweigh what she has to say. And as you know, neither of us was there, which leaves Her Grace's account the sole truth."

He looked at Sabine. "Do you change your story about what happened to the Comte du Ciel?" Louis asked.

Sabine shook her head. "I do not."

"There you go," Louis said, looking back to his brother. A couple of Sabine's guards, including Marcelle, joined the party in the dining room, and though Grégoire and his men were now outnumbered, the young prince's hand never left this weapon.

Grégoire's face grew bright red as the logic sunk in. "You've always thought you were so smart!" he spit out, his eyes blazing in fury. He kicked the chair out of his way and approached Louis, snarling. "In truth, you are nothing but a weakling and a coward, and you should have died along with our brother. The throne is *mine!*" Spit flew from his mouth as he screamed the last words.

His eyes darted around, landing on Sabine. Faron's sword was in his hand as he moved to get between Sabine and Grégoire. Avana had her own knives drawn. "My allies will be here within the week. I will sit on my throne, and all of this protection you hide behind will be struck down one by one. I will deal with you then." He turned from the group, motioning for his two guards to follow him.

Louis snorted as he resumed his seat. "He always was temperamental."

"I don't know that I would be laughing," Sabine said as she picked up her wine and took a large gulp. "He's deranged and desperate. He thought he would simply arrest Avana and carry out whatever other plans he had. Now he's been thwarted."

"At least we know he's waiting for backup," Louis said. "Which is more than he'd confirmed before."

"But who's the backup?" Faron asked as he sat back down.

"We should have just killed him. It still would have been self-defense," Avana said softly.

"We'll try to find out," Louis said. "For now, let's enjoy the meal."

"Oh!" Sabine said, remembering something. "We brought home a large collection of Tristian's letters and books. We know he's been in contact with Grégoire. There could be something there."

"Louis's eyes widened in excitement. "Let's get them, then. We need to know whatever we can."

Chapter Twenty-Six

Faron's mood had only declined in the interim since dinner, but he had done his best to keep his frustration, fear, and anger under control. Yes, he, Sabine, Avana, and Prince Louis had laughed over Grégoire's behavior, and the atmosphere had relaxed into a more playful banter as Sabine and Louis had gone through all the documentation they'd stolen from Tristian. Sabine never let personal threats bother her much, or rather, she hadn't allowed any potential fear to sway her actions. He admired her tenacity, her willingness to sacrifice when she felt the situation warranted it. He also understood she had little choice in the matter if she wanted to continue serving well in her role.

But in the back of his mind, Faron had replayed all the ways the confrontation between Grégoire and the others could have gone badly. Even now, as they prepared for bed, his mind went back to Grégoire and the unhinged look in his eyes. He'd seen the desperation, the desire for power and respect. It reminded Faron far too much of those who had sided with Sargarus in Coralia, and Faron knew the middle prince would lash out soon. All he'd need was the opportunity.

Looking over at Sabine as he removed his vest, he smiled as she brushed her hair. He was tempted to take over the simple task, something he'd found himself doing with more frequency, but somehow, he thought neither of them were quite in the mood for where the action would inevitably lead. Instead, he folded his vest and put it aside before he began unbuttoning his shirt.

"You look worried," she observed, glancing over at him from her seat.

Faron considered redirecting the conversation, to try and keep their night as stress-free as possible. Sabine, of all people, deserved the opportunity to shut out everything beyond their bedroom as evening settled in. He also knew it was unfair to deter her line of questioning. "Just Grégoire. I don't trust him, and tonight, he seemed unhinged. I was very concerned he planned on attacking you, Avana, or Louis for a moment. He still might, unless he somehow convinces himself to change plans. And I doubt he would consider it, given how certain he was of his intention to arrest Avana."

"As I said earlier, he's desperate now," Sabine replied. She put her hairbrush aside, stood, and crossed the room to the bed, where she took a seat. "He thought he would come here, throw his weight around, arrest Avana and possibly you, but he found he couldn't do that. He never suspected he wouldn't get his way just because others protested. I think he believed Louis would back him, no matter what else is happening between them." She sighed. "And of course, all of his latest disappointments follow his attempt to have me killed then married off to Tristian. I am not dead, and my fiancé isn't an ignorant minor lord characterized by over-spending, drink, and cruelty."

Faron chuckled darkly. "You see why I'm worried," he pointed out. His shirt was folded and joined the vest. "You should be proud of me," he added.

"I usually am," Sabine replied.

Faron smiled, momentarily distracted by his future wife. Though she easily complimented him, he could never doubt her sincerity. Her casual position on the bed, dressed in her nightclothes, also frequently caught his attention. "I'm glad to hear it, because right now, I either want to go kill Grégoire or take you and leave, though I think you might protest." He pondered that for a moment. "Honestly, both sound good. I could do both."

"And where would we go?"

"We could figure that out while we rode off together," Faron replied.

"I wish we could," Sabine said. She grabbed his hand and pulled him closer to the bed. "But I have a duty, and I intend to see it through."

"I understand. You must be here for Louis and your people. At the same point, if I threw you over my shoulder and made a run for it, leaving Louis to deal with his brother, would you truly complain?" he asked, only mostly joking.

"I believe I fired you last time you threw me over your shoulder," Sabine quipped.

"This time I'm asking. Or maybe we could say I'm giving you advanced warning? That makes it no longer a fireable offense, doesn't it?"

"Oh, I don't know. I'd been planning on sending you to live in the village when you annoy me from now on," she teased. "And you know from experience how to easily annoy me."

Faron laughed, appreciating her humor when he was feeling so anxious. Sabine's ability to calm and distract remained unmatched. "The isolation would be an awful punishment, but it might be worth it to have you all to myself for the few days it takes Avana and the rest to help Louis kill Grégoire." He reached out as if to grab Sabine.

She laughed and leaned back on her elbows. "You've had me to yourself many, many times today."

He had, and he wasn't close to having his fill of her. "But not under the stars. Besides, it gives you plausible deniability for the death that is sure to happen soon." He moved to settle on top of Sabine, and he grinned as her arms went around him.

"And to think, you wanted to deny loving me. You love everything about me, don't you? You spend your days thinking of how and when you can next have me."

Faron grasped her hip, pressing his hardness against her. "Yes," he growled.

"Tell me what you want right now."

"I want—" Faron was interrupted by a loud banging on the main door to their chambers. He closed his eyes and wondered for a moment if they could just ignore it.

Sabine sighed in frustration and looked toward the door. "I don't think we can ignore it."

Faron huffed and released Sabine. "One can dream," he said as he moved to rise. When he was off the bed, Sabine sat up and smoothed the bottom of her nightdress down her legs.

Faron grabbed one of Sabine's robes and held it out for her. He waited until she was ready then grabbed his shirt so he could redress. Once they were both presentable, they headed out of the bedroom, through her receiving room, and to the door. Opening it, they were surprised to see Marcelle and Finn on the other side. "What's wrong?" Faron asked.

"You won't be surprised by this, but we've reports from the village that Grégoire and his men are drunkenly causing problems," Marcelle replied with a roll of his inky eyes.

"Wait. Grégoire was seen with them?" Faron asked, confusion tinting his voice. Last he had heard, Grégoire was sulking in his room. Faron had instructed those guarding the prince's room to alert him if Grégoire left. Since no report had reached him, it meant Grégoire had snuck out, something foul had happened with the guards, or the prince remained in his rooms and some last-ditch plot was underway.

"None of the chateau staff have laid eyes on the prince," Finn said. "And he may not be there, but the reports from the village say he is. Either way, some of our people need to go down and handle their chaos before it turns into more."

"I agree," Sabine said. "You could always go to his rooms to verify if Grégoire remains inside if you like, but something has to be done about those in the village."

Faron rubbed the bridge of his nose. He had a bad feeling about the reports and what handling the situation would mean. He truly did not want to leave Sabine alone, even in the safety of their room, but at the moment, he and Marcelle were sharing command of the guard when he wasn't guarding Sabine. So, it was his job to check on the village and ensure the people's safety almost as much as it was to ensure Sabine's safety.

"Alright. I'll go check on Grégoire, and if he's in his room, I'll let him know there are reports of his men acting up in the village. Marcelle can gather a group of guards together and ready them to head out. I will join them with or without the prince." He glanced at Marcelle, who nodded, then looked back at Sabine. "Will you please remain locked in your chambers while I'm gone? I can't help if I am worried about your safety."

"I will be fine," Sabine said. "Go make sure my people are."

"I really don't want to leave you," Faron said, pulling Sabine close and laying a soft kiss on her lips.

"I know," she replied, smoothing her hands down his chest. "But the sooner the problem in the village has been resolved, the sooner you can return."

Faron growled softly. "Stop being right." He kissed her again before releasing her and taking a step back. "Stay safe," Faron said and nodded to Marcelle and Finn, the Sirene heading toward the front of the chateau to gather troops, while Faron started toward Grégoire's wing. He hoped the prince was in his rooms, but it would make everything so much easier if he wasn't.

Chapter Twenty-Seven

Faron stood in the middle of one of the most popular taverns in the village, taking in the destruction as the rest of the guards finished arresting Prince Grégoire's men. Tables and chairs in various states of disrepair laid on their sides, remnants of a vicious tavern brawl the Vassetre guards broke up soon after arriving. Behind the bar, broken bits of liquor bottles were scattered across two different shelves as brown liquid dripped in random beats onto the floor below. Another couple of shelves, sitting higher than the others, remained untouched by the surrounding chaos.

The two front windows, broken and tinged with remnants of drying blood, made the usually vibrant, warm room seem dangerous and foreboding. Already, villagers who'd not stopped by for an evening drink loitered outside, peering in with curiosity and fearful surprise. A freckled tavern worker usually tasked with collecting and washing dishes walked around the front, sweeping glass into piles. His youthful face and hard-set mouth contrasted greatly, leaving him looking like a petulant child on the verge of throwing a tantrum.

Faron surveyed the dining area of the tavern, taking in the blood, glass, and liquor as the owner scowled at shackled men wearing Grégoire's crest. Her icy blue eyes, intensified by dark furrowed brows, met Faron's, giving him a look of satisfied annoyance. He couldn't blame her. Beyond arresting the guilty men, he and the guards had done little to put an end to the fighting. The tavern patrons, ranging from teenagers to the very old, had handled themselves well.

"I think that's thirteen accounted for," Marcelle called over to Faron as another Vassetre guard ducked into an adjoining room in search of more people. Faron estimated around twenty soldiers had accompanied Grégoire, so a handful of people were still missing, including the prince.

"No one's spotted Grégoire?" Faron asked, frowning. When he'd gone to the wing to check in on the prince, he'd found the room empty, though several of the windows had been open to the night. Faron wasn't certain Grégoire had left the chateau at all, but as no one in the chateau had spotted the prince, not even the guards at the gate, Faron had to assume he'd snuck away. If he hadn't and Grégoire was still at the chateau, Faron would be pissed beyond measure.

Marcelle shook his head. "That doesn't mean he isn't in the village somewhere. There's other inns and taverns he might have crept away to visit."

"I can see it," Faron admitted. It would have been smart for Grégoire to vacate the area as soon as his men started to get rowdy. Doing so would allow him to claim innocence of any wrongdoing and not end up in a cell. A bad place for a prince to end up. "Get these men to the holding cells, then let's start looking to see if we can find him or any others from his party who might be causing problems for our townsfolk." Faron did his best to ignore the growing feeling of dread. That he had made a misstep somewhere, leaving Sabine in danger. But she had asked him to go and handle things in the village. *For their people*, she had said. So that's what he was doing. Sabine also wasn't alone. Things would be fine.

"You heard the man," Marcelle called out to their people. The Vassetre guards took their time escorting Grégoire's people from the inn, and as the space emptied out, usable chairs and tables were righted by the remaining patrons as the tavern owner began sweeping up debris.

"Send my thanks to Her Grace," she told Faron.

"Of course," Faron said with a nod of his head before leaving. An unseasonable chill hung in the air, renewing the sense of dread permeating his bones. "Where should we start?" he asked Marcelle, though he had a feeling he had an idea of where Marcelle would suggest.

"Do you think he went looking for some company?" Marcelle asked, pulling his cloak closer around his body. "If so, we should head to the docks."

"Spirits, I hope not." The village didn't have a brothel, but there were still a handful of those who were more than happy to trade favors for coin. It didn't matter if that favor included their bodies or helpful information. Besides, Faron didn't think he had enough coin on his person to buy information from them if Grégoire had been to see them, but it was the best place to start.

"If he hasn't been to meet up with someone, he might still be in town. Spirits, he could be on the chateau grounds." Marcelle glowered as they walked through the village toward the harbor. Gravel and dirt crunched beneath their boots as they left the more worn roads. The beaches, rocky and slick, always made for more deliberate steps. Sounds of ocean waves called out over the noises in the village.

"That's what concerns me. He could be anywhere in town, or he might have never truly left the estate at all. Why sneak out?" Faron sidestepped the larger rock which marked the non-commercial passage to the beach. He had to admit, at least to himself, it was possible Grégoire wanted time to himself after the disaster dinner had been. The man had shown his strongest opponents just how unstable he was and might not have wished for several of Sabine's guards to follow him around while he thought out a new plan when leaving out the front door.

The more Faron thought of that possibility, the more sure he was that it was wrong. "I have a terrible feeling," he admitted to Marcelle.

"Any that don't directly concern Her Grace?" Marcelle asked.

"I don't know. I could just be paranoid after the last attack, but something feels off. The prince has been here before, and I assume his men haven't acted so recklessly. I would have been told otherwise. It reminds me too much of Tristian's men acting up so he could…" Faron trailed off. That's exactly what this was. "We need to get back to Sabine." He made to grab Marcelle by the shoulder, but the Sirene sidestepped him.

"We can't all go rushing back at once, especially when we can't confirm where Grégoire is. You head back to the chateau. I'll continue this way just in case," Marcelle replied.

Although the village wasn't huge, Faron would still have a long trek back to the chateau, and he'd be quicker on his own. "You should run into some of the others on their way back by now. They can help you if it's needed. I'll head back once I've confirmed if he's been here or not," Marcelle continued.

Faron nodded and took off at a run for the chateau, offering no argument or rebuttal to Marcelle. He couldn't believe he had been so stupid to not see this as the distraction it was meant to be. He just prayed Sabine was okay when he got there.

Chapter Twenty-Eight

The eerie quiet of the chateau sat ill with Sabine. She sat in her suite, relaxing as much as she could as she waited for the guards to return from their trip into the village. With Grégoire missing from his rooms, Faron had insisted Finn alert Louis of his brother's departure while he and the guards went into the village. Meri had promised to watch over the rest of the staff while the guards were out with Faron, and Avana had been locked away in her room, a measure to let her calm down after the events at dinner while assuring Grégoire would have no access to her.

Sabine had also promised to remain locked away in the quarters she'd shared with Faron, both because her fiancé had asked rather than demanded and because it was the smartest thing she could do with most of her defenses down in the village.

"I should have gone to my office," she muttered as she rose from her chair and crossed the room to one of her spacious windows. She might have read if she thought there was any possibility of being able to focus on the words.

And it wasn't as if Sabine worried. Not really. Faron, Marcelle, and her soldiers were more than equipped to handle every member of Grégoire's party. Especially if they were drunk. The worst any of her people would experience was a scratch. Still, Grégoire's unhinged behavior at dinner, coupled with his disappearance, had her on edge.

The view from the window provided no updates, even with clear skies and bright moonlight illuminating the immediate area. She half hoped to spot the middle prince sneaking around or perhaps the guards returning with the offending soldiers.

Forcing herself from the window, Sabine retreated to the side table displaying her crystal decanter set. She selected a whiskey and poured herself a glass. She'd just brought it to her lips when she heard a pounding at her door. The rapid heavy knocks suggested bad news, though she did not know if that was because of the person on the other side of the door themself or any knowledge they possessed.

She took a sip then placed her glass back on the counter as she considered her options. She could pretend to be elsewhere. Anyone who needed access to her rooms didn't need her to unlock a door. When the banging sounded again, she retreated further into the space, not to hide but to retrieve the dagger she usually carried. This, she tucked into a pocket of her robe.

The door started shaking as though the person on the other side wanted to break in. Again, she did not approach. The knocking stopped just as suddenly as it had started. Silence filled the space for several minutes, and though she did not move from her spot, Sabine started to relax, until another series of much lighter knocks sounded on her door.

Was she supposed to be fooled by this? Her door was locked, certainly, but Lisbeth and Finn would have identified themselves. Faron would have let himself in with the key she'd finally bestowed upon him. Her hands went to her robe pocket, wrapping around the hilt of the dagger as she took a quiet step forward.

Another soft knock sounded at the door, almost tentative, as if the person on the other side was no longer sure she was there. Sabine bit her lip, contemplating what she wanted to do. This person, and she had a high suspicion of who it might be, did not want to leave. She could gamble, remain silent, and hope for Faron and the others to return, but she somehow doubted an unlimited supply of patience waited on the opposite side of the door.

She let out a breath, deciding to answer. "Yes?"

A brief silence followed before a deep voice replied. "Sabine, I heard there was a commotion in town. I wanted to make sure things were alright." Grégoire sounded worried as he spoke. Worried, stressed, and tired.

Sabine trusted none of it. Grégoire was not there because he was worried about her. "Some guards were dispatched to take care of the problem. There's no need to worry."

There was a noise outside the door she couldn't identify before Grégoire spoke again. "If my people did get out of control, I'll pay for any damages."

"I'm sure it will be appreciated," Sabine replied. She moved further back into the space, suspecting she would not be alone in the room much longer. She couldn't exactly flee, as no other exit than her windows existed, and leaving through the window would leave her in worse condition than Grégoire possibly could.

"Would you mind if I came in? I want to apologize for my behavior at dinner, and I would rather do that face-to-face than through a door."

Shit. She did not want him to come in. She did not want to be alone with Grégoire. To do so would be foolish and likely dangerous. She also suspected Faron would be rightfully infuriated if she did something so stupid. "I am afraid I am indisposed this evening, but I do thank you for the sentiment. Perhaps we might speak in the morning?"

"I would rather speak now," Grégoire replied, his voice firm.

Sabine shook her head. There was no way she could allow a discussion. Still, she knew she didn't have much of a choice. She had no doubt Grégoire would eventually get through her door, and she had no doubt of his intent to do so if she didn't agree to speak with him. "I understand," she said. "But I think tomorrow would be better."

"I think we're going to talk now," he said firmly before another louder bang sounded against her door.

Sabine's fingers tightened on the dagger hilt as she waited for Grégoire to force his way through. What a shame since the door had only recently been replaced. Sabine couldn't believe herself, focusing on the time Faron had forced his way in when Avana had arrived to kill her. She felt like this confrontation would turn out differently.

Grégoire gave four more forceful hits against the door before the lock finally gave way, and the prince was able to access the room. Although his height and width fell short of Faron's, no one could mistake Grégoire as weak. He stood there, brushing himself off as if he didn't have a care in the world. "Hello. Sorry about the door."

"You should be," Sabine replied sharply as she took in the damage. She didn't care about sounding or looking angry. "I think very little could justify breaking into my rooms."

"Oh, I'm sure I can come up with something if pressed. Though, I won't be here when they find your body." He glanced down at the knife on his belt. "Pity." He seemed regretful for a second.

Sabine had no doubt of his intention to kill her. Grégoire was a man who yearned for real power, and she didn't think anything could quite stop him in that task. In what was probably a poor decision, she gave a derisive laugh. "And you wonder why you are not king."

"I'm not king because bleeding hearts like you don't understand how this world should be," he growled out as he advanced on her, his knife still sheathed. "Sargarus is right. Humans are the rightful rulers. There's no room for people like you in this world anymore."

She laughed again, mocking and taunting, though she stepped back with every step forward he took. "You are not king because you are a fool," she said, speaking to him as though he were a very young child. "You are not king because you align yourself with people like Tristian." She smiled triumphantly, knowing the man was dead because of her and her people. "Do you know why else you are not king?"

"Why?" he spat out, a gleam of madness shining in his eyes.

"Because I do not wish it."

Grégoire growled and unsheathed his knife. "I was going to make this quick: slit your throat or just slip it between your ribs. But now..." He tossed the knife to the side, ignoring the way it clattered on the tile beneath them. "I think I'm going to enjoy beating you to death. I have enough time." He cracked his knuckles and then shook out his hands. "It won't be the first time I've dealt with someone standing in my way. Just ask my older brother."

Although Sabine had suspected such before now, Grégoire's confirmation of having killed the deceased king only prompted her to continue. She lifted her chin, meeting Grégoire's gaze with her own look of defiance. "The last man who put unwanted hands on me lost his head. I won't promise you the same quick death."

"Your people are gone; you have no help this time." He raised his fists as he got closer, his eyes tracking Sabine carefully.

She could hear her heart beating in her ears, and there was no denying the quicker pace of her breathing. Sabine doubted she could maneuver around the prince without getting caught. Deciding she was better off if he got closer, Sabine played dumb and stepped back closer to the wall, making it seem as though she had no options. Grégoire's eyes narrowed and he quickly scanned the area around her. Apparently, he wasn't as stupid as Tristian had been in thinking she couldn't defend herself.

He took a cautious step closer once he was satisfied and swung. Before he could land a blow, Sabine withdrew the dagger from her robe pocket and sunk it deep into Grégoire's neck. She held it firm, feeling the warm spray of blood hitting her skin, and only once the prince started flailing did she pull the blade out before stabbing him again.

Grégoire tried to scream, but the wound in his neck prevented anything more than a horrific gurgling noise. One hand came up to try and stop the flow of blood as the other tried to weakly grab at Sabine, as if he could somehow stop her attack.

She withdrew the blade again and stepped to the side as Grégoire fell to his knees. Blood poured from the wounds, pooling down his hands and arms and splattering on the tile. "I warned you," Sabine snapped viciously.

Grégoire looked up at her, his eyes filled with hate and loathing. He managed to spit a glob of blood at her before collapsing to the floor, dead.

Good, Sabine thought as she backed away from his body. Blood continued to gather around his head and neck, and she had no interest in getting any more of his blood on her own body. She dropped the dagger on the ground beside his body, certain she wouldn't need it again, then turned to look at her door as she heard approaching footsteps.

Louis stepped into the room, his eyes taking in the broken lock before moving to Grégoire's dead body on the ground and Sabine standing above him, splattered with blood. "What did he do to you?" the prince asked, hurrying forward.

"He said he was going to beat me to death," Sabine replied, not even a hint of regret in her voice. "I got him first."

"Good," Louis said with a nod. When he was close enough, he knelt by his brother, taking in the damage while avoiding the blood. "I was told his men were in the village wreaking havoc. I wanted to make sure you were aware." He stood, looking regretful though angry. "I suppose this was the way things would always play out," he said with a sigh.

Sabine nodded. "I think so."

Another set of pounding footsteps could be heard quickly approaching the room. "Sabine!" Her name was shouted as Faron grew closer. He'd obviously noticed her newly broken door.

"I'm fine," she called back, looking away from the body.

Faron appeared in the doorway to her rooms and, in one quick glance, took in the body on the floor and the blood covering Sabine. "Tell me that's his blood," he said in a half panicked voice as he crossed the room in long strides.

Sabine's expression softened. She understood his panic, and she wanted to soothe it away. "It's just his," she said gently. "I am fine. Not a scratch."

Faron gathered Sabine into his arms once he reached her. "I'm sorry. I should have seen this for the trap it was."

She wrapped her arms around him, hoping to reassure him. "I'm fine," she repeated. "Nothing to apologize for."

"I still should have been here," he told her. "After all, Tristian did pretty much the same thing."

"He did," she agreed.

"You've got to get his body out of here," Louis interjected, disrupting the two. He strolled toward the door and closed it, even if the broken lock prevented total security. When he rejoined them, he spoke up again. "If his guards are all out in the village, now is the best time. You can get rid of the body and claim you haven't seen him since dinner." He motioned to Sabine. "You need to burn those clothes. And be careful of the blood. The more it spreads, the harder it will be to clean up and hide."

"Is Marcelle back?" Sabine asked.

"He should still be in the village. I left him down by the docks," Faron said as he glanced around the room. "You aren't too fond of the rug by the fireplace, are you?" he asked Sabine.

She shook her head. Discarding any material item to cover up Grégoire's death seemed a small price. "If you see him on your way out, bring him with you."

"Of course." Faron quickly grabbed the rug by the fireplace and expertly wrapped up Grégoire's body. "I'll talk to Lisbeth about what we need to get any blood stains out," he informed the two before slinging the body over his shoulder, making sure to keep the head elevated so blood was less likely to drip out.

"It would be better to burn it as well," Louis said. "Assuming those with access to this room are limited and trustworthy."

"They are," Faron assured Louis, though Sabine saw him look to her for confirmation.

Sabine nodded. "Very few people are permitted in here, and I trust those who are with my life."

"Then Faron should get the body out of here," Louis said. "I'll get someone on your lock. It will look like nothing happened. Like you, I trust the person who will make the repair with my life. In the meantime, use that robe to soak up as much blood as possible. Then burn it."

"I'll get this all cleaned," Sabine confirmed. She didn't want to involve anyone else. As far as she was concerned, no one outside of this room needed to know the details of Grégoire's death.

"Good. In the morning, come downstairs angry, as though you intend to demand compensation for the damages in the village. We will all be surprised by his absence."

"If I see Marcelle, I'll let him know the plan," Faron confirmed before making a hasty exit.

Louis turned his attention back to Sabine as the two were alone once again. "I'll leave you to clean up," he shared. He looked at the fire, seemingly checking to make sure it already blazed. "And I'll give you twenty minutes or so before someone shows up for the door."

"Thank you," Sabine replied.

Louis reached out and took her hand, squeezing it. "Thank you. You have continually risked your life for me and my beliefs. I will not forget it." He released her hand before she could reply and hurried from the room.

Sabine did not hesitate to remove her blood-splattered robe and use it to mop up the blood.

Chapter
Twenty-Nine

Thankful for the late hour, Faron carefully crept through the chateau corridors toward the servant exit located at the back. It wasn't the most direct route to the beach, but it would be much more discreet despite the heavy addition of a carpet and a dead body resting on his shoulder. The only issue he expected came as he drew closer to the kitchens. Though evening had arrived, he wouldn't be surprised if lingering kitchen staff gathered under Meri's watchful eye, some cleaning used dishes and counters while others chopped, mixed, and diced, preparing ingredients for tomorrows meals.

He usually appreciated the attentiveness, and not just because he ate well and could trust the cleanliness of the food. The attention to detail in the kitchen spread to all areas of the chateau. He saw it in the way the guards now moved and reacted at training or when they were in the village, making sure everyone was safe and compliant with the local ordinances. He saw it in the way beds were made and linens were laundered. Of course, he saw it in everything

Sabine did. Every scribble on a sheet of parchment, every decision, and even the information she supplied.

Tonight, he could have done with less precision from everyone other than Sabine. Fortunately, if Meri or any of the others straggled in the kitchens, he knew he could talk his way out of suspicion and any delays. Like Finn and Marcelle, Faron often received orders that weren't communicated, or at least explained, down through the ranks. Meri, were she around, wouldn't question anything unless she was alone. Of course, she also refused to hide anything from Lisbeth. Though trustworthy, his oldest friend was prone to more emotional reactions and silly displays and comments as forms of distraction.

Hopefully, Finn might be around or Marcelle would be back, and he'd not have to worry about Meri for now.

As he approached the kitchen, Faron's steps grew slower, softer, and more deliberate. He didn't think anyone who could possibly be around heard well enough to detect him, but his superior elf ears could give him warning. Thankfully, no tired chatter or clanging of pots and pans reached him. As he approached the space, he also saw the interior lights had been distinguished, likely some time ago, as he couldn't smell remnants of smoke wafting from the extinguished tallow candles used in the kitchens. Sabine's quarters and office relied upon beeswax, as did the exterior lanterns outside of the kitchens, though this call had been made by Finn in the name of safety. The rest of the chateau had been fitted with oil lanterns, though neither aroma would have been strong enough to hide burning tallow. Faron breathed a sigh of relief as he quickened his pace and hurried past the doors, leaving his biggest worry behind.

He continued listening as he walked, wondering if any of the guards had returned from apprehending Grégoire's men. Those were the only potential encounters he continued worrying about. Even if arrested and manacled, Grégoire's soldiers wouldn't overlook the obvious transport of a dead body, and they didn't have the justification to keep them jailed indefinitely. Faron paused again out of precaution, making sure he couldn't hear anyone. Perhaps all the guards remained in the village for now, overseeing the cleanup. He resumed walking, going as fast as he dared without causing too much noise or dropping the body.

As he reached the back exit, he took a breath, hoping his luck would hold out. Adjusting his hold on Grégoire, he then reached out to unlatch the locks on the door. A loud *clank* echoed in the corridor, but no other responses answered. Faron took a breath and pushed the heavy wooden door open.

"What are you doing?" a whispered voice asked.

Faron nearly dropped Grégoire's body as Marcelle drew closer to him. Faron scowled, contemplating how he'd missed Marcelle approaching. "Fuck," he growled out, rebalancing the dead prince. "Where did you come from?"

"The harbor where you left me," the Sirene replied.

"Sorry, sorry. You just startled me." That was an understatement; Faron hadn't even heard the other man coming.

Marcelle waved off the apology, which was just as well. "Sirene walk lightly," he said, then motioned to the carpet. "Who are you smuggling out?" he asked, keeping his voice low as he glanced around.

Faron couldn't help but to glance around, although he was positive no one other than Marcelle was near. "Prince Grégoire. He attacked Sabine while we were gone. He didn't even land a hit on her." Faron could not keep the pride from his voice over how well Sabine handled herself during the attack. Still, he couldn't deny, at least to himself, his guilt at not being there for her once again.

"Good for her," Marcelle replied with no trace of judgment in his voice. "Where are you taking the prick?"

"I was thinking about the beach. Either finding a Sirene to take the body or weighing it down and hoping," Faron answered. He wondered for a minute if it was rude to ask the Sirene to take the body, but he also knew this was the best way.

Marcelle's brow furrowed as he took in the plan, but he nodded after a brief moment. "Come with me," he said, motioning for Faron to follow him to the beach.

Faron nodded and followed behind Marcelle, careful of the heavy burden on his shoulders. The last thing he needed was to trip and drop the body. As they descended onto the rocky beach, Faron adjusted his grip, making careful steps down toward the water. Rocks and sand slid beneath his feet, though Marcelle descended without difficulty.

When they reached the water's edge, Marcelle instructed him to put the body on the ground as he knelt and dipped his hand into the briny water. Several long moments passed before Faron spotted the tremors in the water, and an unknown Sirene rose from the black depths. Her body, still humanoid, took on a more bent posture than Faron was accustomed to seeing.

"Marcelle," the woman said in a silky voice. Her long black hair clung to her body, and her inky eyes, already difficult for most to read, existed as though in a void in the darkness of night. She turned to look at Faron, tilting her head to study him. "And elf," she acknowledged.

"He works for Sabine, Raidne," Marcelle explained.

"Ah," Raidne said. The abyss of her gaze landed on the rug. "And what is this?" she asked, a long green-tinted hand motioning to the body.

Faron bowed slightly in respect to the female Sirene. He observed the two Sirene closely as he tried not to look too deeply into her eyes. He knew the Sirene changed when they went into the water, but rarely had he interacted with them in any form other than their most human. The Sirene woman was both beautiful and terrible to behold, and he was slightly terrified of her. After all, it wouldn't take much for them to drag him under, never to be seen again. He wondered, with Marcelle and the woman so close together, what Marcelle might look like in his true form.

Faron had to quickly push away the remembrance of the threat to his life by Sabine's friend to answer her. "It is the body of Prince Grégoire. He perished trying to murder Her Grace."

"Ah," Raidne repeated. "I think Thaumas has spoken of the prince." She walked forward, pinpricks on her skin slowly sprouting dark purple-tinted feathers. "We shall hide him," she decided.

"Thank you," Faron said, relief tinting his voice.

Raidne approached the body, still wrapped in the rug, then knelt as she considered it. She lifted the body with no effort, balancing the weight on her forearms as she rose to her full stature. "I shall send Thaumas when we have disposed of him," she announced.

Faron nodded. "Thank you," he said, unsure if there was anything else he should say. When things were calmer, he should really learn Sirene customs.

Raidne nodded and slowly backed into the water, her body inching down with each step and her feathers melting away to reveal the smooth, water-bound skin.

When she was gone, Marcelle let out a sigh. "You should feel honored. Raidne usually won't consent to meet with those who live on land."

Faron gave Marcelle a concerned look at those words. "She wasn't your queen, was she?" Spirits, he should know things like this if he was going to marry Sabine. Faron suddenly saw a lot of studying in his future.

"No. She's Thaumas's wife," Marcelle explained with a huff of a laugh. "And she only comes to the surface in emergencies. Well, except on rare occasions."

"She is terrifying, and after this is done, I'm going to need to make sure Sabine calls Thaumas off," Faron admitted.

Marcelle nodded. "I suppose an elf could find a Sirene in their truer forms more terrifying," he admitted.

"It doesn't help that Thaumas promised Sabine he'd drown me, and looking at how she moved, I wouldn't know a Sirene was there until it's too late."

"Thaumas is protective of Her Grace," Marcelle said, looking back out at the water. "If he threatened to drown you, only she would be able to convince him otherwise."

"Sabine needs more protective people in her life, even if she can take care of herself." Faron knew there were a lot of people who would give their lives for Sabine, but it never hurt to have more. Though she seemed to be running out of enemies fairly quickly.

"I think his protectiveness has nothing to do with whether or not she can take care of herself," Marcelle said, then he shrugged. "You should get back to the chateau. Our guards will soon return with our new prisoners in tow. You'll likely have to help sort all of them out."

Faron nodded. As much as he wanted to stay and see what Thaumas had to say about the body, he trusted it was gone for good, making it pointless for him to stick around. "Thank you for all your help tonight," he said.

"Our country is safer because of things that transpired tonight. I can only be thankful I was here to help," Marcelle replied. He gave Faron a reassuring smile. "I will catch up shortly. I want to hear the arguments about why we can't arrest royal guards."

Faron laughed before giving a bone-deep sigh, because Marcelle was right. The guards and their captain would raise hell, demanding to see the prince and go on and on about how royal guards were to be treated a certain way. First though, he would go and see Sabine to let her know this was handled. "See you soon." When Marcelle nodded, Faron turned and headed back toward the chateau.

Chapter Thirty

By the time he'd snuck back into the chateau, Faron heard the familiar sound of guards issuing orders in the entryway, echoing through the bottom floor. Briefly, he pondered going to oversee their temporary prisoners being placed in their prison, but Faron decided the move would be too bold given the task he'd just finished. He hadn't checked for any bloodstains on his clothes, but he'd obviously been down on the beach just by glancing at his scuffed, sandy boots. No. He would go back to his and Sabine's rooms.

Returning became an easier matter since he could take the narrow servants' stairs rather than navigate open corridors. He struggled taking these routes thanks to his height and shoulder width, and he'd never have managed the body and rug. He took the stairs a couple at a time, feeling a need to return to Sabine, to ensure she was safe, even with the most obvious threat now disposed of. His heart pounded in his ears, anxiety creeping in on him now that his prior task of body disposal was complete. Had she cleaned the blood? Was her compromised door repaired? Had anyone noticed his departure in the interim? The walls seemed to move closer, threatening to pin in him in. Were they smaller than he thought? Why was it so hard to breathe? Why did he feel like he had absolutely failed Sabine?

Faron sighed in relief as he reached the top of the stairs and burst through the door into the corridor. He drew in great breaths of air in frequent gasps, feeling as though he had never experienced such pure air. His lungs inflated, and slowly, the rapid thump of his heart slowed into something more normal. Something more tolerable. Feeling better, he straightened his shoulders.

Before stepping out fully into view, Faron listened closely for anyone who might be lurking somewhere in the hall. Glad to find the hallway to Sabine's chambers empty, he resumed his journey. Approaching Sabine's room, he paused to note the still abandoned posts where he'd stationed guards earlier in the evening. They'd been sent elsewhere before the attack, and Faron felt anger and stress once again creeping up his neck. Knowing he was in a bad state, Faron decided to go see Sabine. Taking another deep breath, he forced himself forward and to her room. He stopped at the broken door and took in the damage. Thankfully, just the lock and some of the wood around it needed repaired, an easy fix for the night. He spotted Sabine in the sitting area, looking for all the world as though she might have stoked the fire in an effort to find more warmth.

"You just missed Louis," Sabine said by way of greeting. Her nightdress and robe had changed, showing off shades of blue, and though her grim expression spoke of a terrible evening, she looked perfectly fine.

He glanced around the room, seeing no trace of the mess left behind by Grégoire's death. He didn't even smell the metallic stench of blood, though the burning silk in the fireplace more than explained why. "Are you well?" he asked.

"Yes," Sabine replied. "Louis brought someone to look at the door. They will be back shortly."

"Thank the Spirits. I was going to make an attempt if need be, but I am no locksmith or carpenter." He let out a sigh and rubbed the back of his neck, warding off another round of intense anxiety.

"Everything will soon be as it was," Sabine assured him as she stepped forward, closing the distance between them. She reached up, putting her hands on his cheeks. "You look quite upset," she observed. "Did things go poorly?"

"No, they went well. Marcelle helped me dispose of the body, I have a new fear of the Sirene, and we appear to have gotten through this terrible event with none the wiser." Though he had tried for confidence, his eyes slid from Sabine's. How could he pretend everything was okay when he felt anything but? "I am upset I didn't see the soldiers going into the village for the trap it was, and using the servants' stairwell did not help my mood."

"You cannot predict everything, Faron," Sabine said softly.

"No, but considering Tristian used the same tactic, I should have been more cautious." He gave a shrug.

"I would say the circumstances were different," she argued. She let her hands fall from his face, though she gave him a gentle, reassuring smile. "Either way, you look in great need of rest and relaxation. Go wash, and calm. I'll put your boots out of sight until you have a chance to clean them, and we will behave as though nothing more than drunken antics in the village have crossed our minds. Things will be well."

Faron thought about arguing for about five seconds. Sabine could counter any argument he made, especially when he knew she was so much calmer than he felt. He finally nodded. "I'd ask if you'd join me, but with someone coming to fix the door..." He trailed off.

"Hopefully the repair will go quickly, and we can soon settle in our bed," Sabine replied. "I will call for a sleep potion to be brought up for you as well."

His dislike must have been apparent because Sabine's smile widened. "Don't worry. It won't prevent you from waking. It will just help you relax enough to actually find sleep."

"I will consider taking it after I wash," Faron allowed, and he turned to walk back to their washroom. Upon arriving, he turned the tap, allowing water to flow into the sizable tub. Normally, he was amused by the sizable basin, almost as though Sabine had somehow known her future partner would one day fill it.

Shedding his clothes took little time, and a cursory inspection of his clothes found no blood and little dirt that couldn't be explained away by going into town to handle the rogue soldiers. Those went into the bin Lisbeth had set aside for soiled clothing, and he turned to the tub, ready to relax. He paused as he caught his reflection in the mirror. Dark circles under his eyes suggested he needed sleep, but his sickly pallor demonstrated just how upsetting his last few hours had been. He would do his fiancée the curtesy of taking the sleeping draught once he finished bathing.

He climbed into the tub and sank into the hot water, letting out a sound of satisfaction as he submerged himself. After turning off the tap, Faron leaned his head back against the rim, closing his eyes as the ends of his black curls soaked up the water. Faron took a deep breath as he felt his body and mind calming. Minutes passed with him doing nothing else. He realized he'd dedicated very little time for reflection and quiet in his life, but especially since he'd arrived at the Vassetre estate. Sabine hadn't been especially difficult to work for, an obvious observation, as he planned on marrying her. She had been surrounded by trouble, though, and despite her enemies, he hadn't been able to keep his senses around Sabine for any length of time.

A faint, distant knock had him opening his eyes, but the sound of Louis's voice convinced him Sabine was safe for now. Another soft voice he didn't recognize began speaking, but Faron soon confirmed they were there to fix the door. He paid little attention to the light clinking of metal, which he presumed came from repairing the lock, as he closed his eyes again. Eventually, two sets of footsteps left the room, and he heard Sabine's light stride approach the washroom. She let herself in, though he had no complaint. "Did they fix the door?" he asked.

"They did," Sabine replied as she went over to the side of the tub. "You can't even tell it was broken."

"How did he manage that?" Faron asked.

"Magic, mostly," Sabine replied with a smile. "And quite some skill with keys and locks."

"I'm sorry I missed it."

Sabine leaned over and brushed the hair from Faron's face. "Would you like some more time in here?" she asked.

"Only if you're willing to join me. I'm happy to refill the water."

"Absolutely," Sabine agreed. She shed her robe and nightdress then stepped into the water, only waiting for Faron to turn the tap back on before she leaned back against him.

Faron's arms went around her slim waist, and for once, his most immediate response to her naked body pressed up against him wasn't arousal. No. Right now, he felt more at peace than he had all evening long.

Chapter
Thirty-One

Sabine's fork gave a delicate *ping* as she placed it on her plate. The fowl she'd eaten as part of her breakfast served as the main dish, though Meri would send out a couple of additional courses before she would be done. She took a sip of wine from her chalice which had been refilled only moments before by one of the younger servants as she ignored the rantings of Grégoire's guard captain.

Well, not exactly ignoring.

A man of average height, the captain had a beefy neck, red face, and heavy salt and pepper mustache that did nothing to make his bellowed, underhanded threats any more concerning. She didn't glance his way or react to anything he said, but his anger over the arrest of several royal guards and the missing prince had the captain quite put out with Sabine and her staff. He was under the delusion that she owed him any explanation or excuse.

A hand slammed on the table beside her plate, nearly striking her in the process and rattling most of the items surrounding her. "Woman, are you listening to me?" he demanded.

Sabine finally glanced up at him, her expression void of amusement.

"The prince is missing. He was under your roof and in your care. I want to know where he is!" he demanded. He missed Marcelle approaching from the corner the Sirene had occupied.

Sabine did not.

Grabbing the captain by his collar, Marcelle yanked the man back so hard he nearly fell back. "You will refer to the duchesse as 'Her Grace,'" he commanded with an angry authority Marcelle usually did not show. "And the next time you behave so violently around her, I will remove your hand, tongue, and any other offending appendage."

The captain glared at Marcelle but wisely kept his mouth shut. Turning back to Sabine, he straightened his jacket and spat out with the least amount of respect he could, "Your Grace, His Highness informed us he was staying in last night. Now today, we find him missing. Considering how your talks with him have been going, it's all rather convenient."

"When I heard your men were terrorizing my people in the village, the first thing I did was send someone to talk with His Highness about the matter. He was not in his rooms," Sabine replied. She took another sip of her drink. "My assumption, then, is that he went out with the lot of you. If you have misplaced him since, you can hardly blame me." She lifted her glass then paused and set it aside before pointing a finger at the captain. "When you do find him, let him know I expect to be compensated for all of the damage your men caused in the village."

The man's eyes narrowed. "I'm going to assume your people entered the rooms His Highness was supposed to be in. Did they see anything strange? Because I promise, Your Grace, he did not leave with us. It's not his habit to join the men on their outings." He stopped for a moment. "If I remember correctly, your elf refused to allow my men to guard the prince's door. He put your men there instead."

"His name is Faron," Sabine replied. "As to what happened to the prince, I am going to assume you are speaking out of concern that he has not returned from whatever bed and company he purchased himself for the night, and that concern has allowed you to forget you are speaking to the third most powerful person in this kingdom. I am much more tolerant of the lack of respect and the accusations than I should be, but I promise, my guards are not."

The man's eyes flickered to Marcelle but darted around the room quickly looking for a second, larger presence who was currently missing because he was still handling the prince's other guards. Apparently, they had drunkenly attempted to escape their cells, causing injury to two of their own. "My remaining men and I shall go and look for him. With luck," there was a threat somewhere in those words, "the prince will be here. If not..." He trailed off before turning on his heels and rudely storming from the room.

Sabine resumed her breakfast, only looking at Marcelle after a moment. "Marcelle, how do we feel about being threatened?" she asked before she sipped from her drink again.

"I don't think we were particularly impressed by it," the Sirene responded.

"I'm not impressed with it at all," Meri said as she entered the room with another tray. She'd clearly overheard everything.

"I didn't think you would be," Sabine replied. "I am so tired of men trying to threaten me."

"Same," Meri spat out as she placed the tray on the table. "Just because we are the fairer sex doesn't mean we are weaker."

"The question is, what to do about the guard captain..." Sabine said, turning over possibilities in her mind.

"Perhaps, let Prince Louis know when he joins you later," Marcelle suggested. "What with the accusations getting tossed around this morning."

"It's interesting that his first reaction is to blame you." Meri paused in serving the new dish. "Nothing happened last night, did it?"

"You mean other than the disruption in town?" Sabine asked before shaking her head. "I remained in my rooms last night per Faron's request. If anything else happened elsewhere, I've not been informed."

Meri got back to work, but Sabine noted the thoughtful look on her face. "It just seems like maybe there was something planned. Why else would the captain be so quick to jump to the conclusion you've done something to Grégoire?" She gave Sabine a sharp smile. "Too bad we don't have reason to interrogate him."

"After the way he's openly treated me this morning, I more than have a reason," Sabine replied. "I think, though, should the behavior continue, I will turn him over to Prince Louis."

Meri nodded, and Sabine knew she was content that something would be done to the man. "I'm sorry you're going through all this, Your Grace. It's been a lot these last few weeks."

Sabine smiled and nodded. "Thankfully, I have plenty of people around who are more than willing to support me, Meri. The knowledge makes it much easier to contend with whatever comes my way."

"We're all here for you, Your Grace." Meri gave a small bow, finished collecting the dishes, and made her exit.

Louis joined the table a few minutes later, traveling with only one of his guards, who took a position in a corner opposite Marcelle. He looked well-rested and as handsome as ever. Even his golden curls bounced with seeming jubilation over the new day.

"Good morning, Your Grace," he greeted. "You look well."

"As do you, Your Highness," Sabine replied. She speared a sliced melon chunk with her fork. "Your brother's guard captain was here not long ago, making vague accusations about why he has not come to breakfast yet. I thought I should let you know since His Highness hasn't joined us yet."

"Hm," Louis replied with disinterest. A servant filled his chalice with dark wine, and he paid more attention to tasting it once he had it in hand. "I shall speak with my brother about his people's manners. Even Grégoire wouldn't abide soldiers speaking so informally to a member of the nobility."

"At least not to their face," Faron said as he entered the room. Moving to where Sabine sat, he laid a quick kiss on her lips.

"I would agree," Sabine replied, her gaze lingering on Faron for several long seconds after the kiss ended. "I hear my staff gossip about me and my personal guard quite regularly."

"Only good things," Faron said as he took a seat. "Unless it's Lisbeth. She openly argues we are too cute and need to stop." He gave Louis a nod in greeting.

"One would hope newly engaged couples were obviously happy," Louis said, returning the nod. "If others comment, then we can assume you are living up to the expectation."

"Lisbeth and Meri still aren't out of the happy-new-couple phase, and they've been together for a very long time," Faron said with an eye roll. "So they have no room to talk."

"Who has no room to talk?" Avana asked with a yawn. She wasn't quite awake, but that became more obvious when she walked up to Marcelle and planted her face in his chest.

"Lisbeth," Sabine replied, watching as Marcelle looked down at Avana but otherwise didn't respond.

Avana didn't lift her head, so Sabine barely heard her when she spoke. "There's a lot to talk about there."

Faron gave Sabine a confused look but said nothing. He seemed happy to relax after the night and morning he'd had.

"Come eat, Avana," Sabine directed.

Avana let out what sounded like a whine but did as she was told, pushing off of Marcelle. "Thank you for letting me rest on you," she said and headed to the table, taking a seat next to Louis. Her eyes darted around the room before she leaned forward and said in a low tone, "I assume you dumped the body with the Sirene? That was Grégoire you carried out last night, right?" Her eyes squinted as she took in Faron's reaction.

"How?" he growled out.

"My windows face the back exit and the beach. I couldn't sleep for reasons." She trailed off for a second. "I saw you headed to the gate; you were carrying something over your shoulder. I think it was wrapped in a rug, but I couldn't be sure. I'm assuming with the yelling the captain was doing it was Grégoire?" She shrugged.

"Why don't we discuss other topics for now?" Louis suggested, catching Avana's eyes, his expression stern but fair.

Avana looked down at the empty space in front of her, and Sabine could see a blush staining her cheeks.

"The guards in the holding cells have been subdued, but I was curious about your thoughts on what we should do with them," Faron asked, his question aimed at both Sabine and Louis. Sabine saw Avana shoot him a grateful smile, which Faron ignored. Avana began piling large quantities of food on her plate, moving on from the slight embarrassment.

"I'd say treat them as you would any who would vandalize businesses in the village," Louis suggested.

Sabine nodded. "Being affiliated with a prince does not mean you cannot face justice for your crimes."

Faron nodded. "We will have to add in an escape attempt, an attempt to bribe our guards, assault of a guard, and a few other smaller things to the charges."

"Do as you normally would," Louis encouraged with a gesture of his hand. "I will not intervene."

The four continued their meal, chatting and laughing despite the shared awareness of Grégoire's death. At some point in the near future, decisions would need to be made regarding Louis's future as well as the disappearance of the middle prince. Sabine found she couldn't worry too much about it. Louis was as good as king in her eyes, and she couldn't feel sorry for having murdered Grégoire in self-defense.

Sabine was ready to rise and get on with her day when a couple of guards sprinted into the room. "Please excuse our intrusion, Your Highness, Your Grace," a woman with richly tanned skin said as she bowed. "We've received urgent news."

Louis tossed his cloth napkin on the table, his brow furrowed in concern. "What is it?"

"The Coralian army has been spotted less than a week's march across the border. Ships were also spotted off the southeastern coast."

The prince rose from his seat, his face pale but resolute. "We need to get home before Coralia arrives so we can direct a response." He looked over to Sabine, who had also risen from her seat. "You should come. Bring whoever it makes sense to include."

"Of course," Sabine easily agreed, her eyes quickly traveling to Faron and back again.

"Good," Louis replied. "Then, let's plan on leaving tomorrow."

A sneak peek from the upcoming sequel,
Vassetre: Resolve of a Duchesse.

"You are unusually quiet," she said after a long stretch of time that might have been seconds or hours. "Quiet and contemplative."

"Am I not allowed?" he asked, his voice rumbling with a mix of humor and warded-off sleep.

"When it pleases me," she replied, glancing up with mischievous amusement.

"Of course," he countered, rolling his eyes. "Spirits forbid anything happen with motivations other than your pleasure."

Sabine laughed. "My pleasure is quite important. I am always in a better mood when my pleasure receives adequate attention."

"I have noticed," Faron replied, and he playfully moved so he was hovering over her, his long black hair draping around them. "Should I take your conversation topic as a request?"

She laughed then pulled him down for a kiss. "It hasn't even been an hour," she replied against his lips.

"More than enough time," he murmured as he began kissing along her jaw.

Sabine moaned softly as her hand ran up his neck and into his hair. The returned rumble in his throat had her fingers rubbing tiny circles against his scalp. As they fell back into lovemaking, no concern for anything beyond their bed, minutes and hours ticked by without regard.

Later, they lay on top of the bed linens, breathing heavily and covered in a thin layer of perspiration. "I'm starting to think it's not elves. You are just insatiable."

"We can interrogate the next elf we come across if you'd like," Faron replied, laughing lightly.

"You can," Sabine replied, turning her head to grin at him. "I am a duchesse. I'm expected to show more class."

"Oh, of course, Your Grace," Faron teased. He turned on his side and draped an arm around her middle, pulling her close enough he could bury his nose in her caramel hair.

Sabine laughed, content to enjoy him so close. "You really are an asshole," she said.

"I am," Faron readily admitted against her hair. "I can only be what I am, Sabine, but I'd more than suggest you'd be quite disappointed if I changed."

"I would be," she acknowledged. "Your character, your decisiveness, your dedication to what you deem important... All of it draws me to you. If some people read your actions as asshole-ish, that is on them."

"As long as you love it, want it, I don't care what anyone else thinks about me."

"I do, no doubt," she promised. "Though with the reaction you've gotten from some people since we met, it is highly possible your tendencies to not play nicely might leave me a widow."

"I did nothing to earn Tristian or Grégoire's ire. Both men were just jealous I have something they never will. As for your widowhood, I'd not wish for either of us to face such a future," Faron replied. The amusement left his voice, leaving him sounding contemplative and perhaps uncertain. "But I know eventually one of us will be alone..."

"And the one of us left alone will be you?" Sabine ventured. Although they hadn't shared an in-depth conversation on their different life expectancies, the topic had been brought up enough times for her to know how deeply ingrained the fear remained for her fiancé.

"Assuming someone or something doesn't bring your life to an early end, it is absolutely certain elves live longer than humans," Sabine gently acknowledged. "If we both live according to our individual life expectancy, you will outlive me by decades. There is no getting around that. Nor the fact that I will look much older than you very quickly. Those are realities that come with our relationship." She shifted so she could face him rather than let Faron hide his emotions in her hair.

Faron made an unhappy noise, but he nodded, confirming her statement. "There are magics which could link our lives, ensure our lifespans are more aligned, but they are dangerous. I'd never put you in that sort of danger."

"The tales suggest many who undergo the magical processes to link lives often leave injured or die," Sabine replied.

"We could think of it as a last resort, then," he said with a weak grin.

Though he joked, Sabine could see the matter weighing on him, though she had to assume he pondered their reality often enough to have considered magical options before now. "What scares you the most?" she asked.

"The idea of living without you for even a moment," Faron replied in a near whisper. "Let alone the possibility of a near century."

No surprises came with the answer, but then, neither did any real answer. "Why do you find it scary?"

"Because I cannot, do not want to picture a world without you in it by my side. I could not tolerate one breath without you, Sabine."

Book Club Questions

1. Why do you think Grégoire grew so desperate? Was he always on the edge of committing some terrible atrocity, or did his desire for the throne lead him into action?

2. Do you think Grégoire and Tristian truly believed they could force Sabine to marry Tristian, or do you think Grégoire was building a case against the duchesse to justify an arrest or title removal?

3. Did Sabine forgive Faron too easily? Why or why not?

4. Were Finn, Meri, and Lisbeth right to encourage Faron in romantic pursuit of Sabine? Why or why not?

5. How do we account for the different temperaments and motivations between Louis and Grégoire?

6. Why is Sargarus planning on coming to Fythias? Is he using Grégoire, or does he have some greater purpose?

7. Why do Tristian and Grégoire hate Faron so much? Is it because he's Sabine's bodyguard? An Elf? Or is there more to it?

8. Do you think Sabine was too idealistic in hoping the princes could resolve their differences peacefully?

9. Does Lisbeth's zealousness cause undue burdens on others? Why do you think she reacts so strongly to the events around her?

10. Marcelle mentions Thaumas's dedication in protecting Sabine. Why do you think the Sirene remains so involved in his former lover's life?

Author Bios

Kate Jenkins enjoys writing fantasy, sci-fi, and romance as much as she enjoys reading them. She lives in a small town in Idaho with her autistic teen who is her whole world, her parents, and between them, four dogs and six cats. When not hanging out with her son, she loves gaming, especially first-person shooters and asymmetrical horror games she can play with friends. She's a K-pop enthusiast and harbors a secret love of K-dramas and Anime, much to her mother's displeasure, as she's slowly being sucked into them with her. Her favorites tropes are currently enemies-to-lovers, only-one-bed, coffee-shops, time-travel-fixes-it, and soul-mates/soul-identifying-marks. She is hopeful one day she can talk her coauthor into writing these with her.

Morgan Moreau's literary interests span across various genres, showcasing a love for the realms of fantasy, historical fiction, crime, and mystery, as well as contemporary stories. She is an enthusiastic lover of *The Little Mermaid*, as is evident in her vivid red hair, mermaid tattoos, and growing Ariel collection. Morgan also holds a deep affection for pirates, especially those who "wear fine things well," though those in possession of jars of dirt will always hold a place in her heart. She lives in Alabama with her dog, Scarlett, and she looks forward to adopting more puppies in the future. Her current passions include higher education, animal rights, and watching the 1995 *Pride & Prejudice* at least once a month. In addition to her current literary loves, Morgan is a fan of mermaids, vampires, pirates, and superheroes, and she hopes to incorporate these into future works.

Discover more at
4HorsemenPublications.com

10% off using HORSEMEN10

www.ingramcontent.com/pod-product-compliance
Lightning Source LLC
Chambersburg PA
CBHW021046310726
48969CB00006B/1824